D0439638

"Emotionally resonant and profound.
—*Publishers Weekly, starred review*

"*The Falling Boy* is beautifully written, a sort of story in snapshots, some of which take shape as rather formal portraits. It's about what happens when we are looking elsewhere—not only those things that happen to Long's characters but to our expectations as well."   —Ann Beattie,
author of *Picturing Will* and *Chilly Scenes of Winter*

"Each of David Long's story collections is a treasure trove of flawless gems, and in his first novel he gives us the mother lode—a story of love and loyalty, passion and betrayal. Written with the precise language of a poet, *The Falling Boy* accurately depicts life in Montana, with its harsh weather, beautiful landscape, and strong people."   —Chris Offutt,
author of *Kentucky Straight* and *The Good Brother*

"A carpenter's search for his own emotional life—what he feels, and why, and how—is rendered without sentimentality and without condescension, in luminous language and sensual images. David Long has written a novel with the precision and intensity of a short story. *The Falling Boy* is a lovely piece of work."   —Kevin Canty, author of
A Stranger in This World and *Into the Great Wide Open*

"Elegant . . . feels like an update from Updike country, with a Western twang."   —*Portland Oregonian*

"Sentence for sentence, it's perhaps the best-written novel of the year."   —Michael Lowenthal, *Boston Phoenix*

A native of Massachusetts, DAVID LONG has published short fiction in numerous literary journals. His latest collection, *Blue Spruce*, won the Rosenthal Award from the American Academy of Arts and Letters, and was named one of *Publishers Weekly*'s Best Books of 1995. He lives with his family in Kalispell, Montana.

THE
FALLING
BOY

A Novel

DAVID LONG

A PLUME BOOK

PLUME
Published by the Penguin Group
Penguin Putnam Inc., 375 Hudson Street, New York, New York 10014, U.S.A.
Penguin Books Ltd, 27 Wrights Lane, London W8 5TZ, England
Penguin Books Australia Ltd, Ringwood, Victoria, Australia
Penguin Books Canada Ltd, 10 Alcorn Avenue,
Toronto, Ontario, Canada M4V 3B2
Penguin Books (N.Z.) Ltd, 182–190 Wairau Road, Auckland 10, New Zealand

Penguin Books Ltd, Registered Offices: Harmondsworth, Middlesex, England

Published by Plume, an imprint of Dutton NAL, a member of
Penguin Putnam Inc. This is an authorized reprint of a hardcover
edition published by Scribner. For information address Scribner,
1230 Avenue of the Americas, New York, New York 10020.

First Plume Printing, June, 1998
10 9 8 7 6 5 4 3 2 1

 REGISTERED TRADEMARK—MARCA REGISTRADA

LIBRARY OF CONGRESS CATALOGING-IN-PUBLICATION DATA
Long, David.
    The falling boy : a novel / David Long.
       p.   cm.
    ISBN 0-452-27997-6
    1. Adultery—Fiction. 2. Sisters—Fiction. 3. Marriage—Fiction.
    4. Montana—Fiction. I. Title.
    PS3562.O4924F34   1998
    813'.54—dc21
                                    98–9231
                                      CIP

Printed in the United States of America
Original hardcover design by Brooke Zimmer

BOOKS ARE AVAILABLE AT QUANTITY DISCOUNTS WHEN USED TO PROMOTE PRODUCTS
OR SERVICES. FOR INFORMATION PLEASE WRITE TO PREMIUM MARKETING DIVISION,
PENGUIN PUTNAM INC., 375 HUDSON STREET, NEW YORK, NEW YORK 10014.

S.S.L.

P. S.M.

S.S.B.

M.S.-P.

Acknowledgments

*Special thanks to Claire Davis
and Dennis Held, to Hamilton Cain
and Sally Wofford Girand, to
Richard and Hinda Rosenthal, to
Barbara Knutson and the many others
who helped me get it right.*

THE
FALLING
BOY

ONE

Sperry, Montana

SUMMER 1952

Jelly

A freakishly August-like afternoon in May of that year, Mark Singer stands overheated and spattered with light at the altar of the Episcopal church on Third, makes his vows to Olivia Stavros, turns and lifts the gauzy veil from her face. He's just twenty-two. A week later he starts his new job, building houses for Ike Conlon. There's no shortage of work: the present house to finish, another foundation waiting, another after that. Good solid places, not the rickety trash thrown up before the war. The crew's third member is Whitey Burgess. He's in his early forties, with hair the color of suet, the demeanor of a banty rooster. Out of Ike's earshot, he slides the hammer from Mark's hand, says, "Don't *strangle* it. The blow goes up into your bones. Throw the head at the nail." He returns it, grip first. "And take it back a notch, huh?" he says. "You got a long goddamn time to be doing this."

Mark nods, slows down a little.

One morning at break, Ike tells the Falling Boy story. It's early summer, a high dense sky over the valley, cotton blowing from the trees. The boy in Ike's story has been on the job only a few days, and he's young, even younger than Mark. Ike has sent the kid for coffee and rolls, and now he's back, climbing the ladder leaning against the outside of the framed-in house, lugging two white bags, one containing the paper cups, one the doughnuts. He's a goofy, dreamy boy. He starts across the upstairs deck, and—who can say why, except it's his nature to be inattentive—he steps without a word into the stairless stairwell and falls clear into the cellar. Misses the ragged scraps the masons left, but also misses the sand mounded on the cellar floor. Not that sand's all that soft. Two full flights he falls.

It's a summer's day in the story, a day not unlike today. Ike describes the chill that strikes him when he reaches the dark of the cellar, the gooseflesh on his damp arms.

Mark interrupts, asks what the boy's name was. "Maybe I knew him."

Ike and Whitey exchange glances.

"Ricky something," Ike says.

Whitey says, "Remember the whistling?"

"He never let up," Ike says. "You'd tell him, *Put a plug in it,* two seconds later he's going again. In another world, that kid."

"Kind of whistle that's all air," Whitey adds, illustrating, *shee-shee-shee.*

"Anyway," Ike proceeds, "I'm in the cellar now. His left arm's bent funny at the elbow, not good. But the rib cage is working like a bellows, so at least he's breathing."

Finally, Ike says, he reached under the boy's head, and his fingers encountered a gooey slime. He yanked them back, sat on his heels, watched the boy's lips bubble. Then he raised his hand to the shaft of light, knowing what he'd find.

He demonstrates now, sniffing dramatically, says, "I could *smell* the stuff."

Mark's cue to squirm, to act revulsed.

"Naw, naw—" Ike says, his baggy face going merry. "It was raspberry *jelly,* for Christ's sake. The sack of rolls had got up under his head. Saved his fool life."

What's the point of Ike's story? A comment on the treachery

of life, certainly, its *flukiness*. But doesn't it also speak to the vacuousness of certain boys, doesn't it raise the issue of whether Mark is like that, not lost in daydream necessarily, but negligent in some other way, yet to be unearthed? Or maybe Ike harbors plans for him, senses worth?

Mark keeps adding to his inventory of self-instructions: *Don't whistle.*

Don't make him explain things over and over.

Don't be a smart-ass.

Be the man he wants you to be.

This last one is dicey because Ike can be hard to read. Does he mean what he says, or the dead opposite? You're supposed to know when it's sarcasm, mockery, and Mark does, but not every last time. It stings him, not to see what others see, to be the butt of a joke, a rube.

At lunch, he takes long drafts of iced tea from his Thermos, stealthily unfolds his sandwiches . . . sometimes a note from his wife falls out.

Look up at the sky, out toward downtown, can't you feel me loving you?

Or: *Thanks for picking me.*

Or: *Last night!!!*

Ike and Whitey rag him about sex. He's no prude but he won't be disloyal to Olivia, won't give up the first morsel of their private life. Yet, once the two older men are used to seeing her, the composure that attends her walk, the gaze she shines on Mark, they gradually back off, become almost protective of Olivia. It wasn't so crude, anyway, this teasing. Ike's in his fifties. Stocky, rumpled, his face dark and pear-shaped, with old acne pits under the jaw, yet a powerful man, a man instinct says not to cross. He has grown daughters who have left the valley, a wife he calls the Battleship Norma. Whitey's a bachelor. There's a divorcee he sees, and she's in Missoula, 120 miles to the south. Friday afternoons, Monday mornings, her name is invoked to explain his condition.

Perched on the splintery staging, nailing clapboards, Mark hears Whitey and Ike argue politics. The president has just come through Sperry. Spoke to four thousand people wedged into the high school gym, dedicated the new dam up the canyon. Harry S. Truman in the flesh. Stumped for his nominee Stevenson, lambasted Eisenhower for consorting with "special interests." A terrible couple of years for Truman, but you'd never know it. The stores have blue signs in the windows, WELCOME MR. PRESIDENT. The newspaper runs a special edition devoted to photographs, the full text of the speech. "That son of a bitch wouldn't know the straight truth if he sat on it sharp end up," Ike Conlon says.

Whitey's a Democrat from way back. He spits when Ike talks like that. His lips are chapped, cracked. He admires Truman, a scrappy little man like himself. Look how he shitcanned that pompous bastard MacArthur. Whitey and Ike have worked side-by-side for years, except for Whitey's time in the service, yet they're not business partners. Conlon Construction belongs exclusively to Ike Conlon. Mark listens to the skirmishing, the gibes, Whitey on the subject of ordinary working stiffs, Ike throwing looks to high heaven. And he sees how both men assume his allegiance. His twenty-first birthday fell in the off year of 1951, thus he has yet to vote. This year he intends to, and he knows who for, but he's keeping his mouth shut about it.

After its flagrant, disorienting start, the first summer of Mark's marriage proves mild, seasonable. If anyone happened to ask, he'd admit to happiness. He has a job and a wife, an apartment, a savings book. Has a '41 Dodge Deluxe, his father-in-law's old car, handed down as a wedding gift, not a flashy vehicle by current standards, but roadworthy, barely rusted, still has some bristle left to the green upholstery . . . as he drives, he circles his free hand on it until the palm tingles and goes numb. At work, he likes the weight of the nail pouch at his belly, likes sinking the nails. Sixteen-pennies are best: a set, two or three hard blows, one more to clinch. He likes the smell of Ike's cigar if he's not smack up against it, likes the bizarre Popeye the Sailor dance Whitey breaks into apropos of nothing. He likes how rapidly he heals . . . blood blisters, gouges from the hammer's claw, gone in three or four days. He likes the last minutes of the afternoon, the dust suspended in the air. He likes Olivia's solid, accommodating body, her murmurs, the sight of her skin uncovered for his benefit, olive-toned, luxurious, where his own looks blanched, knobbed with bone, though, miraculously, it seems a pleasure to her. He likes the way sex clobbers him, dispatches him into a bottom-less sleep . . . it's as if his body simply shuts down. A Sunday afternoon, say, or an evening after he's cleaned up. Coming to, he floats on a gusher of light, not knowing if ten minutes have elapsed or an hour. But the ordinary nights . . . he likes those, too. He and Olivia lie adjacent in the semidark, and the last thing she says is, "See you on the other shore." It's what her mother said to her and now she says it to him.

The Vagabond Cafe

Mark's private sideshow: observing the four Stavros sisters, into whose midst he finds himself legally bound. Olivia is number three. Not storky and smart-mouthed like Linny, the eldest, christened Evangeline. Not sulky and comical like Celia with her tweezed brows, her jazzy getups, her calamitous history with men. Not fair and even-keeled and tomboyish like

Helen, who's still in high school. Olivia has Linny's profusion of black hair, the same eyes, recessed, dark as coffee beans, with half-moon lids Mark finds unspeakably sexy. But there the resemblance ends. Olivia's shorter by half a foot, carries more padding on her bones, has a natural grace Linny lacks. Where Linny is restless, appraising, wickedly funny, there's a stillness to Olivia, a seriousness that borders on secrecy . . . Mark gazes at her sometimes and doesn't have a clue what's going on inside, if she's here or miles away. It's unnerving, but, Jesus, it excites him, too, literally causes him to shiver. The unknowable galaxy of Olivia. When he tells her this, she says he gives her too much credit. Really, she's ordinary. He doesn't believe it, doesn't believe she believes it. He loves his wife, and loves, too, the idea of marriage. By extension, he loves his sisters-in-law, thinks one of his missions in life is to take an interest in each, and not the wrong kind.

Mark's father-in-law, Nick Stavros, owns the Vagabond Cafe on Second Street, where the sisters work. Their mother, Grace, used to bake breads and pastries for the Vagabond, arriving in the dark each morning, but now that's fallen to Linny. Celia and Olivia wait table during the breakfast rush, Helen comes in after school and Saturdays. Nick's third-generation Greek, born in Chicago, but there's nothing especially Greek about the Vagabond. When the mood struck, he used to run a lunch special of spanakopita or souvlakia, but the Vagabond's clientele never exactly clamored after them. The mood seldom strikes these days. The only Greek touch now is the calendar nailed above the phone . . . Nick's brother Pete sends a new one every December. This year's bears a picture labeled *Porch of the Maidens, Acropolis*. Someone's inked in the names of the four girls next to the statues. The tint is unreal, lurid as Technicolor.

The Vagabond is a skinny, glass-fronted building with a tar

roof. Out front, there's an awning, two gray benches. Inside, a silver pressed-tin ceiling. Fourteen booths, nine swivel stools, two long oilcloth-covered tables in back for friends, off-duty sisters. The building to the east houses the storeroom of Alt's Furniture. The lot on the other side is vacant, a patch of oil-spotted gravel, formerly a barber shop belonging to Wilfred Espy, where Mark's grandmother would send him for his monthly shearing. Espy had been a doughboy in France. Wounded, decorated. His medal with its dull ribbon hung alongside the barber license. He'd become a drinker, his eyes floated like cow's eyes behind thick saucers of glass. He'd begun to nick scalps, the tops of ears. Customers would stir from their reveries and realize the clicking of shears had ceased, see Espy's red face in the mirror, his hands at his sides. One morning the shop didn't open. Later that year, the building was demolished, scooped up into dump trucks and carted off. The resulting slot of ground is barely wide enough to park a car, but someone's coaxed ivy to grow on the Vagabond's homely west wall. And here's another thing Mark likes for no good reason: the ivy leaves against the brick, tremoring in the slantwise light of evening.

The Vagabond Cafe: swan's neck spigots . . . thick, blue-rimmed crockery . . . Cokes made from squirts of syrup and carbonated water. Used to stay open until all hours, steamy glass on a frigid night. Mark would make his way to one of the tables in the rear and loiter with a stack of gravy-stained newspapers, or set up the cafe's chess board and play whoever happened by. If no one came, he played against himself. High on the back wall hung a painting in a thin gold frame: *The Vagabond*. A drifter walking a dirt road. Thatched barns, lonely blue hills, green pastures that reminded Mark of the Twenty-third Psalm. Time seemed to eddy in the Vagabond. The radio played, the kitchen door swung on its hinges, the

Stavros girls came and went, came and went. There was no place he wanted more to be.

Because his own family was a bust: no brothers or sisters, aunts, uncles, no multitude of shirttail relations. His father died a few months before the war, under circumstances less than honorable, a disturbance outside a nightclub. Subarachnoid hemorrhage, the toe of a boot to his skull. To this day the details remain open to interpretation. Mark had just turned ten. Morgan Singer was an erratic, grudge-holding man, a man with a checkered work history, but he was never cruel to Mark, you couldn't say that, you couldn't rightfully say Mark was afraid of him, afraid for his physical safety, only that Mark has made a deep, scarcely conscious vow to conduct his own life differently, more steadfastly, if that's not too corny a way to put it. Without the narrowed eyes, the undertow of ill humor, *You know what pisses me off, you know what gets my*— Unless it's just that Mark's nature is more temperate. Nothing he can take credit for. What would Morgan Singer think of him . . . would he find him tame, too easily appeased? What would he make of Mark's young bride? Ah, let the dead keep their opinions to themselves, Mark thinks in rare moments of petulance.

From fifth grade on, he was raised by his father's mother, Audrey Singer, a dressmaker, seamstress. There was always some stranger getting measured in the front room of the house on East Sixth, always pins underfoot, wispy brown paper wafting around, the odd words spoken, *gusset, placket,* the long section of iron pipe crammed with satiny formals and policeman's coats, re-cuffed pants on hangers. It wasn't until Olivia pointed it out that he thought, yes, how funny, a seamstress named Singer. A plain-faced older lady smelling of Clorets, long-widowed, holding her own in the world . . . always chatting, always throwing her hands up, *What can you do?* Made it clear she wouldn't mother him the way she'd mothered his father. She's told Mark: "I had to be the big know-it-all with him. Had to put on a big front. All he did was resent me for it. I worried myself sick about losing him, then I lost him anyway." No, she wasn't going to bury Mark under a mountain of instruction, he'd have to make sense of things for himself.

Loved him dearly, but drew a line, that was Audrey Singer.

And what of Annette Singer, his own mother who'd run off? "She was young," his grandmother said. "Lacked the wherewithal for the job, the maturity, that was it really. Things overwhelmed her, ordinary things. But I'm not going to poor-mouth that girl. And you listen to me, Buster Brown, you'll have to try not to hold it against her, either."

Audrey Singer said, "If I can, you can."

What good would it be to hate her? How could he hate what he couldn't get a purchase on, for his own memories had eroded, could no longer be trusted. He remembered the reddish hair, too fine, fizzed up with static electricity. The fever blisters. One night she woke him out of a dead sleep, afraid he'd skipped his prayers, one time asked him to keep something for her, made him swear not to tell. A vitamin bottle with a roll of bills inside. Mixed denominations, mostly ones.

"But she's *alive?*" Mark asked.

His tired, well-meaning grandmother who tried to make light of things, *What can you do?* answered him, "Oh yes, honey, I imagine she is."

Didn't need to say, *Don't get your hopes up.*

Didn't need to say, *For all I know, she might be locked up in some institution.*

Audrey Singer, who couldn't quite conceal her relief that the girl, once gone, stayed away.

Is it any wonder he's taken to the Stavros family?

Olivia's mother, Grace Stavros, died in 1947, February.

Linny was twenty, Celia seventeen, Helen not yet eleven. Sophomore year for Olivia. Months later, when they were first in love, Olivia and Mark sat secluded in their booth at the Vagabond, and she gave him the story of that abysmal autumn: Miss Knight for English, Mr. Brieske for math, and after school the gloomy pilgrimage down Eleventh to the hospital. Unless she made a willful detour, she had to walk straight past the mortuary on Montana Street, then under a dripping canopy of horse chestnuts, and up into the waxy corridors of St. Anne's. *Ovarian cancer,* spread to the brain. Mark listened intensely, stroked the tips of Olivia's fingers across the table. It was grim, what she was explaining, but also factual and important, and just touching her electrified him. His memory of Grace Stavros was maddeningly vague. He'd been coming to the Vagabond for years, but she'd seldom been around in the afternoons or evenings. He remembered a tall woman in constant motion: plain blouses, marcelled hair full of bobby pins, a face with sharp angles and coppery freckles, an impatient smile. He couldn't say, truthfully, if Grace had known him by name or not, but he didn't bother mentioning this to Olivia. Seventy-nine pounds at death. It happened that there was a king salmon of that exact weight mounted above the door of Bailey & Sons Sport Shop on Dakota. Mark had passed beneath it a hundred times, noted the gaping jaw, the varnished scales sueded with dust. This, too, he kept to himself.

Olivia's life before him . . . his curiosity's voracious. "I'm boring you, aren't I?" she sometimes asks. Mark says, "You kidding?" The fact is, since he's been with Olivia, almost nothing bores him anymore, almost nothing seems unworthy of marveling at.

But his life before her?

Pickup games, assignments, school days by the hundred,

evenings at the kitchen table with the *zizzing* of the sewing machine from the other room . . . the war years when he and a friend camped out by the radio, Mark thinking aloud, "What if we *don't* win, what *then?*" and the friend, Izzy Tartabull, chiding, mocking him, "Quit talking like that, willya—" Mark shut up about it, his fear not abating, only submerging into that pool of fears he showed no one.

Or the winter he sampled the different churches. The brown-shingled Presbyterian on the lower end of Montana. The less damnation-peddling of the two Lutheran congregations. The Episcopal where he must have seen Grace Stavros in her felt hat those mornings, without knowing it. Here he first heard readings from the Book of Common Prayer, *We have left undone those things which we ought to have done; And we have done those things which we ought not to have done* . . . and the creeds recited in unison, *We believe in one God the Father Almighty, Maker of heaven and earth, and of all things visible and invisible* . . . He was moved by the rolling mumble of voices, the stonework vaulting overhead, the grandeur and confidence. Yet none of it conferred the gift of faith, made of him a believer. He had to, he guessed, come down on the side of things visible.

Or the minor revelations that would ambush him. For instance, looking closely once at the familiar cork-backed ceramic tile that sat beside his grandmother's stove: tiny figures in outfits of a long-departed era, old people hunched miserably in wagons and wheelbarrows, being borne up a flight of stairs to a machine with a crank like a hurdy-gurdy, from which they emerged straight-spined and fair, the women in bright dresses, arms aloft, the men in top hats, pulling jauntily on long clay pipes. Mark looked away, gazed around the empty kitchen in panic, couldn't get his breath for a moment. Or, another time, happening onto the slim drawer hidden behind the molding of her walnut dresser, finding telegrams, much-creased letters in his grandfather's immaculate hand. *My dearest A.* And traces of Mark's difficult father. A birthday card with gold glitter, *You Are My Sunshine.* Wrought-iron fire engine, rubber dagger, knobby chunk of meteorite.

Or all the rest: outgrowing shoes and jeans, having his muscles thicken, his voice crack and drop. The achievements and humiliations, the few times—a week, a month—he thought he might like some girl. It's all there, life before Olivia, but he feels no attachment. It's insubstantial, light as cottonwood fluff.

These days, the Vagabond closes at four, four-thirty. Nick sighs, shuts the grill down, Helen wet-mops, disinfects, off go the lights, the blue neon Vagabond sign. When he lost his wife, the stuffing went out of him, that's the word on Nick Stavros. He's a man of Ike Conlon's vintage, with a head of springy hair, coils of galvanized tin, a brown bald spot like a monk's. Bulging forearms, fingers longer and nimbler than you'd imagine, specked with shiny grease burns. His voice is hoarse, low-pitched, retains a residue of accent, though he and his brothers and sisters were born in the state of Illinois. Sometimes he speaks so low, it's impossible to understand him. Mark says, "I'm sorry, what—?"

"Naw, nothing," Nick answers. "Just jabbering at myself."

Still a handsome man, but diminished, you might be tempted to say *lost.* Hard to see him as a lover, as consumed by love, yet that's what everyone swears. Nick and Grace Stavros, the real article. Stormy on occasion, that union, but name one that isn't.

And Nick's opinion of Mark Singer, first of the husbands?

One day last January, Nick invited him out to McCafferty's Slough to fish through the ice. This was the week after Mark and Olivia announced their plan to marry, surprising no one, but Mark nonetheless expected a formal talking-to. It was a bright, windy Sunday. The slough was ring-shaped, an abandoned loop of the river, segregated from the main channel by an earthen dike. Nick didn't bother with an auger, used a hatchet to bust out an existing hole, chummed the greenish water with niblets. He unfolded a camp stool and sat. Mark followed suit. "Perch in here for the most part," Nick said after a while. "Some whitefish. We used to load up the smoker with them. Bony, but pretty good eating."

Mark shielded his eyes, squinted at Olivia's father, smiled. After an uneventful hour, Nick relocated them to a spot nearer the dike. The sun was already waning. Dead, unfallen leaves made a delirious clacking in the cottonwoods. Nick suddenly put a hand to Mark's shoulder as they walked, pointed at the glassy ice. Two shadows swam beneath their feet, producing a wake of bubbles and stirred-up silt. "Muskrats," Nick said. "They burrow in the bank there." He made a little gesture with the corner of his mouth . . . Mark had seen it made by each of the Stavros sisters. On Olivia it meant: *Strange but true,* or sometimes, *Don't ask.*

Driving home, Nick pulled in at Vanek's Tavern and bought them each a shot of schnapps, lifted his in a wordless salute.

In the short time they were inside, evening came on.

"How'd it go?" Olivia asked him. "What'd my dad have to say?"

"Said he thought I'd make a spectacular husband for you," Mark answered. "Couldn't believe your luck."

"Oh, he didn't say that."

Mark ran his hands down Olivia's sides, let them idle on her hipbones. "Sure he did," he said.

He was left to wonder what Nick *did* think of him. It's a question suspended above his life, and unlike Morgan Singer, Nick Stavros is hard to dismiss. He's right here, still presiding, still casting his shadow. Assented to the marriage, maybe, but Mark can't quite shake the feeling that Nick's about to open his mouth and let fly.

Trojans

Olivia says, "We were fated for each other, you and me. Don't you think?"

Mark says, "So all that time my hair was growing it was just so I could get it cut and then wander next door for a Coke."

"It's worse than that," Olivia says. "Your grandmother had to get over the whooping cough so she could take the train to St. Paul with her sister, so she'd be in the seat opposite your grandfather . . ."

"Good thing he wasn't off in the can," Mark says.

Olivia says, "He couldn't have been because I needed to love you."

They're out for a drive, down the east shore of the lake, Olivia's cotton dress luffing, billowing. They've bought a sack of cherries at one of the stands. It sits between them, the top folded over. The pits they spit out the windows. Now Olivia stretches over and kisses him. Mark stops the car in a patch of deep shade and she kisses him again. Her lips are spongy, damp, flecked with cherry pulp.

It's all just kidding, making fun of the silly way people in the movies hash over their destinies, sniff meaning in every odor that blows by. Olivia can be this way with Mark, light-spirited, happy to go along with the joke . . . even, in her way, flirtatious. All the same, she *does* believe in fate, does believe that everything in the world's connected by a vast root system. The sisters give her flak for being the mystical one, the one with hunches, superstitions, for being a little strait-laced and solemn, so Mark appreciates these times she seems to laugh at herself, to take herself with grains of salt. "We counterweight each other," he says one day without thinking. Olivia answers immediately, "Yes, we do," knows exactly what he meant.

Often, during this first year of marriage, she thanks him for choosing her, as if Mark had stood deliberating before a lineup of the four Stavros girls, then made his selection. If she wants to pretend that's how it was, Mark doesn't mind, he's charmed in a way, though it would be nearer the truth to say *she'd* picked *him*. Or that they'd simply recognized something in each other. Who can explain attraction? Not Mark. What of the fact that each had lost a parent? Were the deaths of Grace and Morgan necessary, and if so, couldn't you say your need somehow caused them? Well, clearly that's nuts. It's like the idea Whitey trotted out one day, that a moth's wing beats could start up a hurricane on the far side of the earth. Don't most actions just fizzle out? Mark wonders: How can you be held accountable for knowing which one thing leads some-where?

You can't be.

Or else you simply are.

One of their first nights in bed, Olivia asks him if he's in a terrible rush to have babies, asks if he'd mind waiting.

Mark says he guesses he can wait, says he doesn't mind hav-ing her to himself. In truth, he's scarcely given it a thought. He expects them to have a family, of course, expects to be a father . . . he'd hate to be the last of the Singers, and isn't there some-thing unnatural and sad about married couples without kids? But the subject of *babies,* no, it doesn't steal into his thoughts the way it does hers. On occasion, a baby would be brought to his grandmother's shop, and Mark would be enlisted to hold it against his shoulder while a hem was pinned. He got so he knew how to pat the back and hum into the convoluted ear, but, in all honesty, he can't remember ever thinking: *Boy, I'd sure like one of these.*

The next time Olivia brings it up, she says she's waiting for a sign.

"A *sign,* now what's that supposed to mean?" Mark asks, but gently.

Olivia peels a tendril of black hair off her forehead, thinks before answering. "Well, I don't know," she says. "It won't be obvious. Signs take a leap of faith."

She hears how this sounds, shakes her head as if to say, "Oh, please don't mind me, Mark."

So Mark nods affably, tolerantly.

Yet he wonders what's behind this reticence, if it's a cause for worry. Is it about *him?* Is she still taking his measure, waiting to see who he is?

In any case, they're careful. A day or two around her period he's allowed the joy of entering her unsheathed. All other times require a prophylactic. Oh, and what acute discomfort, that first sortie to Cahill Drug. He might as well have been wearing a painted sign board: MAN WHO GETS LAID. But subsequent trips, down between the rows of corn plasters and Kaopectate to the druggist's inner sanctum, have already dulled that impression. Now it seems more like a condition he suffers from, a chronic discharge in need of treatment. The druggist fans his goods on the marble counter, makes Mark point and say, "Those ones there." Out of embarrassment, he buys only a dozen at a time, emerges into the glare of another Saturday afternoon, marveling at the vast distance between day and night.

The Singers' address is 112 1/2 Ash, their landlady a widow named Mrs. Kovaric. The apartment is reached by climbing a set of outside stairs, steep, white-painted. In the early evenings, the wooden railing's still warm as Mark balances a grocery bag on it, works the latch, and bumps the door open. The kitchen: open shelves with butcher paper, a range, a round-shouldered refrigerator by Kelvinator. Then the narrow living room, windows on three sides, thin curtains that sail in the cross breeze. The bathroom: low-ceilinged, tub no shower, toilet that runs. One night, Olivia asks if he can't get it to quit. Mark almost answers, "How would I know the first thing about *that*?" Instead, he lifts the top of the tank and watches the mechanism work. It's beautifully simple. He reaches a hand in, straightens a kink in the copper slide. The stopper falls into place, the water rises, the float valve shuts off with a sudden, unequivocal *gulp,* and all is quiet.

He tries it again, calls Olivia, makes her watch, feels her hand at his waist.

The bedroom is tiny, no closets. Olivia's dresses hang in a makeshift enclosure in the hall, Mark's things are folded into bureau drawers. In the evening, he and Olivia climb through the window onto the almost-flat roof of Mrs. Kovaric's porch, and sit in two canvas lawn chairs. The veranda, Olivia calls this. They drink a beer, or iced tea, or vanilla soda. Nothing looks ugly from here, not the racks of garbage cans, not the rust beneath the rotted downspout, the bricked-in windows of the warehouse across the alley. They watch the dusk begin to pool. On the hottest nights they sleep here, under light blankets. One morning near dawn, Mark wakes sharply, and the first thing he sees is a massive consort of birds tearing across the sky. Hundreds, could be thousands, arresting their flight in midair, spraying apart, reassembling into a black knot, veering off at right angles as if they were a single organism. He can't stop staring. Is this what Olivia means by a sign . . . where you feel suddenly vacant and receptive, spoken to? He lies back and strokes her flank, thinks, *Oh man, oh man, oh man.* In a few minutes, he climbs in through the window and quietly dresses for work.

Talk

They talk about money, what things cost. Forty-four cents for Bisquick, eighty-nine for Velveeta. A quarter for three rolls of toilet paper. Meat they get wholesale. It's stored in the Vagabond's deep freeze, flat white packages marked *O & M,* frozen so hard they ring.

"We ever going to be able to afford a television?" Mark wonders aloud. He's watched the one on the wall in the Mint: Red Buttons and big-time wrestling and parts of several Dodger games. Sperry is the first Montana city to be wired for cable. No roof antennas to blow down or tangle with power lines, according to the ads. There are Zeniths in the window of Parmentier's, around the corner from the Vagabond. Sloat's has Admirals and Philcos. A year from now, two years, won't they be cheaper? Which is better: going in debt or saving up? It's interesting, TV, but he's not as jazzed about it as most people. His interest centers on buying a set for Olivia. One night a week she bags up their laundry, drives it to the Stavros house on McClaren Road, where there's a console set Linny and Celia bought Nick. Olivia returns in a glow, smelling of the licorice they eat while watching. But next time he touches on the subject, she says, "Mark, there's no hurry. I have things to read. Besides, I've got you, don't I?"

Yes, of course, she has *him.*

Sometimes they talk about these books Olivia totes home from the library or the used bookstore on Fourth. *Lust for Life,* Pearl S. Buck, the beheading of Anne Boleyn, *The Golden Bough.* If there's a pattern here, Mark's sure not on to it yet. One night he dozes off while Olivia's reading to him in bed. She pokes him, says, "I'm not going to read if you don't *listen,* honey." He tells her no, please don't stop, he loves being read to, her voice is so soothing he can't help himself. "It's my favorite way to fall asleep. Okay, my second-favorite." After a moment, she picks up where she left off: *On the evening of the third day, we came ashore at the village of El Gato Blanco to drop the mail pouch and take on fuel. Captain Mowery instructed us to stay on board. Along the dock stood tin-sided sheds. In their dim interiors we could see the outlines of men and sensed their eyes upon us.* When he wakes again, the light's out, a soft rush of wind is jostling the curtain. It takes him a few seconds to remember where he is.

They talk about trips they'll take. Nothing involving steamboats through the jungle. Olivia votes for Chicago. Nick brought her with him when he took the train back for a brother's funeral in forty-six, and she's never forgotten it, the light-lashed waterfront, the neighborhoods, her privileged glimpse of Nick in his old element, never forgotten for a minute that he chose her, left the others home, wanted *her* to keep him company, wanted to show *her* off to that crowd. This is why Chicago. Mark understands full well, but doesn't care, says, "We can go there first."

And where does *he* want to go?

He wouldn't mind seeing the giant sequoias, he'd like to swim in salt water once in his life. And the East, shouldn't you see the Statue of Liberty . . . Ebbets Field? But it's not the sights he cares about. Somehow, it still hasn't sunk in entirely, that he and Olivia are adult citizens, free to come and go in the world. So if he daydreams about travel, it's about the two of them, two bodies in the front seat of the Dodge. Stopping for the night, renting a cabin, asking where's a good place to eat, approaching Olivia in a strange bed, walking out beside her under a new sky. Well, that's assuming they can save up the dough. Assuming Ike gives him the time off.

And some things they *don't* talk about. The baseball standings, Brooklyn up by four and a half. The funnies . . . Olivia can't see the attraction. They don't talk about what's embarrassing about living together in such tight quarters. Not at length. Each other's noises, rituals. They adjust, they learn, but not all things are said aloud. Mark doesn't believe every stray thought that blows through his brain is so fascinating it needs sharing, doesn't announce each charley horse, each lurch of mood. Some things he *would* talk about if they weren't so nebulous, if he hadn't learned, living with Audrey Singer, to keep his own counsel. The thought of falling sick and not being able to support Olivia, of aging before her eyes, of somehow giving offense and driving her away.

But most nights talk comes as effortlessly as breathing. They talk about the Stavros sisters: old deceits, alliances, hijinks. Celia's always good for a laugh, Celia and her cavalcade of boyfriends. The short one with the skimpy red whiskers, name of Schremp. Toby St. Clair, the lawyer's son . . . broke it off and three months later his wedding's in the paper. The semiclandestine romance with Buzz Castillo, already married. Those and the others.

Often, Celia drops by the Ash Street apartment unannounced, marches in, warbles, "I'm not inter*rupting* anything, am I?"

Olivia lets the teasing roll off her, smiles, madonnalike.

"Oh, spare me that superior look," Celia says.

One night it's Olivia's red pumps she's come for. Another time, she needs to hide out. Someone's looking for her, some man. "You sure you're *okay?*" Mark asks. "You want me to—?"

"It's nothing," Celia insists.

Another minor screwup.

On her way out, she turns to Mark, says salaciously, "'Bye, sweetie." Never fails to raise color in his cheeks.

"You ever have thoughts about my sisters?" Olivia asks when they're alone. "About their *bodies?*"

"Oh, constantly," Mark says, "I have a rich fantasy life." Though, actually, he tries not to speculate too much in that area. Though he's kind of sorry she brought it up.

"If you want to know, Helen's is the cutest," Olivia says. "Very boyish. A nice little chest."

Mark can't help but hear his grandmother's word, *bazooms,* the flagrant commentary on her customers' physiques, *You'd think she'd need a derrick to lift those—*

"No offense to your sister," he says, standing, wrapping her in a bear hug that raises her off the floor, "but I didn't want a boyish girl."

One night, early that fall, they have Nick over to supper. Mark can't remember seeing Olivia so keyed up. "I'm not keyed-up," she insists. "I just want everything to be right." Three times he's back to Lindell's for something. The third time it's paprika. *Paprika.* Nick wears a suit jacket, a tan rayon shirt buttoned under the chin. Olivia's in a skirt and heels. They eat at a card table in the living room. Pork roast, green beans from the produce stand down by the viaduct. Olivia brings out the platter, and it dawns on Mark that he's the one who's supposed to carve. The table wobbles, milk sloshes out of their glasses.

Nick asks what's become of Ike. "I used to see him, he'd stop in," he says. "Not so much anymore."

"We're out south of town now," Mark offers as if it explains anything.

Nick shakes his head. "I can't believe all the houses going up," he says.

Later, he asks how Mark's grandmother's faring.

"She's pretty well," Mark replies, though he can't come up with any news about her that might pass as dinner conversation.

Not the cystitis.

"I made that glaze," Olivia says.

"Yuh, it's good," Nick answers. "Your mother used to make that."

Baked pears for dessert, coffee.

Nick thanks her, thanks them both, but doesn't stay long. Once he's departed, Olivia starts in on Mark. How did he think it went, how did her father seem, why'd he leave so much food on his plate? She says she's afraid he's turning into that old barber.

"*Espy?*" Mark says, remembering the cheeks, so full of broken veins they looked rouged. "No, no," he says, "Nick's fine, he's not like that. Come *on*."

"You never knew him before," Olivia says. "He was bigger. Now everything seems like too much trouble."

How to counter that?

Later, Olivia disappears into the bathroom, remains so long Mark wonders, should he knock, ask if there's a problem? Is she crying? His grandmother's one nugget of advice: *Don't crowd her*. Hard to know just when it applies, though.

Mark slips on his jacket, makes some noise, goes downstairs and takes a walk. Up Montana, past the cannon, the mortuary, past Penney's and the News Agency, up as far as the tin-sided cherry warehouse where he worked the summers before he worked for Ike. The air's turned raw, swirling, laden with grit. He jams his hands in his pockets, angles across the empty street, and starts back, pauses at the window of Schwantes's Jewelry to watch the model train tracing its figure eight, though the cargo of rings and stickpins is locked in the vault at this hour. Down the next block, he steps around the barricaded sidewalk where the Stockholm Club burned. The mounded rubble gives off a mean, scorched-rubber smell as he passes.

The old sign: No Home Like the Stockholm.

He's overtaken by a glimpse of himself deprived of Olivia. A puckery, crepe-skinned replica of Mark Singer, breaking bread with his own grown children, tongue-tied the way Nick was tonight, his life unrecognizable.

A horrifying picture.

He steadies himself, walks on.

Frazil Ice

In late November comes a night of sash-rattling wind, a dump of snow, then ten days of clear arctic cold. The sloughs freeze, the rivers clot with frazil ice. The chimneys of the buildings downtown pour out opaque shafts of steam and smoke. In the house on Ash Street, the thermostat is mounted on the wall of the downstairs apartment, and Mrs. Kovaric keeps the furnace cranked. The hot air blasts from the scrolly registers, flees past her chilly limbs, and shoots up into Olivia and Mark's. It fogs the windows, makes their eyes hot and itchy, parches Mark's already-dry skin so he's constantly scraping his back on the sharp edge of a door jamb. It exits through the beaverboard ceiling, then the roof, where it melts the undermost layer of snow, creating a bank of monstrous, thick-ribbed icicles along the eaves. The street lamp shines through them, spills a tepid green-tinged light across the bed. The stairs outside become treacherous, mounded with frozen drips. Mark pitches down rock salt, works at the worst spots with his wrecking bar, cringing at the idea of Olivia's feet skidding from under her. Each of the coldest nights, on Whitey's advice, he unstraps the Dodge's battery and hauls it up to the warm kitchen. Next morning, surrounded by a fog of exhaled breath, he reinstalls it and the Dodge shudders to life.

The Conlon Construction crew has moved on to another foundation, framed in the house, the first in a circular cul-de-sac where Fifth extends into the remains of an orchard. In the distance, the lake gives off twists of steam that collect in a dense overstory. Ike has an extra layer of coverall, a fleece hat and oil-stiffened wool gloves. Otherwise, he concedes nothing to the thermometer. He keeps moving, same with Whitey. They've dragged in a kerosene heater, but the fumes are noxious, and it's still cold as hell. "You need some meat on your bones," Ike says. Mark nods. It's not for lack of appetite. He's hungry all the time, eats greedily without gaining mass: meatloaf sandwiches on Linny's black rye, radishes, hunks of Swiss cheese, Toll House cookies, sometimes a couple of Mallo bars in the afternoon, the coconut catching in his teeth.

But seldom a note in his lunchbox these days. Olivia is decidedly quieter. It's not exactly unlike her, but what should he make of it? How's he supposed to react? "You want to see a show, Liv?" he asks. Some nights she accepts. They bundle up and walk the few blocks to the Saxon, or the Wren, directly across Second from the Vagabond. Mark feels a pang, an irritation at the sight of the darkened windows where he used to find such comfort. They watch *The Prisoner of Zenda, The Steel Trap* with Cornel Wilde, *The Happy Time,* which has Charles Boyer and Louis Jourdan. Dull, dull, this last one, but Olivia seems contented, laughs now and then, her hand on his as she takes the Coke. Once they're outside, though, once they're home again, she's the same as she was, prone to long stares, looks he can't quite fathom. Some nights, she moans in her sleep, or seems to gasp for air, sometimes wakes him saying she's had an awful dream, and Mark will find himself out in the kitchen making her cocoa. In the morning, she'll try to explain what disturbed her so, but gives up in frustration. Mark's frustrated, too, without knowing why. Not that he puts any stock in *dreams*. You didn't do that in Audrey Singer's house.

One day, early, he swings by the cafe before work. He knocks at the alley door and Linny admits him, surprised to see him that first time, but not terribly. After that he drops by often.

She leads him into the back kitchen, provides coffee. It's blindingly white in there, but for the wide black door of the oven, and Linny's hair in its sloppy braid, crushed against the back of her neck by the apron strap. She's notoriously slap-dash. Eyeballs the measurements, improvises wantonly. Utensils fly, flour sifts out of the air, dusting every surface. By the time he arrives, the bread dough has risen under white towels, and she's on to the coiled cinnamon rolls. They're enormous, the size of catcher's mitts. Then come the pies: lemon, sour cream raisin, German fudge, one called shoofly. He can't imagine being drawn to Linny, physically excited. Too bony, too smart and full of mockery, he could never keep up with her, he's aware of that. But he does like her company, yes. Finds it surprisingly easy to open up to her.

One of these occasions, he sidles the conversation around to the change in Olivia.

"I wouldn't get too worked up about it," Linny tells him. "She always had her moods."

When Mark looks unpersuaded, Linny says, "Don't you tell me you didn't lap it up. The inscrutable Olivia."

Okay, no argument there.

He says, "It's just she seems kind of *spooked*."

Linny wipes her hands, studies him.

"Maybe that's the wrong word," Mark says.

Linny shrugs, rolls her lip. "No, that's about right."

After a moment, she says, "Losing Mother hit her the worst." Nonchalantly, as if it answers everything. "Helen talks about her all time. *Momma this, Momma that*. It's her way of handling it, I suppose. But you watch how Olivia flinches."

Mark's seen it, that flinch.

"One time Liv got hold of a book where the father runs his car off the road and dies, and she started worrying about Dad getting killed. She didn't want him to go anywhere. She was all in a lather, wouldn't let him out of her sight. Finally, he had to sit her down and tell her he was going to keep on driving the car, he had to get places, didn't he? I don't think Liv had ever spent any time on the idea of his dying before then. Well, and then the funny thing was, it was *Mother*. Goes to show."

What exactly does it go to show? Mark doesn't inquire.

Another morning, Linny says, "I think it terrifies her how much she loves you."

She strides to the cooler for a big crockery pitcher of buttermilk, sticks her little finger in, licks, finds it good. "Olivia's very big on love, as you know. Ascribes wondrous properties to it."

Mark nods, feels the heat begin to pound in his temples.

"So what about *you?*" Linny asks.

"I'm big on love, too, I guess," he hears himself blabbing.

Linny's sidelong glance, *Oh, I just bet you are, Mark.*

Sometimes, at work, he'll notice her handprint on his sleeve, and not remember when she touched him.

The Siberian Steppes

Often there come thaws in January. Despite the rancid look of things, the sodden, branch-strewn yards, relief creeps over people. *This isn't so awful,* they think. *No matter what, it's not that far till spring, just weeks*— But this year, no reprieve. A real old-time winter, people say. When Mark happens to report this to Ike, Ike's eyes narrow, he snorts, "Idiots." He launches a tirade about the Farmers Almanac and the horoscopes in the paper, then at lunch he gets himself worked up over a faith healer named Brother LaMott his wife's been touting. "The meek shall inherit the earth," Ike Conlon says, "and the charlatans shall bilk them out of it. Toot sweet." Venting spleen seems to perk up Ike's disposition. Nonetheless, by mid-February, he, too, has had enough winter, enough trying to keep the crew busy when it's too cold to pour new cellars. They do a quick remodel in town, a basement rec room with wet bar, then he furloughs everyone for a couple of weeks, and takes the Battleship Norma off to Reno.

One gray day, Mark borrows Whitey's truck and fills the bed with stove wood from the ricks behind his father-in-law's, spends the afternoon wedging it into the back hallway of the Vagabond. He kills another morning on the cafe's roof, scraping grease from the exhaust vent with a putty knife. He stands to unkink his knees, performs a slow three-sixty: As far as the eye can see, not a blemish in the cloud cover, not a hint of mountain. Might as well be the Siberian steppes. Down below, he catches sight of Augustus France, world's oldest paper boy, mincing along on his rounds, hair like Spanish moss, pouch the same gray as the snow where a car's sat idling.

Mark retreats indoors, sits drinking coffee, watching people, all the boot-stomping, the sloughing off of coats and headgear. Everyone looks hunched-up, beset.

Celia idles by, bristles the back of his neck.

Mark conveys his low opinion of the day, his overall bewilderment.

"What do you expect, hon?" Celia says. "It's *February*. Here, I got this extra grilled cheese. Eat it, willya?"

Mark accepts the sandwich, chews dully, regarding his fellow citizens, wondering what it would take to make them all happy. Same for everyone? Different? Or maybe they're not even worried about happiness, maybe that's the least of their problems. What does *he* know? He watches his sister-in-law Celia succumb to a jaw-popping yawn, watches her tongue the lipstick off her upper teeth, then go after the last bit with her finger. She catches Mark staring, shoots him a look back. Mark hunts around for something to wipe his greasy hands on. Celia's closer to Olivia than Linny is . . . she's the one he should approach about Olivia, and yet he balks at asking, balks at hearing Celia's take on this fledgling marriage.

Not that he's afraid of what he'd hear, not exactly.

A heavy thud as the bathroom door slams. Nick wanders out of the hallway, blinking, retying the long strings of his apron across his belly. "What're you two plotting?" he says.

"Our escape," Celia answers without missing a beat.

"Yeah?" Nick says.

"Yeah. But keep your voice down, huh?"

Nick shakes his head and sits at the vacant chair. "I don't blame you," he says. "I hear the warden's a real son of a bitch."

"Nah," Celia says. "He's a mushheart."

Nick nods darkly, turns to Mark. "And you're in on this, too?"

Mark says he guesses he is.

Nick gazes off, as if he's looking over the frozen tundra. "That's okay," he says. "You won't get far."

Rapture

The sixth of March, dawn, the sky like shredded linen. The wind's up . . . Mark can hear it, feel it straining at the walls, coming in surges, banging things. The rest of the bed is empty. He waits, thinking Olivia's visiting the bathroom, and when she doesn't return, he calls out softly, then a little more insistently, *"Liv?"*

He finds her in the living room, standing at the window in her nightgown. The birches are thrashing, sheets of water pour from the roof. Six o'clock, and it must be fifty degrees out. He comes up behind Olivia, feels her bottom against his thighs.

She taps the upper window, asks if Mark can get it to open.

He pinches the little pegs at the side, pulls, expecting the sash to be painted shut, swollen with dust and whatnot, but it falls with no resistance.

"Oh, *smell* that," Olivia says, up on tiptoes.

After so long, the smells do seem overpowering. Wet pastures, leaf mulch, meltwater in the ditches. Yeasty, almost sweet . . . if he didn't know better he'd think he was smelling far-off citrus trees.

Olivia turns, eyes ablaze, presents her face to be kissed. He holds her, puts his lips to hers, breaks away, kisses her again, harder. She murmurs something he can't hear in the rush of air.

Later, at work, even Ike seems dazed by the warm wind, this chinook. "The old snow eater," he calls it, kneading the loose flesh under his chin. "Havre one time? Mercury came up fifty degrees in a half hour. Saw that with my very own eyes."

"You ought to hear the dogs out by my place," Whitey says. "You'd think it was the Second Coming."

By midmorning, there's a blinding sheen on everything. Ike squints, riffling through the blueprints as if pages are missing. At noon, Mark slides down against a stud wall and hauls his lunchbox into his lap, enjoying as he always does its gravity the moment before he cracks it open. But today all he finds inside is a quart jar of dill pickles wrapped in one of his white socks.

And the note underneath: *Tell Ike you have to come home.*

He snaps the lunchbox closed, shoots a look at his boss, then Whitey. Ike's legs are splayed, the boots waggling as he bites a spear of ham off the blade of his pocket knife.

"I got to run an errand," Mark says clambering to his feet.

Whitey swallows his coffee pensively. "Nooner," he says.

No way can Mark allow Whitey the pleasure of a response. He wedges the lunchbox under his arm. Ike frowns, digs in his bib pocket for a match, lights a stub of panatela, says not a word.

So Mark bounds down the swaying plank to the fresh mud, eyes lowered against the tumult of light, a stray line of his grandmother's coming to him, *The rapture of the running water* . . .

He parks in front of the house on Ash, stands at the bottom of the stairs looking up the dripping white steps, wondering if their landlady is peeping from behind a curtain, but what if she is? He trots up, two steps at a time, calls out, "Hey," as he bursts inside.

It turns out that Olivia *is* sprawled in bed, sheets at her waist. "Don't you look like something," Mark says.

"Hurry up and get in."

Mark's grinning, almost laughing aloud, as if there's an element of prank about this. Olivia's smiling, too, but it's the oddest smile. Agitated, nothing he's ever quite seen before.

"Come *on,*" she says.

But something holds him back.

Maybe it's Whitey's deadpan shake of the head, as if nothing in the world's the slightest mystery. Or the brightness of the room, or the raw, unabashed way she's staring at him, wanting him. Or something else, some unidentifiable reticence, shyness.

"This is our time, Mark," Olivia says, and it's only now he comprehends what's expected of him.

"How do you know?"

She just does.

He stands flexing his hands . . . they're sticky with oil from the nail keg, the calluses feel like globs of hardened glue. "I'm, I don't know," he says. "I'm all—"

Olivia sits up in the bed unbelieving, shakes back her hair. "You can't say no, Mark."

"I'm *not*," Mark says. "It's just that tonight would be . . . nicer."

"We're supposed to *keep* doing it," Olivia says. "Now, tonight, tomorrow morning. You're a lucky dog."

He stands gaping at the plenitude of his wife's chest. If he's ever engaged in a stranger conversation, he can't think when.

"I gotta get back, Livvie," he says, and hearing how lame that sounds, adds, "I told Ike I just had to pick up something."

Olivia snaps, "No, you just had to drop something off."

It's so unlike her, a joke like this. Mark laughs in relief, they both do, cagerly. But Olivia's face goes slack before his does. Her eyes search the bunched-up sheets. Mark reaches over, touches her cheek with his knuckles. "I'll be back before you know it, honest," he says and slips away.

He pauses outside the kitchen, wondering how rude it would be, under the circumstances, to grab something from the refrigerator. For all this, he's starving . . . by quitting time he'll be stupid with hunger. But he leaves empty-handed, delicately shuts the door at the top of the landing, takes a step toward the Dodge, stops and thinks there must be something better to say, more assurance to give. He gets as far as the doorknob before thinking, *Well, no, just let it lie*— He sucks in a breath, looks out over the roofs of downtown, the furious facets of light, starts down the stairs again, misses the first step and pitches headlong. Falling, he has just time to think, *And no bag of doughnuts.*

Useless

He's awake for most of it, the stitching of his forehead, the setting of his ankle. Later, there's a wallop of morphine, and he drifts, not sure exactly what *has* happened, what he's done.

Then Linny and Celia and Olivia are at his bedside, the twilight glancing off the sleeves of their dresses. "And Jill came tumbling after," Linny is saying, and he must be all right, for they're laughing. The sounds carom around in his head as if he's inside a waste barrel.

Celia kisses two fingers and touches them to the air above his head, above the bandage that's obscuring his vision, then she and Linny troop down the hall to smoke, and he's left with Olivia. The good feeling she's gotten from being with her sisters lingers awhile, slowly fades.

He doesn't ask what she said about his being home in the middle of the day. She doesn't volunteer it.

He says, "Ike know?"

Olivia nods.

Soon it's dark. He drifts again, wakes alone. In the morning he hurts everywhere.

By the day he leaves the hospital, the wind has died, the air moves in lazy swirls, filled with birdsong. He climbs the stairs, Olivia to one side, the railing to the other. The apartment lacks a couch, but there's a big green stuffed chair and ottoman, so he settles into this with a stack of old *Looks,* his head not so foggy now, the wailing in his ankle replaced by a pulsing ache, along with the sensation that if he puts any weight on it, it will shatter.

"Why don't you go work your lunch shift," he says. "I can get by."

A moment's hesitation, then Olivia says all right, she will. Promises to be back by two-thirty. Quarter-of at the latest.

He hears the door slap, picks through magazines for a minute. Pictures of waterfowl, a big fire in New Orleans, a piece on shipping in the St. Lawrence Seaway. Nothing holds his attention. He should be at work. He hobbles into the bathroom to empty his bladder, inspects his eye in the mirror. The white is bloody, the lid plumlike. He stares down at Olivia's things, her hair-clotted brush, the atomizers with their blue rubber balls, the crusted wads of cotton and tiny rolled-up tubes of salve. Suddenly, he undergoes a moment of something awful, keener than pain. A remoteness, a blankness. He drops to the edge of the tub and grabs on.

What he couldn't believe—sprawled upside down at the bottom of the stairs, foot wedged fast between the steps and composition-shingled wall of the house, the inside of his skull erupting with white light—what amazed him, and jolts him freshly now, is that he couldn't just bounce back to his feet and resume his day.

It's after three before Olivia returns. Her cheeks are flushed, her fingers icy.

"You *walked?*"

Olivia strips off her scarf. "What can I get you?" she asks.

"Nothing, I guess."

She spins away. He hears her making noises in the kitchen. A spoon on a bowl. After a while, he's aware that the sounds have stopped.

One of them will have to be the first to say something, and he doesn't mind if it's him. He's not so full of pride and stubbornness he couldn't manage that. He thumps down the hall, says, "Liv, you know we could still do it, what you wanted." Says jokingly, "You'd have to promise to take it easy on me."

"No, too late," Olivia responds, her voice stonily resolute.

Mark offers nothing in return.

That night, he sleeps in the chair, his leg on pillows. He wakes shivering, blankets off. There's music coming up through the floor, a great tide of strings, rising and falling, rising again. But faint, as if strained through a layer of earth.

In a week, he can negotiate the stairs, but still can't put enough pressure on his left foot to operate the Dodge's stiff clutch pedal. The sidewalk in front of the apartment is dry, the snow berm along the boulevard reduced to slivers of sooty, pitted ice. The Vagabond's too far, four blocks down, three over, but some afternoons he hikes to the corner store, where they sell sodas, sits outside on a slatted bench watching the traffic, the packs of school kids slamming in and out, ringing the bell atop the door. One day Mrs. Kovaric marches by in her long coat. A tall, fierce woman, a face out of a daguerreotype. Olivia pays the rent every month, so Mark's hardly given her any close attention. He almost stands now, almost falls in beside her to ask about the music he heard. It seems too intimate a question. He lets her go on alone.

Eventually, he has Olivia drive him out to where Ike's working. A misty rain is falling. Whitey's truck is sunk to its hubs in muck. A zigzag line of planks runs out from the house, but they're slick and he'll never make it in the cast. While he's considering this setback, he notices there's a new boy on the crew, wobbling under the weight of a long two-by-ten. Thin as a broom straw, with a cloth cap and two jug-handle ears.

In a minute, Ike slogs over to the car, bends to Mark's window.

"Who's that?" Mark asks, nodding toward the new recruit.

Ike glares at Mark, says, "You didn't think I was going to hold your job for you?"

He waits for Mark to look stricken, to act as if the ground's gone out from under him, before letting his face down, laughing darkly. "Naw, Christ," Ike says. "That's my cousin's kid. He's useless."

A Stream of Blackbirds

Olivia has a talent for thinking about things that are beyond thinking about. For instance: Who is it they didn't make the day of the chinook?

Better, in Mark's opinion, to ask questions that have answers. Such as: What if they never make love again? As Ike Conlon says, you don't have to be off square by much to screw up everything down the line.

March passes, the evenings stretch out, loiter pleasingly. Celia blows in after supper one night, decked out in black capris, a man's button-down shirt with the tails untucked, patent leather belt cinching her middle, shoes that show off lacquered toenails, coral pink.

"How you doin', Superman?" she asks Mark.

Mark puts out his arms, mimes leaping into space.

Celia slings a canvas bag off her shoulder and extracts a chess board. A dime-store set, backgammon on the flip side. "I was thinking you could give me a little lesson," she says.

It occurs to Mark he hasn't played at all since he's been married, not once. Olivia doesn't care for games, cards, Monopoly, finds the rules arbitrary, takes losing too much to heart. All but charades, which they sometimes play at the house on McLaren Road, and which Olivia's surprisingly good at. Totally absorbed, transformed . . . where Mark remains stubbornly self-conscious, clumsy.

"So who's the new guy?" Olivia asks.

"Wouldn't *you* like to know," Celia answers. "Actually, he's very nice. Staying at the hotel." She looks back and forth between them, says, "Well, I can't have him thinking I'm a moron."

"We wouldn't want that," Olivia says.

Mark balances the board atop the green ottoman, apologizes for being rusty. Celia sits cross-legged on the floor and he talks her through a few games, explains some common openings. After a while, he lets her play without commenting. She fingers the wooden pieces, calls them her guys, her brave little warriors. Her moves are almost brilliant in their daffiness, and every time she leans forward, she bathes Mark in her musky perfume. Across the room, Olivia's returned to her library book. He hears the cellophane crinkle, the pages flip, sees her foot bobbing out of the corner of his eye.

Moments at a time, he's virtually at peace.

Another night, Helen and a girlfriend drop by on their way to the tennis courts. She blesses his cast with the racquet, tells him to hurry up and heal.

"I'm hurrying," Mark says.

Then it's Linny who comes, toting a sack of Ballantine Ales, wearing the opener on a lanyard hanging inside her shirt. She retrieves it, pops the caps with a flourish. It seems she's had one or two already. She and Mark and Olivia gossip back and forth. Outside, the twilight dissolves into evening.

Linny slouches in her chair, long bare arms slung over her head. "This place," she says after a silence. "I have *got* to get out of here."

"For where?" Mark asks.

Linny's cock-eyed laugh. "God if I know. *Points unknown.*"

"You wouldn't leave Dad high and dry," Olivia says. "I know you wouldn't."

Linny shrugs, says, "Dad's a big boy." She reaches for another ale, finds the bag empty, makes a clown's sorrowful face.

In none of these visits can Mark detect any chastisement, any doubting looks from the sisters, so Olivia's said nothing, for which he is grateful in his bones.

Tonight, he insists on walking Linny down to the sidewalk. The ankle's stronger, he says. Plus, he gets to feeling cooped up, needs to move.

Once they're outside, the two of them, Mark says, "You really *going?*"

Linny's voice, subdued, "I sure as hell hope so, kiddo."

Mark desperately wants to keep her there a minute. Linny must sense this, because she takes out another smoke, tips her shoulders against the fluted column of the streetlight.

Mark waits for a car to drive by, for the quiet to sift around them once more. "If a woman's fertile," he asks, and to his great surprise isn't a hundred percent mortified. "If she's fertile, how long exactly until she's fertile *again?*"

Bless her, Linny's of no mind to make him pay for his ignorance, for the ungainly way he's put this. She studies him languidly, touches his forearm, says simply, "It's not exact, Mark. It's not always the same down to the minute. But twenty-eight days."

"Twenty-eight," he says.

"*Yes,*" Linny says. "Yes, Mark," her eyes drifting, shutting.

By now, Mark and his wife are back to sleeping in the bed together. Mark beside the open window, wearing boxer shorts, his shoulders bare. Olivia's in a pale flannel gown that stops at her knees.

A night passes, another night.

Then it's the third of April, 1953, a Friday. All morning while Olivia's at work, Mark thinks: What if she moves away to the cool part of the bed, what if she just plain *lies there,* just suffers his hand on her? What if she says, "You had your chance"? Deadly thoughts. He shoves them aside. Later, they're back. He shuns them again. After lunch, he hauls a chair onto the porch roof, the *veranda,* and sits in the almost-warm sunlight, dull-headed. Chunky, white-bottomed clouds float by. He begins to picture Olivia rounding the corner, bursting into their alley. Face radiant, hair flying out behind like a stream of blackbirds. He watches the way he used to watch the window of the Vagabond for her, his heart buoyant, uncontainable.

Long minutes.

He thinks: *Now . . . now . . .* convinced he can make her appear. When she doesn't, he abruptly stands, spilling the chair. He feels stupid, sick, remembers the wave of disconsolation that struck him as he walked uptown the night they'd had Nick to supper. Only then does he hear footsteps behind him, inside the apartment, only then does he realize she's taken the long way.

At supper he picks at his food, tastes nothing. He's jumpy, nerved-up. At one point, leaning in the doorway to the kitchen, watching Olivia lift their plates from the suds, he almost asks, "Liv, are things right with us or not?" Instead, he says, "It's funny, when I'm not working it doesn't feel like a Friday. Doesn't feel like anything."

No reply from Olivia.

A minute later, he says, "Wouldn't you like to go out?"

"Where?" she asks, eyes on the dishwater.

"I don't know. Just a drive. We haven't done that in ages. Wouldn't you like that?" He pictures them bumping across the knobby boards of the Old Steel Bridge, low sun spiking between the girders. Below, on the river bank, driftwood fires, people fishing.

Olivia hangs up the apron, goes to find a sweater, but just as they're out the door, the phone rings. One of the sisters, Celia most likely, judging from the sound of Olivia's voice, "Can't you tell him . . . no, I understand, but can't you tell him that—"

Mark waits outside on the landing.

Ten minutes, another ten.

By the time she's finished, the sunlight's all but gone and the evening's turned breezy, chilly. It seems pointless to go driving around in the dark.

Later, when it's time for bed, Mark dawdles in the bathroom, runs the razor over his face, inspects his teeth in the mirror, his tongue, his nails, waiting until he's sure Olivia is under the covers. He flicks off the lights, checks the door, sniffs at the burners on the stove, listens for Mrs. Kovaric's record player. Nothing, nothing. Finally, he walks stocking-footed into the bedroom, yanks off his shirt and sits half-dressed on the edge of their mattress.

He doesn't move for so long Olivia says, *"Mark—?"*

Without having meant to, he starts explaining about his day. The vigil on the roof, his failure to make her materialize. The queasy, desolate way he felt.

"But I didn't know you'd be looking for me," Olivia says, reasonably enough.

"I know you didn't."

"How can you blame me then?"

"I'm *not* blaming you. That's not it at all. What I'm trying to say is, you could make something out of it, you could read into it, if your mind worked that way." He doesn't wait for her to object, hurries on, "But the only part I care about is how much I *wanted* you to come. I couldn't stand it."

A rustle of sheets. Olivia's arm drapes around him from behind, her face settles against his shoulder, skin on skin. "Is that true?" she asks.

"Of course," Mark says.

"You're positive?"

He says, "I don't want you thinking you made a mistake with me."

"I don't."

"Sometimes it seems like it," Mark says.

How difficult, this first year of marriage, for Olivia to admit confusion, to admit that life is only the way it is.

Her hand rises to his cheek, to his lips. Mark lets them go slack, lets the fingertips explore his teeth, back and forth.

"Don't you want to get in?" she asks.

Yes, he does. He does.

TWO

AUTUMN 1960

Helen's Dance Card

After the fiery summer they've had, the valley's air clogged with dust and smoke, the sunsets lurid, it would make sense if the autumn that finally comes is fierce and abrupt, as if the year's supply of fuel had been exhausted. That's not what happens. The season turns like the ending of a single day, growing slowly cooler, darker.

Helen has taken to staying at the Vagabond after Nick goes home. She scrubs around the grill where he missed, checks the greens in the cooler, gathers up the grubby aprons and wipe rags and stuffs them into a laundry bag, sets the thermostat for the night, then sits at the counter under a single light and reads the paper. She has grown into a mannish young woman, twenty-four next month, slim-hipped, hard-muscled through the shoulders and upper arms. Though she's the one ginger-haired sister, her eyebrows are thick, black as unsweetened chocolate. Her bangs stand out from her scalp like the bristles of a brush. She has no boyfriend, no burning interest in one. It may have crossed minds to wonder if Helen likes boys, men, at all, but it's not that.

With Linny gone to California these last years, Olivia and now Celia married, Helen's the only one left at home on McLaren Road. She and Nick have fallen into a quiet partnership. When she arrives later to start his dinner, he'll ask what took so damn long, he was starting to wonder. She'll touch her cheek to his, give her standard answer, "Just getting things set for tomorrow." Nick will nod, unable to summon up any reproach. This is Helen, after all, the one he's never lost a night's sleep over.

So it's a day in late October, the afternoon about finished, a gusty wind kicking through Second Street, flapping awnings, lofting grit and doughnut papers into the air. Ivy leaves shoot off the Vagabond's outer wall like sparks from a grinding wheel. Helen's never one to sit around ruminating. Even at this hour, when she craves a short rest, sitting's a challenge. Her left hand opens and closes as she reads. Kennedy's people still sparring with Nixon over a fifth debate. Patrice Lumumba under custody of U.N. troops in Léopoldville. A monkey slated to ride a satellite around the earth . . . for an instant, a chimp's wincing face appears in her mind's eye. Tuesday's *Evening Record,* she reads it straight through, front to back, the brevities, the want ads, lingering over the obits. The short ones are a cheat. Born, died, service under the direction of. Celia says she's got a morbid streak, but Helen shrugs. She's only curious, respectful. In the longer notices you see the whole life, quirks of circumstance, paths taken. Some she scissors out and pastes in a notebook at home. Frederick Munter. Elijah Hodsdon. Mirabel Zahrobsky, an artist's model. Even Celia doesn't know about this.

When she's done she drops the paper in the bin by the wood-stove, makes her final inspection. The truth is, she hates to leave the Vagabond, hates to think of it deserted for the night.

Collapse setting in. Vacancy.

Tonight, she's scheduled to baby-sit for Olivia. Last fall, Mark moved his family into a powder blue ranch house off Paxson Road, which they're buying from his boss. Olivia is good about not asking too often, so Helen generally says yes. She likes the boy, Davey, who has Mark's good looks, his natural sweetness, but there's something about the girl that puts her off. A small cold version of Olivia, wouldn't sleep more than two hours at a stretch for the first eighteen months, and even now she frets, her good moods as fragile as new ice. Helen scoops a handful of candy corns from the bowl by the till and drops them into her sweater pocket, hopes Olivia won't complain about her doling them out to the kids.

Beyond that, as Celia might say, nothing's on her dance card. She's a constant goad, Celia: "Aren't you sick of this, hon? Don't you want anything *else?*" Helen insists she's fine, really, the current arrangement happens to suit her. She's not bored in the slightest. She likes having Nick to herself. Likes her routine, likes falling asleep exhausted and not waking in the night. Likes that nine times out of ten the world behaves the way you expect it to. And when the light shifts and you see down into the heart of things, she likes that, too. There's no point in forcing such moments, in renouncing the ordinary life they disturb. Nor any point trying to explain this to Celia. *Olivia* would know exactly what she was talking about, but it would embarrass Helen to say it aloud. Helen, who's never credited with deep thought.

At last, reluctantly, she picks the truck keys off the hook, slings the apron bag over her shoulder and heads out the back hall.

Before she reaches the door, it opens. Helen says, "Sorry, we're closed."

It's a woman's figure in the doorway, scarf-bound head outlined against the fading light of the alley. "Cool your jets," this intruder says. "It's *me.*"

And so, with no more pomp than this, the legendary eldest Stavros girl again sets foot in the Vagabond. Helen's not the type to wrap anybody in a hug, but instinctively she touches Linny on the sleeve, squeezes until she can feel Linny's muscle firm in response.

"I was just going home," Helen manages.

Linny slips past her into the darkened cafe. Helen turns and follows.

"God, am I *bushed*," Linny says, undoing half dollar-size buttons down the front of her coat. But the cafe's already chilly and she leaves it on, showing a sliver of rayon dress, maroon, cordovan.

Few tasks daunt Helen, yet she's never had an easy time talking to Linny, one to one. Feels dull-witted, naive . . . a ten-year-old girl who lost her mother.

"But you're all right—?" Helen asks.

"It's just I've been driving since the middle of the night," Linny says. "Think you could put on some coffee?"

"Oh, sure," Helen says. She hesitates, though. "I've got to fix Dad his supper," she says. "I guess I could *call* him, or why don't we just go home?"

But it seems Linny doesn't want to leave the cafe, doesn't want to see people, not just yet.

Helen's not sure how to take this. She backs off, studies her sister, says, stalling, "I can't believe it's you."

"In the flesh, kiddo."

Helen sees about the coffee, keeps her head down until the machine has begun to gurgle.

At last, she turns back to Linny and says, "No one thought you'd skip the wedding."

She catches the look in Linny's eye, the momentary blankness: *What wedding?*

So it was true she never got her mail.

Celia's marriage had come up without much warning. *Sweet Jesus, why wait,* that's always been Celia's general attitude. They'd called Linny repeatedly, sent letters. Nick wasn't about to stew over Linny, not in public, but he fooled no one. Celia managed to convince him her sister was simply holding out to make the grand, last-second entrance. Maybe a new lover in tow. "Yeah, that's about right," Nick said. "Can't you just picture it." The wedding was in late August, a spectacularly hot afternoon, relieved by a three-minute cloudburst that danced on the flagstones. When Linny didn't show, Celia made a fine display of lambasting her in absentia. How else to stay on top of the day's mood, to keep everybody laughing? Nick put the best face on it he could, went around blotting his head with a folded handkerchief, telling the girls how nice they looked in their dresses. Only Olivia seemed truly out of joint. "I can't *believe* her," she griped to Helen. "Of all the thoughtless stunts."

Linny sinks onto one of the Vagabond's wobbly stools, stretches her long torso to snag an ashtray, asks, "It wasn't you got married, was it?"

"*No.*"

"Dad then. Some young thing sink her claws in him?"

"You know who it was," Helen says. But Linny's smiling that elusive, lopsided smile of hers, shaking her head, and Helen can't help but join in.

"Wonders never cease," Linny says.

Royalty

A six-pound roast of lamb, rubbed with rosemary, garlic, lemon. Hubbard squash from the Skonnards across the road. Nick's pole beans from the deep freeze. Olivia brings a relish tray, Celia a cheesecake dripping with caramel. Nobody lets

Linny lift a finger. They station her at the far end of the table like visiting royalty, slip her a goblet of burgundy. Nick runs the carving knife through the sharpener, *shoop, shoop,* eyes his firstborn through the archway . . . Linny taking in the chaos over the rim of her glass, sipping, saying naught. What a piece of work. Her hair's flat black, like primer paint, cropped brutally short, shortest haircut he's ever seen on a woman, outside of a magazine. Makes her neck seem a foot long, her mouth wide and lethal. Plus, her earlobes are pierced, ornamented with silver hoops you could stick your hand through.

Those years when she was just out of school, he'd be prowling the downstairs, sleepless, sciatic nerve howling, and he'd find Linny in the kitchen, fingers adrum, feet splayed on a chair. Two in the morning, three. The lank black bangs, the look he knew down in his marrow, for they were simpatico, harbored the same grave suspicions about the world behind the world. "You ought to be in bed," Nick would tell her. *Yeah? Me and who else?* She'd do him a gaudy French inhale. Nick would succumb to milk and brandy. She'd tell him anything, Linny. *I was creaming my pants* . . . Jesus, she could be crude. But he was done trying to clamp down on her, none of that mattered any longer. Pretty soon they'd be choking with laughter. Even after Grace was gone and Linny started running the bakery . . . there were mornings they staggered in to work like a pair of giddy zombies.

Precious few laughs available in those days.

Helen slams the oven door, jockeys the roast onto a platter and Nick carries it out. "Everybody siddown," he announces.

When the table fills in around her, Linny acts embarrassed by the trouble she's put them to. Oh, but greatly relieved, too, don't think Nick can't read that through her camouflage. That she's still worth it, still worth making exceptions for.

To her left sits Thomas Balfour, Celia's prize. Rather an elegant, long-faced man, an antique dealer and appraiser. He's considerably older than she, middle-aged, the only one of the men wearing a coat and tie. He lifts his glass to Linny, looks her straight in the eye, says what a pleasure it is to finally know the remaining sister. Calls her Evangeline. No one else would, but somehow it strikes the right note of ceremony.

"And here's to you, Thomas," Linny fires back. "I hope you know what you're in for."

"He knows *enough*," Celia says. "And don't you go blabbing. Loose lips sink ships."

Thomas smiles. Not a guy who surprises easily, Nick's come to believe, unless it's the astonishment of having latched onto Celia. His first wife was killed in a famous train wreck, a trestle collapse that sent a string of Pullman cars into a tributary of the Ohio River. It was in all the papers. He and Elinor were childless, a fact he mentions with regret, though not so often you doubt him. What a turnaround for Celia, after her luck with men. Look at how they're always touching, on the hand, the shoulder, how she comes up behind him on the sofa, cranes over and plants her lips on his big dome of forehead. Goes, *mwah*, gets away with it.

"We certainly missed you at the wedding," Thomas says.

No one's digging into *that* can of worms, not at the table certainly, but Thomas's tone is reproachless. "You're staying on awhile?" he asks.

Linny's been cagey thus far, deflects direct inquiry with that throaty laugh of hers. She tells Thomas, "My plans are fluid," waggling her empty wineglass.

Gallantly, Thomas refills it.

Nick observes these proceedings from the opposite end of the table. Saws at his lamb without comment, scowls at the mint jelly as it comes by, vile stuff. Helen's at his right shoulder, and across from Helen are Olivia and the kids and then Mark.

Amelia's still in a high chair, and she looks ornery tonight, too, eyes wild and red-rimmed, nose chapped from constant wiping. Olivia's hardly taken a bite, attending her, retrieving the stubby spoon from the rug again and again.

"Come on, honey," she tells Amelia, "keep it on your plate, I *mean* it."

After Davey's birth, Olivia gradually thinned down, as Grace always had, but it's obvious the twenty-five pounds from Amelia are lodged there intractably. Olivia's the one who seems a throwback to earlier generations, the one who got the Stavros face, *Full Moon over the Peloponnese,* Nick used to call it when she was little. All attractive women, his daughters, even Helen with her abrupt, tomboyish features, but only Olivia would you be tempted to call beautiful. Now her face looks swollen, she complains. Boneless, slitty-eyed. "Ah, don't be so damn hard on yourself, sweetheart," Nick tells her. She doesn't listen. Makeup's no help, she says, says Mark swears it makes no difference to *him,* but she doesn't believe it, and who wants to look like that, like a sow? Other times, just *having* a body seems a bother to Olivia, a distraction from important things, matters of the spirit. His thirdborn. Loyal, proud, easily offended, the daughter reputed to love him most intensely. Of course, Nick plays no favorites, refuses to choose. Even so, isn't there another who has access to the blackest chambers of his heart?

Celia's been recounting a rather involved story at her older sister's expense, her foray into acting, senior year. Linny and her pal Wendy Ochs, two vamps on five-inch heels. The infamous cast party. Linny soaks it all up, tolerant, amused, but Nick catches the look she flicks Celia at a certain point, and Celia breaks off, exercises discretion.

"You ever hear from Wendy?" she asks after a moment. "I used to see her around."

Nick did, too, saw her downtown. He recalls the sauntery toed-out walk, the unruly laugh. Always wanted to be a night-club singer, wanted people to adore her. He remembers Grace wondering how good an influence Wendy was, and him telling her, "Yeah, that's what her folks are wondering about *Lin*."

"She still owns the house," Linny says. "Her dad died a couple winters ago. Old Otto, dropped over in the snow. She comes back once in a while. Takes the rest cure."

If it nettles anyone that Linny's contacted Wendy Ochs, when she's so nonchalant, so derelict about staying in touch with *them*, no one says a word.

Keep it light.

But, for the most part, Linny's silent this evening, falls back on her ploy of getting others to talk. Listens to Celia's new husband, chin on her fists: *I'm all ears, Thomas.* She even brightens Mark Singer up. When she catches Nick staring, she makes a face at him as if to say, *Ain't I a marvel?*

And his own fleeting, mock-grudging look in return, *I'll give you that.*

Helen clears the table, serves the kids strawberry ice cream, brings the coffee around. Mark wolfs down a second whopping wedge of Celia's cheesecake. Nick says no, Christ, you want me to explode, then has some anyway. He tips back in the chair, belly like a globe of the world, surveys his riches before they scatter.

The Singers are first to leave, Amelia riding on her father's hip. Nick gives Olivia a squeeze as she exits through the vestibule, says his good night, but she's exhausted, pulls away. Celia and Thomas go next, and finally Helen's lured downtown by Linny, who's gotten her second wind. "Don't stay out late, huh?" Nick almost says, an old reflex. Linny kisses her fingertips, presents her hand to the air. When he's alone again, Nick slips on a jacket and steps into the yard. A misty night, fog rolling among the spruce trees. He lights a cigar, leans against a rick of larch rounds, smoking.

There's something he hasn't said, something he means to take up with everyone, but why spoil Linny's dinner with it? Some weeks ago, the Vagabond received a rare visit from G. K. Alt, who owns the furniture store to the north of the cafe. Alt eats at the Sperry Hotel, as do his salesmen. Thirty years he and Nick have run their businesses tooth by jowl, and Alt's barely had a word for him, even at Grace's passing, which could not have escaped his attention. His brother's an officer at the Cripps Bank, his cousin a fixture in the legislature. The building around the far corner of Alt's once housed the law offices of Shirtliff & Boggs, but they've erected quarters at the lower end of Montana, nearer the courthouse. Alt snapped up the old building, leveled a portion of it, built his store a new entrance, laid down blacktop for parking. And it turns out that Alt owns the vacant lot where Wilfred Espy's barber shop once stood.

Now he wants the Vagabond.

Nick shooed him off. But, not long afterward, Alt's lawyer, Fred Terrell, stopped by and tendered Nick an offer.

Nick refused it outright. "He needs space so bad why doesn't he go out and build on the highway. It's just *my* space he wants. You know the trouble with people like Alt, they want it all."

Terrell smiled indulgently. "Give it some thought," he said. "You'll do that, won't you?"

Nick shooed him off, too. But he'd be back. And, after that would come visits from the health inspector, the fire marshall.

Screw them each and every one.

Yet, maybe he *does* want to get out of the business. Not a thought he can cosy up to. He elbows it away. Later it's back, tugging at his sleeve.

What would he do then? What about *Helen?*

He bends, spits.

It's been thirty-six years since he and Grace parted company with the city of Chicago, the miserable muggy summer of 1924. She had only her mother to worry about, Nick his seven brothers and sisters, a battery of cousins, barrel-chested old Stavros uncles, aunts of surpassing rectitude and nosiness. Nick had been driving truck for his Uncle Cato, fetching soiled linen, delivering clean. He hated every minute of it. Cato's mouth stank of rotting molars, his son was a nincompoop, abysmally lazy and vice-ridden by Cato's own admission, but would, in any case, take over the business. Nick's own father was a meat cutter, employed by one of the other brothers. Sweet, people acknowledged, but not so gifted with ambition, with self-interest. Nothing like Nick's grandfather, the old Athenian, who was a complex man—educated, restless and sharp-tongued, had a lust for American commerce, didn't start off in the muck and ooze below the bottom rung of the ladder, where the common run of Greeks found themselves, the Ionians, the Macedonians who were only good for lifting crates. Nick and his own father got on all right, but he favored the daughters, had little to offer Nick or his brother Pete beyond the occasional baffled smile, the bland injunction, *Go see what your mother needs.* Which strain would surface in himself, Nick was left to wonder, chronically, the father's or the grandfather's.

By that summer, Nick had Grace beside him saying, *Let's just vamoose, then. Why don't we?* What about Mrs. Fraleigh, Grace's mother? No, you had to hand it to her, she threw no net over them. *It's not me you need to be thinking about, you two. Go if you want, I mean it.* A raucous, free-thinking soul, loved a joke. Nick sees some of her in Linny and Celia, regrets her early demise. In the wrong place she was: beside the plate-glass window of the Carthage Delicatessen when a gas main blew. To this day, Nick recalls the shock of this news, then the subsequent shock of learning that she'd taken out life insurance, naming Nick and Grace. It was what allowed them to build the house on McLaren Road.

Still, when you think about it, isn't it amazing they ever made the break? Family legend says it was a sweet August evening when he and Grace impulsively laid over in Stillwater, Montana, instead of pressing on to Seattle's King Street Station. Hazy, alfalfa-scented air, crickets. All day, they'd been watching the mountains approach, a blue mirage rising from the rolling plains. They passed into it at last, with a visceral thrill. Grace was possessed of an intuition, she said. Nick was ridiculously in love, loath to argue with his new wife's currents of foreknowledge, because otherwise she was down-to-earth, no defender of nonsense. Wildly freckled, her features severe, implacable, a tall woman, more striking than pretty. Nick barely came up to her eyebrows . . . but in bed she'd ask him, "Are you my big bull, Nickie?" What a thing to remember. So there they were in Stillwater, surrounded by luggage. "I don't know," Nick said, "this place looks like it's *asleep*. How you supposed to make a living?" Everywhere he turned, Germans, Scandinavians, no one who looked remotely like Nick Stavros. "You think they're going to just welcome us with open arms, these people?" The whole thing struck him as foolhardy, an invitation to get kicked in the seat of the pants. "Fear not," Grace said. Within the week, they'd bummed a ride to Sperry, the next town to the south, and happened onto jobs.

The Vagabond Cafe was operated by a man named Cecil Jordan. Trim and spectacled, with a bow tie and a shock of prematurely ashen hair, he was perhaps fifty-two when they first met him. The story that's survived says Jordan, being a man without family, took a shine to Grace and Nick, found them hard-working, stalwart, took Nick for a man he could talk to, could trust without reservation, not your run-of-the-mill, feckless young bumpkin who'd never seen a goddamned thing. Nick did his best not to disillusion the man. He and Grace rented an airy upstairs room on Dakota. Grace set out pots of geraniums along the stone sill, made curtains from bedsheets. "We doing the right thing?" Nick kept asking her. "We could keep moving, you know. It's a big country."

Grace told him not to *think* so much.

"But are you happy?" Nick asked. "I want you to be happy."

"Nick, I'm happy," Grace said. "Trust me."

All right, he trusted her. What choice did he have?

So Grace learned to bake, Nick how to be a grill man, how to order produce, how to not be conned, who to watch out for. After several seasons of apprenticeship, Jordan suddenly offered to let them buy him out, gave a generous price, offered to carry the paper. By then, Grace was pregnant with Linny. Two more years and Celia arrived, the same autumn the stock market fell. An exquisite time to be running a business. And yet, Montana's economy hadn't been rosy for ages, and people still had to eat, did they not?

All this is fact, but family legend is selective, neglects to mention that Cecil Jordan had been in love with Grace. Irrevocably, privately. In his politics, a vitriolic man . . . Nick would see him go steely with rage at what he called the big-money interests, the bigots and hypocrites who had the country by the balls . . . an anger that undergirded the Vagabond's reputation as a harbor to strays, a reputation Nick's taken pains to preserve. Yet, in his personal life, Jordan was richly circumspect, gentlemanly. After the sale, he resettled in Great Falls, ran a boarding house for retired railroad men. Nick and Grace would get a picture postcard of the Missouri River now and then. Nick tacked them up by the phone. *Thinking fondly of you both*. He's long deceased, since before the war. Cancer of the larynx, a miserable way to go, in Nick's opinion.

"You better drive over there and see him before it's too late," Grace told Nick, and Nick, though he quailed at the thought, went. Jordan's voice box had been removed, and it was only then, reduced to what speech he could produce by gulping air and expelling it in the approximate shape of words, that Jordan revealed his feelings for Grace. Nick should have been aghast, probably. But, somehow, he put aside the questions that churned to mind: how much she'd known about all this, whether Jordan's lips had ever touched her, and if there'd been an incident, or incidents, how she'd resolved the situation without his ever suspecting. So Nick understood, at last, the truth behind Jordan's departure from Sperry. He looked the man in his cloudy eyes, felt himself convulse with an uneasy gratitude.

What could he give back but Grace? He began to describe the pregnancy currently in progress . . . Helen this was, the last daughter, though he didn't know it yet. Frankly and without embarrassment, he told Jordan how remarkable Grace looked when she was carrying a child, how it stirred him up to watch her undress. The third and fourth months when she swelled and glowed and made unusual requests of him. He'd never revealed this to a soul. Probably the last thing on earth you'd want to get into with a dying man, but not in this case, Nick felt.

"He was bad, wasn't he?" Grace asked on his return.

Nick shook his head. "*Bad*. I don't think he can eat much anymore."

Grace seldom wept—when she did it tended to be in frustration, not sadness, *I've done everything I can do, Nick* . . . She didn't weep now. She had a slack, drifting look. He could see her biting down on the flesh inside her cheek.

"He asked after you," Nick said. "I said you were good."

Grace came and lay her chin on the meat of his shoulder.

"I told him about the baby," he said, and let it go at that.

Two months later, a call to the Vagabond from one of Jordan's tenants.

Nick hacks, spits again.

The cigar tastes hot, rancid. He stubs it on the end of a log, squeezes the tip, drops it in his jacket pocket. He's got no excuse to be outside in the raw air now, but for a while he doesn't budge. Feels like a night ghosts are about, if you believe in that sort of thing, which Nick Stavros most certainly doesn't, not for one instant.

Ah, buck up, he tells himself, *Nothing's wrong with* you.

And Linny's home.

Balfours

The fog is worse in the low, marshy ground near the lake. Thomas switches to low beams, slows to a creep. The Thunderbird has bucket seats, which prevent Celia from burying her face against him, but she does the next best thing, leans his way, rubs his neck, bristling the hairs at his collar.

"So what'd you think of my sister?"

"Oh, I liked her," Thomas says diplomatically.

"Yeah, well, don't like her *too* much."

She can feel him smiling in the dark. God, she loves this man.

"She didn't seem all that offbeat," he says. "The hair maybe. Plus the fact I had no idea what she was thinking."

"Uh huh," Celia says.

She's the only one who's seen the big-city version of Linny firsthand, having visited her in San Francisco the spring of 1956. And again, less agreeably, the following year. Linny was

waitressing at a restaurant called Lago Maggiore, a few streets
north of Chinatown. Family-style tables, odd paraphernalia
hanging from the ceiling. Banners and model airplanes, doll
heads of papier-mâché. After work, she took Celia to the
clubs, where they met her friend Claude, an Algerian who
loved American jazz. He played piano himself, or maybe he
was a bassist, was that it? Linny had a splash of some sauce on
the front of her blouse. "You are *wounded*," Claude said,
stanching it with almond-colored fingers.

"Throw my ashes off the bridge," Linny said. She made
Celia and Claude promise.

Then Claude told a story about a man who was scattering
his lover's ashes into the sea when a wave swept him to his
death. This was followed by a long discussion of whether or
not the event was tragic, or only blind chance. Linny weighed
in on the side of random catastrophe. But was it true, Celia
wanted to know. "You made it up, didn't you?" She was a little
drunk by now.

"No, I swear it," Claude said, feigning innocence. His
accent was thick as brambles. After a while, he told Celia he
knew someone, a friend, would she be interested?

"I don't know, sure—" Celia answered. "Why not?"

Linny laughed helplessly. Celia could always make her
laugh, since girlhood she could. A little clowning, a little cau-
tion flung to the wind. You use the tools you have. The friend
never materialized, but others joined the table. When the band
broke, the party went outside, split, reformed, strolled through
a gumbo of night smells, ducked into other clubs. Squawky, jit-
tery music. None of this was Celia's style—she'd have preferred the heat and spark of southern California, or the desert,
Las Vegas, but the idea of carrying on with Linny, riding about
in cabs in the middle of the night, yes, it was suitably thrilling.

Misery in the morning, that, too. "Here, have some
codeine," Linny said. Celia took a slug, but she never minded

hangovers that much. They made her feel she'd wrung the good out of a night. Linny's apartment was up under the eaves of a row house, the light mercifully subdued. In the afternoon, they hiked down to the bus. Everyone they passed was Chinese, old women with parcels, resolutely climbing the steep, pebbly sidewalks.

Linny said she was going to start taking classes. Some screwy mix of subjects, accounting and poetry, human relations. Wasn't going to spend the rest of her life with a tray on her shoulder.

But the next time Celia came, she got the impression that Linny hadn't exactly been expecting her. The apartment looked untended, things were stuffed in boxes as if she were moving, though she denied it. And she'd quit the restaurant, or perhaps been fired.

"You're not out of money, are you?" Celia asked.

Linny wouldn't discuss it, which had to mean she was flat broke. *Celia* had money, she'd been saving for weeks. She'd broken off with another boyfriend, and this one she'd had real hopes for. She was in the strangest way, moved through her days in a cloud of euphoria and dread. All the way from Montana she'd envisioned another wild time with Linny, let herself concoct a daydream about living with her. The first five minutes vanquished that.

"Well, look, hon," Celia said, "take what I have. It's a couple hundred."

Linny refused.

"At least clue me in?"

She didn't expect Linny to divulge much. Linny was vastly better at hearing confession than darkening the air with her own. Linny shook her head. She looked beat, disgusted with herself.

Celia soldiered on, asked if Linny was still seeing Claude.

Oh no, she'd never been "seeing" Claude, he was just a

friend. Hadn't Celia known he was a homosexual? Anyway, he'd been deported months ago.

"Somebody else then?"

No answer to that.

Celia tried her best cajoling.

"No," Linny said mirthlessly. "Not seeing anyone else. Not at present."

Celia asked, "Should I just *go?* Is that what you want?"

"Well, now Christ, you don't have to do that," Linny said.

But Celia stayed only another day, rode home in a deep funk. Whatever arrangement had fallen through for Linny, Celia never learned of it. But let it be said: She never blew Linny's cover, never countered the upbeat evasions Linny salted her letters to Nick and the sisters with.

Anyone can have a down time. Who knows that better than Celia?

Abruptly, out of the fog, the canted signpost that says BAL-FOURS. Thomas steers down the lane, stops before the main shed, where he stores pieces that need work. Regluing, lacquering. This had been his Aunt Caro's place, a log house on a slight rise, the flats at the head of the lake stretching out behind, crazy with shore birds. He'd intended to sell it and move away. Then he'd met Celia Stavros.

"Give us a kiss," she says.

Thomas complies. His fingers are dry and cool on the planes of her face. She loves kissing him. The balance point between patience and urgency. "Let's stay out here and neck all night," she says. Thomas humors her, though warm rooms await them.

But, following him up the walk in the damp air, she thinks of Linny again: *It was all up to me tonight, up to me to take her back. Could have made her pay, didn't.*

It's this gratitude she has from living with Thomas, it spills over.

Here It Is November

One Saturday when Olivia and the kids are in town, Mark straps on his toolbelt, hauls out the extension ladder and climbs to the roof. Months ago, he added a pair of dormers to the attic, turning it into a room for Davey, so they could finally move Amelia into one of her own. But he never got the siding on, or the windows caulked, and here it is November. The day's cool and still, the mountains starkly dusted to four thousand feet. His head swims with numbers . . . there's ten days before the property tax goes delinquent, the Chevrolet needs a clutch and shocks, he has a twenty and a five stuffed away for Olivia's Christmas, but no idea what to buy. Last time, he bought earrings at Schwantes's downtown, squares of ripply sterling, classy he thought, but after the first week she never wore them, preferred the old ones apparently. Too often these days he feels cheap, small. He tells himself, forget it, concentrate on what you're doing. Moments at a time, this works.

A creek wanders past the back of their mongrel property. On the far side lies a salvage yard surrounded by a ten-foot wire fence. An acre of abandoned machinery. Davey's fiercely attracted to the place. Evenings, Mark has to walk him down to where a bouncy plank crosses the water, then they slip through a seam in the fence and the boy's in seventh heaven. Truck frames, pontoons, enormous gear sprockets, the bucket of a steam shovel, nameless fabrications of old metal . . . they look as if they've risen out of the ground. Davey goes after them with his horseshoe magnet. Iron, not iron. Olivia doesn't want him playing in there, but what the hell, it's fascinating.

Just don't bring him back here with his head split open.

I'm always with him, Olivia. I'm watching him, for Christ's sake.

Sometimes her worry over the kids strikes Mark as extreme, an indulgence. Other times, they seem to irritate her, having them always be there. Not that Mark questions her love for them, or *him,* for that matter. She's loving, she's responsible. It's just she acts kind of disoriented sometimes, acts surprised that getting what she most wanted hasn't freed her from the pursuit of happiness.

This house on Paxson Road isn't one of Ike's. Far too cramped and shoddy to be a Conlon house. No, it came Ike's way in a defaulted deal, and he's been closemouthed as to the particulars, so Mark's never decided which motive had the upper hand: giving them a boost or unloading the place. In any event, owning a house, even *this* house with its woes, gives Mark an unholy thrill. Along the property line to the east, four strands of wire on white ceramic insulators, fencing in the neighbors' nonexistent horse. A crab apple tree leans over it. Now that the leaves are gone, the apples seem to glow in the flat light. They keep catching Mark's eye, sending him into a stare.

It's too cold for the caulk to work right, even squeezing two-handed. Should've warmed it in the damn oven. He sits back on his heels, pondering his next move, and now the caulking gun tumbles from his hand. He's startled to hear a yelp from below, squints over the roof's edge and sees his eldest sister-in-law standing in the grass.

Twirling the caulker like a six-shooter.

Mark climbs down.

"And where's the fam?" Linny asks.

"Penney's, to the best of my knowledge."

Linny's been back a month now. She helps at the Vagabond, taking the odd shift, as if for her own amusement. After she'd left Sperry, Nick hired a woman to bake for the cafe, a Mrs.

Hunkala, who was actually, according to Nick, a hell of a lot more faithful to Grace's old recipes than Linny had ever been, but she'd lasted barely a year. After her, two others came and went, and now the Vagabond buys its breads and pastries from a commercial bakery. But the subject of Linny reclaiming her job doesn't arise, and nobody pushes. Is this a visit, a permanent homecoming, a rest cure like Wendy Ochs's? No one's gotten much out of her. Celia's jokey wheedling hasn't worked, nor Olivia's sober-faced implication that Linny owed them an explanation for being incommunicado, nor have Helen's straightforward inquiries, "Is anything *wrong*, Lin?"

"I'm absolutely terrific," Linny insists. "Never better."

Today she's in corduroy slacks and a black sweater. Walking has rouged her face, and her spirits *do* seem good. In any case, Mark's not about to pry. That would be the way to learn what there was to learn: Don't ask.

"I'm interrupting you," she says.

Mark casts a look back up at his work and suddenly it seems laughable.

He shrugs, says, "Some mansion."

Linny lets it pass.

"What do you make of old Thomas?" she asks.

"He's okay," Mark says, fearful Linny's already sniffed out a fatal weakness in the man. Actually, Mark likes him fine, admires his easy way with people, his generosity. A few Sundays ago he showed up here with his truck, unannounced, delivering a walnut bed frame for Amelia. A sleigh bed. "I know she's not ready for it yet," Thomas said, "but she'll like it when she's a bit older." Olivia thought they should offer to pay him, seemed slightly annoyed . . . she could be like that, proud about money. Thomas gently refused. It was a piece of his aunt's, he wanted them to have it. There are lessons to be learned from watching Thomas, Mark has come to believe.

"Must have been the wedding of the century," Linny says.

"Yeah, it was pretty amazing," Mark says. "And sweltering, *man*."

"Always hot when the Stavros girls get married."

Mark smiles at this. "So far," he says.

They stand talking in his backyard a few minutes longer, a kind of loose banter. Finally, Mark thinks to ask if Linny *wanted* anything, if there's a message for Olivia.

"Oh, nothing special. I was just a little—" She shrugs. "Stir-crazy, I guess."

Her old crowd's dispersed, Mark knows. Married, drifted off. If she means to stay in Sperry she'll have to start fresh.

But she won't stay, he thinks. Not a chance.

She refuses his offer of coffee. "Another time," Mark says.

"Sure, another time."

Then Mark's on the roof once more. He cuts a length of batten, taps it in place, pulls a finish nail from between his lips. He looks up and sees Linny striding away against the field grass. When he remembers to look up again, moments later, she's gone.

Heaven

An evening out, but when it comes time to get ready, Olivia is still feeding Amelia, and Mark discovers there's no sitter lined up—apparently, Olivia never intended to go. "Thanks for telling me, Liv," he's about to complain, but thinks better of it. She'll just say she doesn't feel sociable, she'll just narrow her eyes at him. Why isn't he more *observant?* His hands slap to his sides, he pivots, leaves the kitchen, showers, the hot water interrupted only briefly by Olivia running the tap. When he appears again in the kitchen door, she says he looks very nice, and his irritation founders.

"So I'm just squiring your sisters," he says, as if it's burdensome, not the pleasure it is.

"Your reward will be in heaven," Olivia says. A reply she often gives, nothing to take seriously, though with Olivia it's hard to tell. Lately, she's been going to the Covenant Church with new friends from up the road, the Watnes, Sonja and Fred. Sonja has a twitchy, submissive look. She and Olivia seem to get along, but Mark's never received a bit of warmth from her. Fred's the pushy, sanctimonious type, works for one of the electrical wholesalers . . . Olivia seems to think that since both men are in the trades they have lots in common. One evening last summer the Singers walked up to Sonja and Fred's for a cookout, and Fred made them all join hands around the creaky picnic table so he could say a blessing, and used the occasion to slip in a jab at his older boy: *And Heavenly Father, let Scotty keep his hands off his little brother.* Mark's been to the Covenant Church a few times. The place gives him the willies. The blue plywood walls, the folding chairs that keep you from getting comfortable. But it's not that, the austerity, it's how everyone digs at you, *Are you one of us, Mark? Have you asked Jesus into your heart,* how much time they waste on whether you're in their club or not. Lately, Olivia's quit bugging him to come. A relief, but also, in a way, a worry.

Mark bends and kisses his wife on the forehead. "I'd just as soon have it here," he says. "My reward."

He turns to his daughter, who smells of egg custard, kisses her, too. He walks outside and hollers to his son. Davey's tossing chunks of shale into the creek. Not lobbing them like bombs, nor winding up and pitching, but flicking them with his wrist as if they were darts. Mark pictures a pyramid of stones accumulating on the silty creek bottom. "Building your own bridge?" he inquires.

The boy stops for a second, tries to gauge if his father's serious, takes in Mark's dress-up clothes.

"Your uncle Thomas got us tickets to a concert," Mark explains, pantomimes a fiddle player, tells Davey he'll see him in the A.M.

The boy offers a little cupped-hand wave he probably should have outgrown by now.

Nick is spared tonight's proceedings—he's east of the mountains with Ike Conlon. One autumn in the mid-fifties, Ike asked Mark to ask his father-in-law if he'd care to come deer hunting with him. Other than duck season, which he honored irregularly, Nick hadn't been out since before Grace's death. Ike owned a cabin on the Musselshell, out by Ryegate. "Jesus, I don't know," Nick said. "That's a hell of a ways to go to shoot something." But Mark could see he was teetering, and contributed the nudge. Every year since, they've gone, Ike and Nick and another old cohort of Ike's named Berton Fuchs. Mark's not invited, not that he expects to be. Besides shooting birds a few times with Nick, he doesn't hunt, never acquired the taste. Still, he wouldn't mind being able to say no thanks.

When he pulls into the long gravel drive at 412 McLaren Road, the lights are ablaze. Helen's waiting outside, bareheaded, squinting at the clouds. A drizzle's starting to coat his windshield. She slides in, giving off a pleasant soapy scent, says, "Guess who's running late."

"We're okay," Mark answers. Driving over, a good mood has descended on him for no particular reason. They sit waiting, playing the radio. Brenda Lee, the Everly Brothers, "Cathy's Clown." Then "Running Bear."

Helen says, "That's icky, that song."

"You're kidding, you don't like it?" Mark's teasing, hoping

to lure a smile from her. "Poor old Running Bear," he says mournfully, "off into the Great Beyond."

Of course, Helen's right, it's a weeper. The radio's full of them these days.

"Give her a *honk,* will you."

Mark waits a moment longer, leans on the horn, and Linny finally lopes down the walk, her overcoat trailing its belt.

"Scoot over," she tells Helen, and Helen slips over next to Mark, and off they go, three across in the Chevrolet.

Ordinarily, concerts are held in the big auditorium at the high school, but a play's in progress there, so tonight's affair was booked into the Saxon downtown, the oldest of the movie houses, refurbished this past summer. Scrollwork replastered, new carpet with camellias, garish new paint job.

Though it's after eight, the lobby's still ajostle with people. Linny wades fearlessly in, calls back over her shoulder, "Like a fox farm in here."

What can Mark do but laugh?

There's Thomas down front, waving them to their seats. They squeeze in, Helen first, then Linny, and Mark on the aisle for the leg room, though now that he notices, Linny's legs are every inch as long as his. Celia catches his eye, mouths over, "Livvie get a better offer?" Mark shrugs, mouths back, "Tough day, I guess . . . the kids."

Then robust applause as the soloist emerges from the wings, a short, wan figure with bulging cummerbund. Chin aloft, he waits for silence, announces the first piece in an accent Mark can't pin down . . . must be Dutch, to guess from the name, Vandenbos.

"A tour of the sticks," Linny whispers. "What a treat."

But Mark detects no sign of contempt, condescension toward the citizens of Sperry. The man fits the instrument to the flesh of his jowl, his eyes fall shut, and the air explodes with notes.

Mark lays his head back, lets his gaze rise to the ceiling. A firmament of iridescent blue, spattered with gold stars, so shameless it sends a shiver whistling through him, or maybe it's only the Tchaikovsky. Despite the soaps that played all day in his grandmother's house, she possessed a great rack of phonograph records, thick vinyl recordings that came in the mail. "Your father said this stuff gave him a migraine, so I quit listening to it when he was around. Wasn't worth the aggravation," she told Mark when he was twelve or thirteen. "But now I'm going to enjoy myself. You'll just have to suffer through it, Marco." And so it reminds him of winter nights on East Sixth Street, snow ticking the windows, reminds him of falling asleep determined not to be the kind of man Morgan Singer was. And he can't help thinking, too, of the Ash Street apartment, Mrs. Kovaric downstairs with her hi-fi, and the bizarre way she died. Choked on a chicken bone the year Amelia was born. Olivia had been the one to find her—she'd gone down with the month's rent, spotted their landlady's lisle-clad legs through the kitchen curtain. She and Mark skipped the service. Olivia was big and pregnant at the time, and they'd barely known the woman. It hadn't even occurred to them to go, really. But it's funny, the mood he's in tonight, he wonders why, feels a spurt of shame.

After the Tchaikovsky, a dance suite, some Aaron Copland.

At the break, Celia dashes off to stand in line outside the women's room, and before Mark can get a word with him, Thomas is swallowed up by friends, older men, their wives . . . Mark's out of his league there, and instinctively he backs off. He notices Linny head outdoors under the marquee to smoke, Helen at her side. He follows. The rain's a steady blur, five degrees colder and the air would be clotted with snow.

Linny says, "What do you say we run and get a drink." She sticks a hand over her head and darts into the rain. Mark and

Helen splash along behind. Around the corner, and into a dim slot of a bar called Churchill's. All sooty stucco and cross beams, portraiture of bulldogs.

Linny orders herself a scotch, beer for the other two. Collapses at a table as if they've made it through a typhoon.

"Well, this joint hasn't changed one whit," she says.

Mark nods affably. He's never set foot in Churchill's before tonight.

Helen drinks her beer off as if it's orangeade, blots her mouth on her wrist, says, "We ought to get back."

But Linny's just lit another smoke, and there's no rushing her. Helen waits half a minute, says, "I'm going."

Linny answers, "Okay, we'll be right behind you, kiddo."

Once Helen's gone, Linny shucks the coat off her shoulders, asks Mark if he'd mind getting them another.

Waiting at the bar, he takes a leisurely glance at his sister-in-law. Plum-colored dress, cut high on the arm. She's resting on her elbows, one hand hidden in the opposite sleeve, a pose he's seen in a picture somewhere: Woman lost in thought, absently shielding her chest. Of course, Linny has her clothes on, and unlike Olivia doesn't have much chest to shelter. But it's her expanse of neck he finds himself staring at, thinks again of Mrs. Kovaric with the chicken bone lodged in her gullet, as Audrey Singer would put it. Thinks, *Your whole life aimed at that. If you only had a clue . . .* Thinks of what they'd have to say down at the Covenant Church, *Called away to life everlasting.* Mark's instinct is to be reverent, but that gloating sound turns his stomach.

He draws a long slow breath, pays for the drinks, eases himself down to the table again, says, "There you go."

Linny smiles, sips.

"Do I seem any different?" she asks abruptly.

"How do you mean?"

When she doesn't elaborate, he volunteers, "Not really."

Such a surprise when Linny says something straight.

"I have to trust you to tell me," she says.

"I don't know if I'm the right one to ask."

She shakes her head, lays her hand atop his. "How can you be so sweet?" she says.

"I'm not," Mark tries to say. "I'm—"

"*What?*"

Just as unsettled beneath the surface as you. But he knows that doesn't begin to be true. Still, he's not the docile work-horse she thinks he is, is he?

Old Wreck

Not for the first time, Olivia remarks that the life she lived as a girl orbited securely around her father. How could she fly off into oblivion with Nick Stavros as her anchor? "But for Mark," she says, "there was just, well, a vacuum."

Mrs. Singer listens, Olivia's voice fading in and out like a radio signal. She sees Olivia check whether this last comment has given offense, but Mark's grandmother lets her off the hook. None intended, none taken. Over time, they've grown easy with each other without becoming terribly close, Audrey and Olivia, the two Mrs. Singers. It no longer matters that Mark's grandmother wished he hadn't leapt headlong into marriage, that she viewed Olivia as the instigator, that the girl's devotion to Mark seemed almost *peculiar,* too single-minded to be entirely real. All water under the bridge. She's grown used to Olivia's overblown way of phrasing things, her streak of earnestness, her expectations. Sometimes they shop together, sometimes drink coffee at Mrs. Singer's, while Amelia plays in a corner of the room inspected for pins.

"Morgan would have been fifty this winter," Mrs. Singer says matter-of-factly.

"Mark barely mentions him," Olivia says. "You can't not remember, I tell him, you were ten. *I remember him fine,* he says, *I just don't think about him. I don't* dwell *on him.* It's not like Mark to be secretive, but I can't believe he doesn't think about him anyway."

Actually, as Audrey Singer is well aware, Mark *can* be rather secretive. Not devious, not calculating like his father, but given to stubborn eddies of thought, oh yes. Doesn't Olivia know this? But as regards her point, Mrs. Singer has to agree. You can see it in everything Mark does, how furiously he's avoiding the site of an old wreck.

What Mark won't reveal about his father, Audrey Singer feeds Olivia in little doses, as the spirit moves. "He was the kind of man who couldn't leave anything be," she says. "He just couldn't turn around and walk away, always had to say that one more thing. Always had to pick at the scab." She tries for candor, for Olivia has every right to know these things, the same as if the Singers had a history of diabetes, heart trouble. She tries, but the instinct to stick up for her wayward son proves too strong. "Now you shouldn't get the wrong picture, Olivia," she says. "He wasn't mean in the sense of being a bully. He just was never at peace. You could look in his eyes and see it. No job was good enough for him, nothing you did for him was the right thing. He was a contrary boy, I'll tell you that."

She talks into the flat gray light of the afternoon, watching her granddaughter-in-law. "Well, thank goodness Mark's cut off another bolt."

"Thank goodness," Olivia says.

The facts surrounding Morgan's death have always been a sticking point for Mark. Olivia says, "When we were first going out he told me his father had been in Tacoma on business and was attacked by a gang of men outside a hotel. I imagined it was a robbery attempt, something of that nature, but after we were married, I got the idea it was more like a bar fight. He said Morgan had been kicked in the head by some soldiers."

"I suppose he was afraid you'd think less of him," Audrey Singer says.

"I wouldn't have done that."

"No, of course not."

Morgan Singer was a big believer in luck, she explains. "He thought he'd used his up, here. He was always talking about moving on, cleaning the slate. Somehow he'd convinced himself they'd hire him at the Navy yard out in Bremerton. He'd only been staying because of Annette. She'd never been anywhere. A sweet girl in some ways, Olivia, but let me tell you, everything was too much for her. She was a little boat in big water. Morgan had been gone several times before this, and she was on me like flypaper: *He's not coming back this time, we're never going to see him again.* Oh, I had to settle her down, believe you me. But the truth was I didn't know what Morgan would do myself. I'd think: Maybe this *is* the time he won't be back."

In the midst of this recitation, a blur darkens the window, becoming the figure of a sheriff's deputy. She has a sudden irrational foreboding, bitter as tar, as if he's come on a terrible errand. The bell over the door sounds, rocks back into silence. But he's only here to pick up the two pair of uniform pants she's let out. Her dressmaking days are mainly gone, still she has her customers, a procession of mending and minor alterations to see to. She's seventy-four, but won't give it up. *What on earth else would I do,* she asks Mark, *sail to Tahiti?*

She comes back to the table, sits heavily. "I always think they've got bad news," she admits. "Even when I know better."

Olivia looks stricken, and says, "Do you know I had the exact same feeling just now. What do you suppose it means?"

"*Means nothing,*" Mrs. Singer answers, perhaps a little too sharply. "It's just your thoughts at work. I wouldn't put the least stock in it."

She reaches for a vanilla wafer, her indulgence, along with the occasional cigarillo, now that she's an old lady. "But you know," she goes on, "that's not how I heard about Morgan at all. It was over the phone. I swear life makes no sense sometimes."

It's nearly time for Olivia to round up Amelia and meet Davey's bus, but she doesn't move yet, so Audrey Singer picks up the thread of her story again. "There was an inquiry, of course, but they never could establish exactly who the villain was. Morgan had been pestering a table of soldiers all night. He'd gotten shoddy treatment over at the shipyard and had to take it out on someone. There were witnesses to that, but nobody would say what happened outside. No charges were ever filed."

She gives Olivia's hand a pat, says, "Can you imagine kicking another human being in the head?"

Olivia says no, she can't.

"I'm sorry Mark has this to think about, not much of a legacy, I'm afraid. But we all have something, don't we?"

"He was about the same age Mark is," Olivia says.

"Is that so?" Audrey Singer says, though this fact hasn't escaped her attention. *If there's a worse mystery than time,* she thinks, *I don't want to know about it.*

Another day, more on Annette. Olivia's mother-in-law, whereabouts unknown. A good-size girl, Audrey Singer says, nearly Morgan's height, buxom, but slope-shouldered, hair bordering on red, never fixed up quite right. Might've been pretty if it weren't for looking scared to death fifty minutes out of the hour. You wanted to take your thumb and smooth down her brow. What had Morgan seen in her? What besides sex, for her talents did seem to lie in that area. Not that she was the sultry, seductive type, no, you wouldn't say that. Audrey Singer's private guess is she liked feeling useful, generous with her body. And perhaps what Morgan liked was calming her, for Mrs. Singer can recall the look of repose that would steal over Annette when Morgan spoke to her: *Annette, let's not be like that, all right? Let's just take it easy now, honey*— Perhaps that was it.

One weekend some months after Morgan's funeral, Annette had sent Mark to stay here at the house on East Sixth. His things were wadded in one pasteboard suitcase. "Oh, she was coming unglued," Mrs. Singer says. "So *distressed* by what had happened to her, didn't recognize her life. As if *I* were a disinterested party. Can you imagine? And Mark never lived with her again, not one single day."

How could that be?

Just was.

During the war, Annette had departed Sperry for Spokane where she had a friend from school. She intended to find work. "Letters arrived once in a while," Mrs. Singer says. "I had to screen them. The last two or three I couldn't show Mark. Had to rip them up. Sad, wandering things. The bizarre promises that woman made."

"And she's never come back," Olivia says. "I just find that very difficult to believe."

I know you do, Mrs. Singer thinks, and she feels a tenderness for Olivia. This girl is nothing like Annette . . . she's good to these children, she's trying, she is.

If the afternoon's conversation has taken a melancholy turn, Mrs. Singer is careful to bring it around at the end. "You be sure to kiss our boy for me, and tell him I wouldn't mind if he stopped by himself," she says as Olivia zips her daughter into her jacket.

Olivia promises.

Alone once more, Mrs. Singer finishes a nasty bit of tailoring she's been avoiding, turns on *The Edge of Night,* though lately the story's gone astray, in her view. This business with the brother-in-law, implausible. Oh, the sofa feels good, but the next show is a bore, and you can't just sit. An invitation to disaster. She turns the set off, goes into the kitchen and inspects the cabbage soup bubbling on the slow burner, splashes in some red wine, has a little herself. The streetlights have come on.

It's always tiring talking with Olivia, picking at people's motives, as if they added up, as if knowing more made you happier. Audrey Singer's own included, her instinct for self-preservation, hard as a bit of gristle.

All evening she's susceptible to memory, and there's no point in shying away . . . only renders it virulent. She conjures up her husband Aaron, withstands his old complaint that she is unmoved by his illness, that she will gladly go on living in his absence. She brings forth Morgan, poor Annette. Has she done right by anyone, she wonders. By *Mark?* Sweet Lord. Has she left him wanting, ravenous for somebody else's noisy family?

Audrey Singer receives these visitors, listens, but only so long.

She takes a glass of vermouth, reads in bed, then sleeps. She wakes once in the dark. Her heart is a steady engine, unfazed by the night's work. It's past seven before she wakes again, plants her feet on the floor, parts the curtains to see what kind of day it is.

Weightless

Mark walks the tire ruts up to the road, his breath chuffing out. It's not truly bitter, a cold you soon adjust to. A few stars to the south, in and out of clouds. He passes their neighbors', a gawky brick place alone in a field. During the fall, he'd sometimes see an old woman working outside in tall rubber boots and watch cap, pruning with long-handled shears, wheeling a cart piled with refuse. He waved once, received the same attention she'd give a passing magpie. Tonight, the house looms like an unrepentant shadow. Head down, he walks along the snow berm where a plow blade has scraped up dirt and rags of grass, reaches the edge of town, turns left into a short street that dead-ends behind Sperry Post and Pole.

And there's Linny's car, the black Morris Minor. Cramped, austere, wrong-side drive, one of the odder specimens you'll see in this town that favors trucks, roomy American sedans. Mark climbs in. He removes his hands from his warm pockets and Linny gives her face for him to kiss. Briefly bares her long neck.

This is the extent of their physical contact, perhaps a minute of kissing, her hand lightly on his leg, for balance. In all honesty, he's not so wild about kissing Olivia anymore. Grown numb to it somehow . . . must be the same for her. They never kiss for the sake of kissing. What would be the point of that? But kissing Linny is something else. Slippery, flavorful, new each time. To look at the two sisters you wouldn't guess this, not in a million years. It makes him squirm, and yet, strangely, endows him with patience, makes him as weightless as the light on waves.

She straightens, her face drifts away. She says, "That was lovely, Mark."

This has been going on a couple of weeks now. Linny acts like it's the most natural thing in the world. She was so funny the first time, *Don't tell me you've never imagined kissing me.* He couldn't just say, *No, actually it never crossed my mind.* So what did he answer, her good-natured brother-in-law, so out of practice in saying other than he means?

Didn't think I'd live so long . . .

And Linny's little nod, as if he'd done considerably better on a quiz than she'd anticipated.

Three-quarters of an hour they drive the back roads, out around Burns Lake, up Orchard Ridge, Linny handling the car with none of Olivia's reserve. She downshifts avidly, slews through the gravelly corners, knees poking up, all the time talking and talking. Mark manages to convince himself this is the point of their meetings, Linny's craving for an audience that's not the sisters.

And he accumulates an earful these nights. He can't keep half of it straight, no longer tries, lets it cascade over him. Begins to recognize names, women she waitressed with, a nurse she knew from somewhere, a pair of hookers . . . and men, Simon, Jack, Claude, whose relationships to her, to each other, confuse him. They've all come from somewhere else, they've assembled there, where ordinary rules of conduct no longer apply. She gives her intinerary through districts of the city, describes a stabbing she witnessed, the kite flyers and jazz players, the pungency of certain narrow twisting stairwells, Santucci's on Columbus Avenue where she buys her biscotti. She breaks off, frowns, says almost sharply, "Why do you let me *run on* like this?"

"No, I like it," Mark says. A true, though partial, answer.

"Well, don't tell me anything of your own."

"Don't worry," he says.

Doesn't say, *There's not that much to tell*.

Sometimes, long silences.

Linny says, "But you get this, don't you, Mark? How I had to go where there was some fucking *life?*" And Mark Singer understands she's been pleading a case from the start. He takes an eerie pleasure at being the one singled out to receive it, though he knows he's only getting a glimpse, a glimmer, knows he's not the final judge of this evidence, only an interested party, a potential ally . . . always the need for allies if you're Linny Stavros. At the same time, increasingly, he's subject to a crushing fear, a horror of his own paltry life. What's he ever done but stay put? Why no commensurate hunger to roll around in the world's dirt? And where have these last few years *gone* . . . you add day on day, you'd think they'd weigh more.

One night, she doubles back into town, pulls into a gash of shadow behind the Park Inn, runs inside for coffee. Waiting, Mark wonders how it looks, him riding with his sister-in-law. But that's stupid, no one sees, and, anyway, it's hardly a crime. Later, dropping him in the cul-de-sac by the pole yard, Linny says, "Thursday?" and he nods. She smiles, ready to be done with him, says blithely, "Good night, Mark." He watches her taillights until they're gone. Across the tracks, the stack at the mill pours out a shaft of steam, stinking of oil and sawdust. He starts home, glad for the air on his face, the bite. He keeps losing his rhythm, scuffing into a trot, as if he had to be somewhere, which he does.

Olivia never questions him when he returns from his walks, thus there's no need to hedge. Most often, she's reading, so he says nothing, hangs up his jacket, looks in on the kids. He listens a moment to Amelia's ragged mouth breathing, climbs to Davey's attic room and turns the light out, stares briefly out his window at the shadows on the snow.

He seldom disturbs Olivia when she has her nose in a book, but now when he asks what it's about, she gives him an odd stare: *Why so curious?*

"It's just a story," she says.

"True?"

Olivia nods. Yes, true. Holds it up for him to see: *Life Under the Pharoahs*, Leonard Cottrell.

When they crawl into bed, Mark doesn't press himself on her, worried she'll ask what's gotten into him all of a sudden. If it comes to pass they *do* make love, it's her idea. The heat is turned back for the night and they're buried under a ton of blankets. In the pitch darkness, Mark claws at them, rakes them to the floor so he can catch his breath. He hears Olivia panting below him, recovering. Not for an instant does he imagine it's Linny.

Ballast

Never fails to surprise Nick, how he slows down in the cold, the stingy hours of daylight. How stubborn his appetite becomes, as if he needed the extra ballast. Middle of the morning, he finds half a salted nut roll in his hand. He parks it on the shelf by the cannister of black pepper before Helen can shoot him a look. Later it's gone and the wrapper's wadded in his pants pocket. By the same token, though, business picks up. The Vagabond's patrons eat with a crazed, glassy-eyed desperation. Every morning he makes a thick cream soup, a cauldron of chili. By two o'clock the pots are soaking in the deep sink. Buttermilk pancakes, oatmeal, towering stacks of cinnamon toast, pecan rolls, double the number of potatoes for mashing, double the gravy . . . custard pies, pudding cake, bricks of fudge brownie. Starch as the antidote to gloom, that was Grace's theory. You're anemic, you crave liver. Same principle: the wisdom of the body. Nick shrugs. *Who the hell knows?* She was always on good terms with her own physical plant, Grace, always raring to go. Her colds never lasted. Her cramps were nothing. No abscessed molars, no impetigo, migraine, pinched nerves in the neck. No arsenal of patent medicines. No seeping malaise. She was blessed with feeling good, and more power to her. In the perverse way of things, doesn't it make a certain sense that it's Nick who's left, Nick with his aching legs, his crabbed thoughts, his searing gut, which nevertheless demands these heavy foods? In Nick's case, however, just stuffing his mouth never did the trick. A black spell would descend on him in November. Not every year, nor always in November, but often enough to make him wary, vigilant. A foretaste of doom collected in the back of his throat, as pungent and recognizable as the smell of the incinerator. His concentration sifted away. A heaviness bore down on his shoulders. "You know what I feel like?" he'd ask his wife. "A hod carrier."

Grace had no patience for malingerers, for people's moods. Her advice: Snap out of it.

"Don't I wish."

"No, you *don't* wish, Nick. You welcome it with open arms, it gives you license."

"The oracle speaks."

"I don't want this rubbing off on the girls."

"Now, Christ, Grace," he said, "it doesn't *rub off* on people. It's either in them or it isn't."

Old grievances. Let them lie, let them lie.

Outside the twin windows of the Vagabond Cafe, another dim bulb of a day in Sperry, Montana, one of a run of days that would scarcely register on a light meter. Late afternoon,

Nick tells Helen he's headed to the bank, worms the deposit pouch into his waistband, grabs his coat. Linny looks up from the back table where she's been idling over a broken-spined paperback. "I'll come," she offers.

"Yeah, okay," Nick tells her.

A listless snow dusting the streets, wisping behind cars. Linny takes his arm, adjusts her stride. "The scarecrow and the bulldog," she says with a twist of the mouth.

Nick snorts, keeps walking.

Upstairs, over the News Agency, a ceiling light coming on, a hand yanking down a paper shade. Figures in hats, upturned collars. A woman parking down the street from the Opera House, walking the length of the block, breaking into a stiff-legged run, purse to her breast, disappearing through the side door of the hotel.

"My, I wonder what *she's* up to," Linny says.

Suddenly, the way his mind operates these days, Nick thinks of an August evening when Grace was alive, the two of them strolling the fairgrounds, Nick in high spirits, his gaze happily going here and there among the summer dresses, and then Grace giving his hip a sharp bump. "I'd kill you," she said.

"Ah, you wouldn't either kill me. That's all hot air."

"I'd disable you, buster."

"I'd take it as a sign of affection," Nick said.

He bought her a cone of shaved ice and syrup. Later, home, she climbed atop him. He had to clamp a hand over her mouth, "You want to wake the whole goddamn neighborhood?" But was she truly jealous, Grace? Nick sometimes alluded to his love life before her tenancy . . . she couldn't have cared less. Apprentice stuff, beneath her concern. It was the Stavros marriage that counted. She promoted it shamelessly, referred to it as one of history's great passions. Nick rolled his eyes to heaven when she talked that way, though he didn't disagree.

Yet, she wasn't a possessive woman, wasn't honeycombed with suspicions, wasn't covetous. A paradox, he thought. It was as if she knew she wouldn't have a long life . . . beneath what she said lay a bedrock of detachment.

Nick can't avoid thinking of Emily Cotton now. She used to frequent the Vagabond, years ago. Grace's age, or slightly younger, but smaller, petite, with hair glossy black except on the left side where she had a streak of white, as if a single incandescent thought had burned a path out of her skull. Sometimes she sat with legs tucked beneath her like a schoolgirl, shoes slid off onto the linoleum. A plain band on her ring finger. Sometimes she was in the company of women Nick knew to be secretaries, often she was alone, but never huddled with a man, to the best of Nick's recollection, so he imagined she was on her own, whatever the reason, the ring perhaps for show. If he wasn't cooking, he might come out and exchange a few words with her, one foot up on the bench seat. He often visited with his customers. Nothing unusual in that. "Mrs. Cotton," he called her and she didn't object. Once he overheard her on the Vagabond's pay phone. Her voice was so playful, generally. Now she seemed to be pleading, begging, "But don't you think you could . . . no, I'm not saying that, I'm not, but I don't see why you couldn't . . . no, that's *cruel,* after what—" When Nick entered the hallway, her forehead was against the plaster. An awkward moment, Nick unable to squeeze past her. "I hope there's no trouble," he said. She opened her hand and put it on his chest, a palm the size of a ginko leaf. "Just an unfortunate . . . situation," she answered. Nick found himself moved to pity, and though pity ordinarily carried no erotic charge for him, he had a fierce urge to take her in his arms, to lift her off the floor. And then what? He'd not been unfaithful to Grace, not remotely, except in the mind's eye . . . and even that, muddled images of female flesh, legs and backsides and breasts, he didn't see how it caused any harm, so long as Grace was the recipient.

"I'm sorry to hear that," Nick said, his voice low.

A week went by, two. When he noticed Mrs. Cotton again at the cafe, he granted her privacy, remained in back tending to things. But soon he started running into her every time he turned around. There she was at the dime store buying beads, at the bus depot where he'd gone to pick up the new motor for one of the ceiling fans. Nick tipped his hat, amused. *We meet again.* One evening he went to a ball game, and she was high up in the stands behind the plate, wearing dark glasses, smoking, sitting alone with her knees crossed. He was sure it was her. He climbed the steps, made his way along the row. "You know any of these boys?" he asked. She said she didn't. "Well, it's too hot to stay indoors," Nick said. Yes, that was true. There was a breeze. "Would you care to sit down?" she asked him. Nick looked around a moment, sat. She told him her father had played on the town team. A shortstop, an excellent base runner. "Here?" Nick asked. No, no, she said, not around here. Nick tore open his bag of peanuts, offered it, shook a few out. All chance encounters these were, yet it did seem peculiar, it did seem as if there was more to it than that. Another night, two or three weeks later, Nick went to a smoker at the Stockholm Club, drank some vodka, shot some nine ball with Albert Sowerwine, but ducked out early, the camaraderie sitting poorly with him for no discernible reason. He left his car on the street and walked down the alley. The air was hot and still, yet cooler against the damp underarms of his shirt than the fetid atmosphere of the Stockholm. Some boys were circling downtown in the back of a truck, whooping and cranking a hand siren. Nick watched them pass. He let himself in the rear of the Vagabond, raised a hand to his evening crew who were closing up. No doubt they were surprised to see him, but never mind that. He went into the little room where he kept the accounts, shut the door. He opened his desk drawer and withdrew the telephone book. It was entirely possible there'd be no listing. But there it was: *Cotton. E.* No address given. It was possible, as well, that the ringing would fall on vacant rooms. Yet, almost at once, she picked up, and if she was surprised to hear from him, Nick couldn't detect it. He apologized for the lateness.

Mrs. Cotton said not to worry about that. She was something of a night owl.

"Ah," Nick said.

He said it was none of his business, but he wondered if her situation had gotten straightened out.

She said it had. She thanked Nick for his concern, asked if he was at home.

"Naw, downtown," Nick said. He tried to reconstruct his intake of vodka, was it only three? He felt clearheaded and spry, but vodka could do that. "Well," he said, "I was just thinking about you, that's all."

"They were good thoughts?"

Nick covered the mouthpiece and cleared his throat. "Tell you the truth," he said, "they were very pleasant."

"They *were.*"

"Yes," Nick said.

He tipped back in his chair, heard the spring groan. His office was windowless and smelled of the rubber slicker hanging behind the door, and of shredded twine and Borax and the gummy flystrip twisting indolently overhead.

"Maybe you should tell me about them," Emily Cotton said.

Nick said he wasn't sure if he could do that.

"Why don't you try."

Nick suppressed a laugh, but it overcame him.

He told her what the blaze of white hair did to him, what furies it loosed. With increasing fearlessness, he described the attack of desire that had struck him in the Vagabond's back hallway, the impulse to hoist her into the air, to engulf her. The momentary illusion of her heels jamming into his back. He supposed she'd either hang up now, revulsed, or else ask if he wanted to come over . . . and how could he do that?

She did neither. She waited a second, as if to see if he was truly done, then said, "All that about me, Nick?"

Nick swiped a hand across the stubble on his neck. "I don't know what I'm saying," he said.

"Oh, I think you do," she told him.

There was a knock on the office door. Nick smothered the phone to his chest and blinked out at his workers, told them to go on ahead, he'd lock up, good night, good night.

To Emily Cotton he said, "I don't want to make more trouble for you."

"You needn't worry about that," Mrs. Cotton said.

How many more of these hour-long calls did they have? Maybe three, spread over weeks? If they left him stirred up and forgetful, Grace took no notice, as far as Nick could tell, and, anyway, this seemed to have nothing to do with her. When he and Mrs. Cotton saw each other, they waved as before, smiled in the manner of acquaintances. Then, all at once, he stopped running into her. The weather had turned early that year . . . maybe she'd left for the winter. Nick made a quiet inquiry or two. Her telephone was no longer in service. It was possible he'd look up one day in spring and spot her in her booth, but when spring did come, laggardly and wet, the river roiling within a foot of flood stage for weeks, the war in Europe eating holes into people's peace of mind, Emily Cotton failed to reappear. Nick dug at himself. *Jesus, what was I thinking.* There was a song on the radio about that time, Rufus

Desmond's "Lost Love." Linny went around crooning it end-lessly, thirteen years old and already ridiculing the plangent chorus . . . *in the last late light of day, I'm thinking of my law-aw-aw-aw-awst luuhv.* "I wish you'd knock that off," Nick barked at her. A mistake, of course. Now all she had to do to get his goat was droop her eyes and soundlessly mouth, *lawst luv.* Nick had no lost loves, not then. He certainly hadn't loved Emily Cotton . . . what he'd known about her wouldn't have filled his breast pocket. He'd lost only the possibility of love, scarcely an embryo of love. Was that anything to go sleepless over? When he had far more than he could ask for in Grace, when the idea of hurting her nauseates him, even now, this very afternoon when Grace is beyond harm? Another paradox. Since his earliest twenties, he'd equated being a man with how much brute contradiction he could stomach. Lately, amazingly, he finds he's sick to death of it.

At Cripps Bank, Nick hands over the Vagabond's deposit, stands yawning while his tally is double-checked. Not even the stern fluorescent tubes overhead are up to the challenge this afternoon. Despite a formidable application of face powder, the teller has sooty, ghoulish crescents beneath her eyes.

Linny tugs at him, whispers, "Let's beat it, huh? C'*mon.*"

So they're out on the street again, Nick sorry he can't con-jure up another errand for the two of them.

How strange Linny's here at all. He won't hazard a guess as to how long before she's off again, or what the flash point will prove to be. In the evenings, they share the sofa. She watches his shows with him, *Naked City, Peter Gunn, 77 Sunset Strip,* or else goes out in her car, or some nights takes off walking, eccentric, beret-headed. Sometimes he ventures a few words, "We don't hear anything for two or three months, I feel like calling the missing persons" . . . but they come out sounding like teasing, like admiration. Linny gives him the palms-up,

That's it, that's the state of things. "It's not like I want to run your life for you," Nick says. "But you could have a little more consideration, you hear what I'm saying?" Oh yes, she hears, and she knows Nick sees past the dodging and playacting, sees her as no one else, but even he's at a loss to say what it is in Linny that's failed to pan out.

They cross at the signal. A few more cars now as the afternoon draws to an end. Cones of light sweeping by. The snow's no heavier, but neither has it quit.

Good Night, Mark

One night Linny's not there.

Mark waits, shifts from foot to foot in the cold. The cottonwoods clatter and whoosh overhead. After a while, headlights sweep into the short street, but before he can step toward them, they veer into a drive and are extinguished. Fifteen more minutes and he gives up. He's relieved in a way. Walking home, he talks to her, says, *I mean, this is lunacy, isn't it?* Says, *I don't know what this is exactly, but I can't keep doing it.* Once he reaches the blacktop, the wind's in his face. The clouds have blown through and the temperature's plummeting. He comes within sight of his house, sees the scraps of exhaust flying from the furnace vent. But by the time he's let himself into the garage, the relief's become irritation, a razory desire to know where the hell she is.

Even in winter, the place stinks of turpentine, wasp spray, bundles of roofing felt. It's gravel-floored, cramped, their junk dangling from spikes. Wading pool, canvas lawn chairs, hose.

The overhead door's so dented it jams in the track and they seldom bother with it. Mark's loitering out here, fists under his armpits, thoughts at a standstill, when Olivia opens the kitchen door and snaps on the light. She looks at him blankly, asks what he's doing.

"Can't leave the Chevy out tonight," he manages.

"Bring it inside, then."

"That's what I'm doing," he says, hoping the keys are in his jeans pocket. Mercifully, they are.

"You want me to help with the door?"

Mark accepts.

The two of them grip it from the bottom. "Don't cut yourself," he says instinctively. Rising, the door makes a hideous wincing sound, somehow worse in the cold, but it curls up far enough for him to sneak the car in, the blue Bel Air that has replaced their old Dodge.

He sheds his jacket in the kitchen. "Look at you," Olivia says. "Your cheeks are like radishes."

"It's so hot in here. What've you got the thermostat on?"

"It's just you've been outside."

Davey appears in the doorway wearing his droopy mukluks. He comes and coils an arm around each of their legs, asks to be read to.

Mark waits a second to see how Olivia will respond, then says, "Okay, run and get the train book."

"No, you come up."

Mark says all right.

The train book is a gift from Davey's Aunt Helen, and it has him enthralled. Glossy photographs by the dozen. There's no story, so gradually Mark has invented names for the trainmen, given them wives, favorite ball teams, six-year-old boys waiting at home. Davey laps it up. One night they paused at the picture of two Great Northern engines, tender, and vast string of boxcars snaking across a wooden trestle. On a whim, Mark said, "Looks like they're *stopped* out there, doesn't it?" Ever since, he's required to have the engineer climb down and stand on the tracks with the wind whistling up his pant legs, the river miles below, a wrinkle of light.

"He's not scared," Davey offers.

"Scared?" Mark answers. "Oh, he's scared. But what can you do? The train doesn't run you get out and walk. And it's *exciting* out there, think of that."

Then adds, "Not that I want *you* walking out on a railroad bridge. Understand?"

He lets the story end there, lets Davey drift off. But one night, still posted by the bed, his own eyes closing, he suddenly sees the face of the man on the trestle and it's Thomas Balfour. Thomas staring into the roiling murk, bare-headed in the rain, weeping.

Tonight when he climbs down from the loft, he's ravenous for some reason, makes for the icebox, tears off a chunk of ham and eats it over the sink. He can hear the water running in the pipes. Olivia's bath. It's only nine-thirty. He pictures himself calling over to Nick's, wonders what the chances of Linny answering are. Slim to none. He's in no frame of mind to trade small talk with Nick, doesn't relish the idea of asking if his eldest girl's at home. More likely, Helen will answer. It's easier to picture talking with her: *This is Mark—I got to ask your sister a quick question, she handy?*

He goes for another bite of ham, finds a piece with some of the crisp glaze, salty and sweet both, cups a handful of water from the tap, wipes his mouth. There's no way Helen would question him, *What about? What kind of question?* Thus, no need to conjure up innocuous business he has with Linny.

Still, what if she does?

He hears Olivia calling him from the bathroom. Waits a

moment to see if she's serious, then goes to her, opens the door on a wall of steam, asks, "What?"

Olivia sunk to her chin in the oily, sparsely bubbled water. "Where's your razor, honey?" she asks.

"What's the matter with yours?"

"I forgot to buy blades."

"I hate it when you use mine," he says. "You never clean it out."

"Just this once," Olivia says. "Could you reach it for me?"

He gets it from the medicine cabinet, gives it over, handle first, like a knife. Olivia sits up, streaming. "You're the one that likes smooth skin," she says.

No rebuttal to that.

He leaves her in the tub. Back in the kitchen, he grabs up the phone, dials, and in the moment it takes to ring, thinks, *What if she's just plain gone?*

But all of this is pointless worry: Linny answers, almost instantly.

"What happened to you?" he asks, then realizing his voice sounds a little frantic, accusatory, backs off, says, "Did I get it wrong, about tonight?"

"I couldn't come," Linny says flatly.

When she doesn't elaborate, Mark asks, "Couldn't or wouldn't?"

"I don't know," Linny says. "Does it matter?"

He considers telling her how it felt to stand out under the rattling trees, but says nothing.

"I've been taking advantage of you," Linny says at last.

"It's okay."

"Well, no," she says. That throwaway laugh. "That's one thing it's not."

He lets this go for now, asks, "Were you going to call me or anything?"

"Look, Mark," she says. "I'll see you in a few days. We'll have a talk."

He hates how that sounds, hates the whole way this call has worked out. Hates that she thinks he's not up to the ambiguity of their situation. And that it may be true.

He hears the gurgle of water exiting the tub, figures he has a minute or two before Olivia reluctantly gives up the tropical atmosphere of the bathroom.

What he should do is tell Linny sure, they'll talk in a few days. However she wants it is fine. Yet he can't resist adding, "I wouldn't come if I didn't want to."

All Linny says is, "Good night, Mark," the same way she does in the car. Jokey, weary, private.

Later, under the covers, Olivia's body lends its heat to the bed. He associates the way she smells with the word *jasmine*, but has no precise idea what jasmine is or where in the world it derives from. The wind is pouring against the bedroom wall, catching a loose strip of facing at the eaves. Beneath this noise, almost subliminally, he thinks he hears the clunk of his daughter climbing out of bed, waits for the rasp of her door hinge, which fails to come.

He tries to relax, can't.

After a while, Olivia says, "What's the matter, not sleepy?"

"I'm okay," Mark says, "I'll drift off," though his legs are crazy with energy. From her tone he guesses she wants to talk. Many nights, she waits until he's ensconced in bed, his guard down, then expects him to discuss things they didn't discuss earlier, expects him to make decisions. How's Ike been treating him, for example. Maybe Mark should think about going off on his own. Ike had his own crew by the time he was Mark's age. It's complicated, Mark answers, exhausted. But will he give it some thought? Yes, he'll think about it. Lately, she's been agitating for another baby, wants them to be of one mind.

Amelia was such a handful from the start, wouldn't sleep, wanted to nurse all the time, then wouldn't drink . . . Olivia's breasts were constantly raw and infected no matter how careful she was, no matter how she kept them smeared with lanolin. "I can't believe you're hot to do that all over again right away," he says. Olivia answers, "It's been three years. I wanted to have a family, Mark."

Mark asks, "What do you call *this?*"

But tonight, drowsy from the bath, all Olivia says is, "Try not to thrash around, okay, honey?" And when, after a decent interval, he doesn't respond, she says, "Good night, Mark."

Steam

All through the holidays, Mark watches Linny for an indication of her thoughts, rehashes their talk on the phone.

What do you want me to do?

Nothing. I don't want anything.

Yes you do. You do.

No, honestly.

Christmas Eve, Christmas dinner. They're constantly thrown together, but never alone, not for more than a moment or two, and Mark can't bring himself to contrive errands. He's willing to wait. If he waits this may yet prove to be weather that will blow through.

New Year's Day everyone convenes at McLaren Road to watch the Rose Parade. Celia arrives in a long red skirt and ruffled top, makeup toned down to a little blush, faint smudges of color on her lids: Thomas's influence taking hold. She kisses cheeks, bends and gives Davey a balsawood glider, which he sails from the landing halfway up the stairs, sliding

the wings into different positions. There's hot cider, sandwiches cooked under the broiler, the last tray of Helen's
Christmas cookies, stray chunks of fudge, rum balls in pow-
dered sugar. The men stay to watch football. Thomas, Nick,
Mark Singer. The others drift away, Celia and Linny to the
second floor on some mission, Olivia and the kids to the sledding hill by the crescent slough. Helen lugs out the stepladder,
the liquor boxes that store the tree ornaments. No one ever
accused Helen of having an artistic streak, but it's she who's
taken custody of Christmas.

"You like a hand?" Mark asks.

Helen thanks him. No, she'd rather take care of it alone. So
the pine cuttings come down from the archway and mantel, the
creche gets disassembled, the ropes of popcorn and wizened
cranberries are coiled into a bread sack. A few of the oldest
ornaments are left, Grace's. Clear glass balls with pastel
stripes, heavy in the hand, some with the wire hooks Nick
made during the war when you couldn't buy hangers. Helen
treats them like soap bubbles.

Mark's never been one to lay in and watch football by the
hour, not when he could be out doing something. Seems child-
ish, wasteful, yet today he's grateful for it, relieved to be in the
older men's company. They see part of a lackluster Sugar Bowl
game, then the Rose Bowl, Washington–Minnesota. Nick nods
off in the third quarter, snores like a slow bellows. Thomas
seems to know all about the Huskies, points players out to
Mark, claps his hands on his corduroys, says, "Wasn't that
sweet, oh my." Oddly, Mark finds himself caring, rooting. Nor
does the Irish creme hurt. He and Thomas have been dosing
their coffee with it all afternoon. By the time the game ends,
Mark's in the strangest way.

Jazzed, ethereal, fearless.

Celia and Thomas have one last party on the docket and she

manages, in low tones, to cajole him into action. He gives Mark a smile, thanks him for his companionship.

Mark says, "You, too."

At last, Nick stirs, blinks at the empty chairs, runs a hand down his face, says, "I sleep a year?"

"Let's get you some *air*," Helen says. She coaxes him upright, furnishes his coat and muffler. The day has faded. It's not snowing, but it's that kind of light.

Mark watches them go, trying to remember if he was supposed to catch a ride home, or what?

After a moment, Linny appears in her bathrobe, barefoot, hair wet and combed back in wide furrows. "Everyone clear out of Dodge?" she asks.

"Appears that way."

Linny backhands a yawn, scuffs away.

Mark assumes she's in the kitchen, but hears nothing. Eventually, he goes to see. Past the stacked boxes, the pine boughs heaped on the carpet. Then upstairs, where he has only on rare occasions ever been, and never while Olivia still lived at home.

Linny's in the room she used to share with Celia, now a spare room. The beds have chenille spreads, watery blue with flowers that show up gray in the thin light. Linny's sitting on the edge of the one nearest the window, looking out. Mark stands a moment, then sits beside her. The bed frame offers a mild complaint, accepting his weight.

She won't move until he touches her, he thinks, waits to see if that's correct. He slides his hand inside the robe on the off chance she's wearing something underneath it, feels the flat plane below her collarbone. Her breast is tiny, as he knew it would be. The skin is cool and taut, the nipple like a glass bead.

"How can I do this," he says.

Linny shrugs out of the robe. "Or you could ask how I can."

Not once in his life has he felt such hunger, not as a teenager, nor in the first sanctified days with his wife. He is all over Linny, and she him. When he is almost done, she knows it, and pulls away abruptly, just long enough to confuse him, then crams him into her mouth. Nothing in his life has prepared him for this. Then he is bucking and falling against the headboard.

It's marginally darker when he's next aware of the world.

"Nick and Helen," he says out loud.

Linny rolls herself off his chest and quietly sits up. "They're either here or not here," she says.

Mark recognizes the icy wisdom in this, gathers himself together without succumbing to a frantic scramble for shirt and shoes.

"Kiss," Linny says.

Mark kneels and touches his lips to the salty skin of her breastbone. Then he is out in the upper hallway, and down the staircase, empty-handed, not the least alibi on his tongue.

Nick's house is nearly dark.

Mark switches on a table lamp, then the white fluorescent ring in the kitchen ceiling, then the porch light. He jams his arms into the sleeves of his overcoat, lays a hand on the newel post, wondering if he can keep himself from sprinting back up to the second floor. A moment later, the back door opens and his father-in-law stomps in, picking bristles of ice off his mustache. Helen's right behind him.

"Still here?" she asks.

"I was waiting for Liv," he says. "I guess they went straight home."

"I'll give you a lift."

"No thanks," Mark says, ducking out. "I'll be fine."

It's the better part of two miles, and he hasn't got a hat, but he sets off at a lope, pictures his head giving off steam.

Elephants

The house they're building: perched on a grassy ridge south of Sperry, now snow-covered, licked up into frozen waves, the road bladed through the scant topsoil into gravel, nine switchbacks. There's been just enough thawing and freezing to give it a treacherous glaze. Whitey's acquired an old Willys, four-wheel drive, but has to chain up anyway. It's dark when he honks outside Mark's place on Paxson Road, still dark when they stop at the bottom of the new driveway and set out the chains, a royal pain, another affront to the working stiff in Whitey's eyes, this bruiser of a house atop the hill. Above it all, looking down. Where do some people get their money? The owner, Norman Sibley, is from out East, retired already in his late forties, Whitey's age, or semiretired, does something in banking, stocks, investment capital. All you know about the owners is what you hear. How they look nosing about the worksite, how the wives act.

"You'd rather be out of a job?" Mark says.

Whitey doesn't honor this with a reply, other than a quick exhalation, a wipe of his nose with the back of his glove before tromping on the gas, charging up the incline, the cleats biting, grabbing. He's given up on Mark, Mark's absence of politics, his blindness, but on some other level they get along, it seems. Mark's hung in there, hasn't whined, been overtly stupid. It's true his good nature is more than Whitey can abide some days, but that's increasingly rare, and, without knowing precisely when, Mark has passed out of his apprenticeship. It's not clear if he and Whitey are friends. They *work* together, two hundred fifty-some days a year, and it's not as if Whitey clams up around him, you know what's eating Whitey, and there've been times they stopped at Vanek's or the Diamond T on the way home, escaping the chaff-hazy summer sun for as long as it takes to drink one, maybe two cans of Rainier, but the idea of them doing something together on the weekend, taking his boat out, for instance, or of Whitey dropping by the house for supper, it's barely imaginable. So maybe they're not exactly friends, and maybe this doesn't much matter.

The house *is* big, no question it's the largest thing Ike Conlon's ever built, the largest private residence. The front is all glass, a bank of custom-made windows, facing the lower valley, the river snaking toward the lake, its earlier channels sloughs now, diked oxbows, bright reedy water with thick stands of cottonwood in the centers, and farther out, the Swan Range, poking directly up from the valley floor. Better, according to the Sibleys, to have the afternoon sun reflected and not straight in your eyes. Behind this glass is a cathedral ceiling, twenty-eight feet at the apex. By now, like the rest of the builders, Ike's abandoned rock lath and plaster for Sheetrock. He contracts out the mud work, and the tapers have choice words to say about this place, not only the height but the eccentric jutting angles. Diabolical. There's a loft off this big room, a balcony reached by stairs spiraling around a knobby shaft of ponderosa pine. The one tree on the ridge before the bulldozer arrived, and now it stands in roughly its old spot, minus bark and limbs, rubbed with several gallons of tung oil supplied by Mrs. Sibley.

The end of this mammoth room is all fireplace, the opening big enough to do jumping jacks in, something out of an English castle, a terrific heat waster. Not that it matters with baseboard heating all around, nor is this fireplace made of brick or slabs of local shale, but cobbles of igneous rock, river stones, handpicked every last one, Whitey insists. You can't rule anything out with these people. Two groaning dumptruck loads, hauled up to the ridge back in the fall. There's another fireplace in the master bedroom, and one in the kitchen, more modest, so in all three chimneys rise above the steep pitch of the roof. Octagonal terra-cotta tiles for the kitchen floor and two of the bathrooms, stacked in the foyer, waiting, in the way. And the garage: four bays, a shop, another set of guest quarters upstairs, full bath. So far it's just a slab covered by VisQueen weighted with rocks. Below the house site, where there'd been a slight plateau, the bulldozer has carved a wide bench, and into it a hundred-foot gouge that will become a pond. Grassy-banked, cattails, morning mist, oversize goldfish, which Whitey says are nothing but carp. *Carpus delicti,* he cackles. Mark can't help laughing. But it looks ruinous now, the dirt clotted, frozen in raw clumps, the boulders resting askew, gashed by the cat's blade.

Whitey negotiates the last switchback, the front tires bucking, stuttering, then pulls up in the rutted drive. No one's around yet. He douses the lights, leaves the engine running, digs the Thermos from under his seat and doles out coffee. It's windy out, not bitter cold, but dead gray, the first light meager, grudging. That's another thing about Whitey, he's a real java hound, takes it thick, rimed with black scum. It's almost worth leaving the house early, these ten minutes, like lingering under the sheets, warm, his thoughts gliding around lazily in their confinement.

"You heard about that wreck," Whitey says.

Mark nods. It's been in the paper, on the TV news out of Missoula, though the incident happened just west of Sperry. Small plane nosedived into Camas Lake, straight into the ice, like a grosbeak hitting your plate glass. Pilot thought to be completely disoriented, though how could you not know you were flying down, wouldn't you feel the blood in your face, your chest on the straps? It's amazing what people will go up in, Mark thinks, these little planes, Tinker Toys and lacquered canvas. You hear about people flying back from east of the mountains, headwind so stiff they're glued to one spot, must look like kites from the ground, having to land on U.S. 2, trying not to clip the power lines. But this Camas Lake incident is strange, the plane borrowed, a woman still buckled into the second seat when they winched it out of the ice. A young woman, nineteen or twenty, and the pilot missing, an older man, married . . . two sets of luggage in back, and the plane not so badly mangled as you'd think, survivable maybe. Something fishy about the whole thing.

"You think he's in the lake?" Mark asks.

Whitey shakes his head, *No, he's long gone . . . long gone.*

Windy that night, too, so the man's tracks would be obliterated in a few hours. Mark's natural curiosity is for what really happened, what was *behind* it. He puts himself there for a minute, spooks himself. Not so, Whitey. It's all just more stupidity as far as he's concerned, entries in *Whitey's Book of Human Folly,* which includes, for instance, the story of the man who cut off his own dick with a rotary lawnmower. All one afternoon Whitey goaded Mark and Ike with it, making them guess how you could accomplish a feat like that, announcing finally: *He's too cheap to go down and rent himself a hedge trimmer . . .* And Ike: *Aw, Jesus, I believe it, I do.* Bizarre deaths, maiming, serious but not serious. It all stems from Whitey's being in the war, coming ashore in France in one of the later waves, July, mop-up duty, but ending up in the Battle of the Bulge the next winter, one of two men in his platoon not to take mortar fire or sniper's bullet or freeze to death, an incredibly shitty winter, all in all, these deaths being real. What people do to themselves he has only this blackly funny contempt for.

But not even Ike talks to Whitey about the war, even after this long. You just stay off it. Ike who was too old, and Mark only a ninth-grader by V-J Day, later exempted from Korea by virtue of his grandmother, family hardship, though he had classmates who weren't so blessed.

Whitey unrolls his window, knocks the sludge from the bottom of his metal cup and screws it back on the Thermos. His face hasn't aged well, it's all deep creases from squinting, screwing his mouth up to spit, thin reddish white skin, English-Irish-Scotch like Mark. Is that how *his* face is going to hold up? Lights come jouncing over the remaining stack of two-bys, the cement mixer, the mounded gravel. Then a pair of doors slamming, like duck hunters firing almost simultaneously. Ike and his nephew Roddy. The day commences.

All morning Mark works alone, cutting in tongue-and-groove pine paneling for the room off the balcony. There's a tall, mullioned window with a half-moon top, also a steel-and-glass skylight. Neither has arrived as yet, which has Ike fuming, so the openings are covered with black crackling plastic and Mark has to rig up a work light so he can see. It's marked "Office/Gloria" on the plans, belongs to Mrs. Sibley. Roddy's portable radio is playing downstairs, almost out of earshot, thank God. He and Ike are starting on the kitchen cabinets, Roddy who has no discernible talent for finish work, no patience, except blood's thicker than water, he's Ike's sister's youngest, not a bad kid unless he drinks, something wrong about how he metabolizes alcohol, in one scrape after another until they pinned that down. So here he is under Ike's wing, and Mark doesn't beat himself up over it, not all the time anyway, not this morning, damn grateful as he is to be left alone up here with a halfway fussy job to occupy him, no one gunning him, a decent stack of ten-foot one-by-twelves, and so far, sighting down the length of each, only one with a warp, and he'll cut that down for the short pieces under the window.

He straightens from the miter box, jerks back at the sight of Mrs. Sibley, hugging her arms, eyeing him. A pale blonde in a flannel shirt, dungarees with a crease from the laundry, thin sharp-boned face, intensely blue eyes. Younger than her husband, forty maybe, forty-two, though Mark's no expert. The kind of woman the tradesmen love to mock once she's gone, but she seems to like Mark, seems glad to find it's *him* finishing off her room. Or maybe that's stupid, maybe they're all just worker bees to people like the Sibleys.

Mark says, "Your office—"

She's edged close enough to him that he can smell the scent spilling from the open neck of her shirt, which even in the forty-degree air releases a flurry in his groin. Jesus, isn't *that* embarrassing? "Yes," she says, "my *office*," investing the word with a twinge of meaning that just eludes him. She flattens a hand against her chest, steps compactly over the rubble, runs a finger on the tongue of the last board he's tapped in place.

"Well, if it's your room," Mark says, without forethought, "maybe you'd like to nail this in."

Her first reaction, automatic, razor-quick, is to throw a look back over her shoulder, eyes cut, nothing flirty in that look, but immediately she brightens, says, "You don't mind?" Takes the hammer from him, her hand white and waxy-skinned on the blue rubber grip.

"You toenail it in through the tongue, then it doesn't leave a hole," Mark says, "same way you do a hardwood floor, basically. Just don't hit it in all the way, do the last part with a nail set and you won't ding up the wood. This pine's easy to damage."

What's he doing running off at the mouth like this, like a kid?

But she listens seriously, nails up this board while Mark watches, then he cuts another and snugs it in and she nails it, and one more after that, then they're both aware of Norm Sibley down in the big room calling, *"Gloria?"*

She returns the hammer, says, "I guess that's enough," sweeping the sawdust off her sleeve. Says, "You're—?"

"Mark."

"Married, Mark? Kids?"

Mark nods yes. Married, kids.

Sibley again, "You up there, Gloria, for God's sake? Let's get a move on."

She gives Mark a last look, cornered, brows bunched, says, "You're an angel, Mark," and slips away, leaving Mark disoriented, thinking, *What was* that *all about?* The work not so stupidly pleasurable now that he can picture the room in use, *hers* . . . the desk, the long expensive drapes, a couch or daybed of some kind, a rectangle of sun from the skylight stealing across it. Sibley not invited up here, in her office, though he can go anywhere he wants, it's his house, isn't it?

They stretch out for lunch in the kitchen, Ike, Whitey, Roddy, also Russ Mikelson, one of the electricians, a cheerful balding guy Mark's always liked, and a stone-faced older man who's helping Russ today, shirt says *Skippy* in red script, which strikes Mark as pathetic, undignified, like what his grandmother once said about John D. Rockefeller's son, *Called Junior all his life, can you imagine?* . . . and leaning in the door frame one of the tile guys popping potato sticks in his mouth, dabbing the grease on his pant leg, a short, curly-haired man named Salvi.

Mark unfolds his wax paper, finds a slab of meatloaf, gelatin, congealed fat, sniffs it. He's not hungry, walks outside, takes a ferocious steaming leak into the hole along the foundation, steps around the torn-up ground to the valley side, watches a yellow van make two or three passes at the hill then give up. There's a patch of broken cloud over the lake, but more cloud above it, dingy, pocked like rock-salted ice.

When he comes back inside, Mikelson is telling a story

about two tourists from London, England, which Mark sur-
mises is in response to Whitey's bringing out the plane wreck
again. Roddy's laughing, a snorting, horsey laugh, face bobbing helplessly, and Mark drifts away, hoping no one's paying
him any mind. What a long day, not even half-past twelve. He's
managed not to think of Linny for any extended period of
time . . . that old joke, don't think about an elephant, and your
mind's suddenly giddy with elephants, trunks blaring, nothing
you can do about it, like your tongue going to a broken tooth
all day. But that's not exactly true, is it? You *can* turn away
from thoughts, you don't have to give them dominion. So he
allows himself only tastes, Linny with the flat afternoon light
on her jaw, the smudge of shadow, her white shanks like pin-
wheels, *Happy New Year, Mark . . .*

Mark hears his name invoked in the kitchen, hears it carom
around the big room, nothing yet to soak up sound, all plywood and rock still, "Hey, Singer—" Ike climbing heavily to
his feet, first stogie of the afternoon wedged between two
sausagelike fingers, "Wha'd you and the missus have going?"

"*Gloria,*" someone says.

Mark says, "Gimme a break."

Boots crunching on the subflooring, like a poker game bust-
ing up.

"I'll give you the break of your life," Ike says, but he's
already lost interest in the subject of Mrs. Sibley. He bends and
hacks at the phlegm in his chest, then heads off toward the
bedrooms where Mikelson has disappeared.

Mark hauls out his watch, Timex on a cheap expansion
band, catches the hairs on his wrist so he keeps it in the snap
pocket of his overalls.

12:39 becoming 12:40, sweep of the tiny hand.

He panels around the windows, then the other long wall,
which is only wainscoting with a chair rail, then trims around

Mrs. Sibley's walk-in closet. Suddenly now he *is* hungry, light-headed, feels a twinge behind his eye socket, ignores it. He's not exactly wasting away on Olivia's cooking, thirty-four inch jeans snug on him, wore thirty-twos when they were married. It's not fat yet, but your constitution changes, one morning you discover you're padded out like Ike. *Prosperous,* his grand-mother's word for it, though she knows better. Mark's not going to let that happen, no way, but he needs something right now or this headache's going to get roaring. He scares up Roddy downstairs, ripping some maple with the table saw. Kid eats like a greyhound. Mark happens to know not a morning goes by that Ike doesn't stop at the Handy Grocery on the way to work so his nephew can stock up.

"Where's the big guy?" Mark asks.

"Him and Mikelson had to go straighten something out," Roddy says.

"In town?"

"Yeah."

"Down the old bobsled run."

Roddy grins at this, shakes his head, says, "Yeah, boy."

"Look," Mark says, "you wouldn't have anything left over from lunch?"

"What's wrong with yours?"

"Didn't agree with me," Mark says, though he doesn't intend to get into it with Roddy.

"Might be something," Roddy says. "What's it worth to you?"

I'm in no mood, Mark thinks, but you might as well play along with Roddy. "Depends what it is," he says.

"I think I got some Snoballs. And sunflower seeds."

"With the shell?" Mark asks.

"Uh huh."

"Spits," Mark says.

"Yeah, spits."

"What'll you take for them?"

"I was going to hang onto those," Roddy says.

You fuck.

"Buy me some Wild Turkey," Roddy says.

"Well, that's one thing I'm not buying you," Mark says.

"A bag of tall guys."

"I wouldn't give you a beer if you were in the middle of the desert."

Roddy says, "You're no fun."

"Guess I'm not."

Roddy shrugs, digs the seeds from a paper sack and tosses them over, says, "You owe me, buddy."

And upstairs again, a wad of seeds in his cheek, the salt sharp, leaking down his throat, almost intoxicating, it's only 2:56, then 3:22 before it sinks in with any authority that he'll be no better off when the day's over. Might as well be at work. An old joke of his father's that ends *Everybody's got to be someplace,* overheard, sexual more than likely, that dark insinuating laugh. He doesn't consciously think of Morgan Singer, but what can you do with this stuff that tears loose and bobs to the surface, except let it float away. Mark leans over and spits out a bolus of stringy husk, tasteless now, looks for his tape, which for some reason has disappeared from his apron, toes through the pine scraps. *Jesus,* where do things get to? No, he thinks, you can just stop pulling out your watch because the end of the work day is no salvation, and once he takes this wisdom to heart, the last ninety minutes of the afternoon dance away like spatters of grease.

Only three weeks since the solstice, but already it's not pitch black as he climbs back into the Willys. There's a steely glow on the lake, an eerie cessation of wind. Whitey jams the shifter into low and they start down, five miles an hour, sliding, grabbing, the gearbox keening.

The Old Town Tonight

Gray days, spits of dry snow, fog roaming the fields. Strews of tempered glass and chrome where two streets come together. A fisherman trapped under the river ice in his heavy coat, an old Finn named Aho. A sheriff's deputy accused of feeling up two runaway girls. At Parmentier's, a white sale. Pinkeye hop-scotching through the grade schools. One night a welter of sirens, and it's the Farmer's Union elevators on fire, the sky over downtown so fiercely lit it shows out to Paxson Road, a salmon-colored canopy of light.

Mark and Olivia and the two kids are drawn outside into the twenty-degree air, Amelia in her sleeper, feet slopping in a pair of Mark's rubber boots, army surplus, Davey coatless, dancing on his toes. He asks, "Can't we go *see?*"

Mark's on him in a second, refuses so aggressively, Olivia touches his arm, says, "Mark?"

"I'm sorry," Mark says, "we're not driving over there and watching somebody's trouble. It's bad enough we're standing out here."

They can smell it, not the sweet gunpowdery fallout that washes over after fireworks, this is a rank smell, charred wheat heads and melted zinc, incinerated feed pellets, the old painted wood of the offices, fissures in the silolike concrete releasing noxious billows of lime, tank mold.

"And anyway," Mark says, "Heldco's right there." A welding supply company. The back lot packed with cylinders of compressed nitrogen, propane, could take out that whole end of Railroad Street, row apartments, scruffy old rental houses. Good thing it's nowhere near the Vagabond, or his grandmother's place on East Sixth, but still, *somebody's*. He says no more about this in front of the kids, but finds himself clenched against the concussion, imagines, though it's silly, that the city is under seige.

Waits, nothing.

Inside again, Davey lobbies for hot chocolate, and Olivia, making up for Mark's outburst, goes to fix it. Nestlé's with that dog Farful on TV, *chaaawk-lut*.

Later, Olivia approaches Mark, asks, "What's with you?"

"Nothing's with me."

"Sure fooled me," Olivia says.

He draws a deep breath, ready to justify himself. Lets it out again instead, drops his hands.

Olivia stoops and retrieves the crocheted yellow blanket Amelia drags around the house, folds it, lays it on the back of the sofa, before catching Mark's eye again, and she's not really put out with him, he sees, not gunning for him. Only tired, says with a sigh, "Hot time in the old town tonight."

It so takes Mark aback, her joke, her chagrin at how they're spending another Friday night, that he finds himself holding Olivia in the middle of their low-ceilinged living room, rubbing her back, hands up and down on the soft flesh.

Saturday morning the Singers troop down to the cafe for a big breakfast, and there's Linny in her white blouse and apron, working the counter, the back booths.

Short-haired Aunt Linny, white crockery platters stacked up her arm.

"And you want a pancake," she says to Davey.

"Three pancakes," he says.

"They're pretty big."

"How big?"

"Oh, like hubcaps."

"One's plenty," Olivia tells him.

"And bacon," Davey says.

Linny writes *bacon*. A load of eggs and sausage for Mark, who's ravenous this morning. Wedges of toast, tomato juice for Olivia.

The Vagabond's busy, noisy, the food slow to arrive. Mark keeps his eyes to home, converses with his wife. Davey's like an altar boy in here. Next to the junkyard, he loves the cafe more than any spot his life's yet taken him. Mark remembers his own adolescent fascination: the fluted chrome, the door that swings both ways on its hinges, the painting of the vagabond in moody blues and greens . . . must date back to Cecil Jordan's time, Mark realizes now.

They feed Amelia from their own breakfasts, but soon she wants out of the high chair, stands fidgeting on the spongy vinyl. Olivia finally agrees to take the kids down to see the ruins of the elevator, while Mark has a last cup of coffee.

Collecting plates, Linny leans into the booth, says, "You look like a pasha." Smile a little commotion in one corner of her mouth.

Swipe of the white rag. Her veiny hand.

She disappears into the kitchen leaving Mark to contemplate the damp oilcloth before him, to stick his head up and eye his fellow citizens.

Someone coughing, hacking.

After a moment, he launches himself from the booth, strides back past the pay phone, through the swinging door. Nick takes Saturdays off, so it's Billy Krona at the griddle, white cap jaunty and serious on his skull like Nehru. Mark nods, raises a hand. They were in first grade together. He veers around a stoop-shouldered girl shredding lettuce at the long table, past the coolers into the old baking room, stacked floor to ceiling with cartons now. There's Linny, head bowed, Winston searing the edge of the high, canvas-topped table where he can remember pies on wire racks.

"Found me," she says.

"All week—" Mark starts to say, but Linny puts her mouth on his, doesn't release him when his sense of timing pulls him back.

"Squeeze me," she says, and Mark squeezes, hears the knobby vertebrae crunch. Sound of a canoe's armature.

Finally she asks him, "You doing okay, Mark?"

"Sure."

We'll see, Linny's face says.

In a moment she says, "You better go." But keeps two fingers tucked in his belt.

"You're not going," she says.

Mark gently extracts himself, stands just out of arm's length, smiling.

"Come here," Linny says.

"I have to go," Mark says.

"No, I have to tell you something."

"What?"

"Come here."

Mark brings his face back within the shadow of hers. "All right," he says, "tell me, then."

"Remember Wendy Ochs?"

He nods, gets an indistinct picture of Linny's old sidekick. No reason to pay attention back then. "I didn't really know her," he admits, not wild about reminding Linny of the difference in their ages, remembers vaguely the subject of Wendy Ochs coming up at Linny's homecoming dinner. "So, she around?"

"Well, as a matter of fact, she's out of town at the moment," Linny says, tipping her forehead to his. "And I'm sitting her house."

"As of when?"

"As of this instant."

"Ah," Mark says, thinks, *Yes, but when can I possibly—?*

Delivered of her news, Linny ducks away from Mark, says, "'Bye, love." Brief fleeing silhouette in the door to the kitchen.

The smell of scorching fibers, Mark brushes her cigarette onto the floor, snuffs it with his toe. He wipes a hand across his face. Slips then into the hallway and out the rear door, waits near the garbage cans for his Chevrolet to come nosing through the alley.

Ragged formations of ducks against the lusterless sky, partial letters. Pigeons affixed to the gutters of G. K. Alt Furniture. Snow beginning to fall, melting as it hits.

But another week elapses before Mark arranges to be gone from his house. A chunk of afternoon, an unspecified sequence of errands Olivia won't begrudge him. Long hours he's been working, and here it is the dregs of January.

At the south end of Sperry, the section known as Grover's Addition, the streets stop at Davis, all but Sixteenth, which continues along an embankment giving onto marshland. A trailer or two, an engine repair shop in a pale green Quonset, here and there a nicely made older house with a sweep of lawn, rock gardens, pruned-back stands of lilac, and still, in the winter of 1961, a few undeveloped lots graced with red and white CRIPPS REALTY signs. Then the street ends in a potholed turnaround. The last place, through a gap in a caragana hedge, is the Ochs house. Tidy, tin-roofed, overseen by blue spruce.

A reel-to-reel's slowly unwinding on the table in the front room, piano jazz, music Mark knows zilch about, usually makes him feel like he's missing the joke. But this isn't so harried and cryptic, it's almost soothing. He doesn't ask who it is. Wouldn't be a name he knows.

Linny's wearing jeans, a fuzzy angora top. "You want some tea, Mark?" He watches her drizzle honey into hers and stir lazily.

He stands behind her chair, lets his hands play down the

front of her sweater. "Do you know how nice that feels," she says. "Do you have any idea?"

Out the side window, he watches the idle motion of the spruce branches. Supposing, now that they have all the time in the world, it's no good? Supposing he's not what she wants after all?

Gauzy curtains in the bedroom, rag rug on the varnished floor. A space heater purring in the corner. The sheets white, turned down, scalloped hems with tatted eyelets.

"Let me *see* you," Linny says.

Mark's never gotten used to walking around naked in front of women, showing himself off. Though he has solid shoulders, a torso that has thickened, become furred with sandy hair. Though he is thirty years old, no boy.

"How'd you get this?" she says, flicking her nail on a rill of scar above his hipbone.

"Don't remember," Mark says. "Must've been at work."

"So careless."

Then her tongue on it.

And soon thereafter, her hands thrown back over her head, gripping the spindles of the bedstead, blue-white showing at the bottom of her eyes. Her ribcage heaving, belly a shallow basin, moist.

"Don't you dare stop," she says, full volume, for who's to hear?

But Mark's a lost cause.

Then, some minutes later, Linny searching out his hand under the bedclothes, steering it down to where there's work to finish.

He dozes, dreams chaotically, and when he wakes she's sitting on the edge of the bed, dallying with his chest. He squints the clock face into focus, sees that it's not even four, falls back in sweet relief.

"How's my soldier?" she asks.

"At ease," Mark says.

Turns out not to be the case.

When he catches his breath again, he sits up, swings his feet onto the rug.

Linny says, "I think you need to wipe yourself off a bit."

"A shower."

"You don't want to smell like soap, either," Linny says.

In the bathroom, he works at himself with a blue washcloth, wringing it out several times, bends and scoops water into his mouth and cleans his teeth with one finger. When he reappears, he finds the bed made, Linny at the table once more, resting on her elbows.

"I gotta tell you," Mark starts to say, "I don't know how often—"

"No business now, okay, love?"

"All right," he answers.

Sits, says nothing.

"You could tell me what a fabulous lay I am," Linny says.

Blood flushing his cheeks. It's like there's some etiquette he always misses.

"I'm *kidding*," she says. "You want a sandwich? Coffee?"

"No."

"Anything?"

Mark shakes his head.

"Well, then." She takes his hand, intertwines their fingers, kisses the ones that aren't hers.

He is no sooner out the door, boots crunching gravel, than he wants to be back inside, and no sooner seated in the Chevrolet than he's possessed by the intuition that the car won't start, that it's conspired to give him what he wants. He sits a moment, eyeing the knot of keys dangling from the ignition.

He retraces his path, Sixteenth to Davis, cruises through

town, where the stores he hasn't visited are locking up, dousing lights. He heads down Railroad Street, sees that the bulldozers are still at work behind the police barricades, five-thirty on a Saturday evening, mounding up rubble, splintered siding, spars of galvanized metal, a set of concrete steps upended, the rest of it clumped and sooty, unidentifiable. And the three grain tanks in ruins, caved in at different heights, blackened as old chimneys.

How can you not stop and watch?

Molting

Nick steps from his office, grabs his coat off the peg, throws a quick look at Billy Krona tending his flock of lunch orders. Odd kid, Billy, couldn't tell you who the governor is, but he's a genius at the griddle. Has a sixth sense, impeccable timing. Nick ducks into the bathroom and runs a brush through his fringe of curls. *Friar Tuck,* Grace used to call him. He inspects the corners of his mouth for coffee residue, scratches with his nail. Had a sour stomach since he got out of bed this morning, like a hot poker some days, others just a rosy glow. He spits, runs the water, flicks off the light. Calls back into the kitchen, "Anybody's looking for me, tell them don't bother."

It's a decent day out, considering. Leavings of winter. Grimy awnings. Another couple of weeks the pothole crew will be out throwing shovelfuls of blacktop. The willow branches on the flood plain catch his eye driving to work. Already that smoldering shade of orange. But you can still get fooled, this late. That time with Grace, coming back from Missoula. A shopping expedition, one night's change of venue, back during the war sometime. Saved-up gas coupons. The storm unannounced, wet snow, slick as snot. They couldn't make it up the Ravalli hill, the car slewing all over. Couldn't see past the hood ornament. Damn lucky not to be creamed by a truck. Then a tussle with Grace: Drive around the long way, through Dixon and Moise, or wait it out? Grace often impatient, implacable. *Let's keep moving, Nick.* What did they end up doing? He can't remember. Made it home somehow, went on living.

That other storm unannounced, too.

Grace's.

Nick walks down the Opera House block, waits at the light, clandestinely fingers the keys on his key ring, the familiar serrations. Long skinny key that starts the Dodge, stumpier one for the truck, worn-down brass key to his office and the sturdy Schlage that opens the Vagabond's alley door, one for the safety deposit box, one for the rear of 412 McLaren Road (to the best of anyone's knowledge none exists for the front), the double-sided little key that fits the shed's padlock, then the three mystery keys. Ought to throw them out, never does. Ten keys, and around again.

"You and your rosary," Grace used to say.

He stares up Montana Street. The brick front of Kauffman's is buried under a facade now. It sports verticals of some lightweight alloy, oddly spaced doodads of trim. The old Bagley Building, 1904, still houses the Masonic temple on the second floor, but downstairs it's all glass and aluminum, diagonal struts, like a row of javelins at rest. And the JC Penney's. Jaunty new fronts everywhere, give you a headache if the sun ever comes out.

Same with the hotel lobby, he thinks, entering. Lowered ceiling, acoustic panels. Orange plastic chairs out of a cockpit. Used to have a big mural of the steamboat *Lucille,* cargo stacked on the dock, men shaking hands.

Gone, too.

Nick climbs the half-flight and stands a moment eyeing the
dining room. Milky light from the curtained windows, glow-
ing sconces. He makes his way to Alt's table: Alt and his son-
in-law Luther, Rex Johnsrud of Brevity Insurance, and Dr.
Tutveit, a squinty, bluff sort who puts you in mind of Teddy
Roosevelt. Luther's picking at Swedish meatballs. Porterhouse
for Alt, stuffed pork chop for the sawbones. Stuffing the con-
sistency of damp sawdust, Nick observes.

"Why, Nick," the doctor says. "How's the boy?"

"Holding my own," Nick says, standing behind the empty
chair.

"We're too old to hold anybody else's," Johnsrud says. The
man actually has gray skin, deep smudges around the eyes like
an elephant. Good Republican.

"Speak for yourself, Rex," Tutveit says heartily.

Alt turns to Nick, tells him have a set.

Nick obliges.

It's widely known that Luther knocked up Alt's oldest girl,
Alicia. On leave from Fort Lewis that spring. Narrow-faced
girl, mirthless, not clear how accidental it was. Nick receives a
bolt of pleasure every time he lays eyes on Luther, to think he
never had to absorb any unlucky sons of bitches into the family business. Must be Mark's age, Luther, three kids now, crew-
cut retreating into an obvious W. Not such a whipped dog look
these days. Settled into his fate, world of dinettes, breakfronts,
Hide-A-Beds. He used to frequent the cafe when he was a
younger buck. Cokes with extra shots of syrup, great rafts of
fried potatoes. Now he stays away . . . Alt's unspoken protocol.

Nick folds his hands on the linen before him.

"Get you a drink?" Alt asks.

Nick shakes his head no. "I thought we could talk," he says.

Alt smiles, says, "Come around the office, why don't you."

"I'm here now."

Tutveit consults the wall clock, wards off a monstrous belch with his fist, shoves back his chair, and says, "Time to lance a boil. Gentlemen."

Moments later, Johnsrud, too, surrenders his napkin and jumps ship.

Luther raises his eyes in his father-in-law's direction, but Alt shows no interest in running him off.

"Ever had a boil lanced?" Alt asks.

"Not that I recollect," Nick says.

"Sounds unpleasant. But then, of course, there's the relief." Luther explains that once, as a child, he'd had a mastoid drained.

Alt ignores him. "Still having trouble with that roof, Nick?"

You'd be the last man on earth I'd tell, Nick thinks. Though, in fact, the Vagabond's flat tar roof has begun to leak again, despite repeated patching. There's a panel of saturated plaster on the west wall where the wallpaper is molting.

Alt goes on, "The cafe's been looking a little down at the heels lately, if you don't mind my making that observation. It occurred to me your heart wasn't in it any longer. Or maybe there's a financial situation of some sort. I wouldn't want to speculate on that."

It's not clear to Nick why he *has* come, though he's known from the moment he woke that today was the day. Maybe just to hear Alt out once more, then tell him to piss up a rope. And a fine pleasure that would be.

Men like Alt.

But as Alt talks, Nick feels something let go and roll soundlessly away. His stony combativeness, or what's left of it.

It's truer than he would've believed that he is tired. Sixty-two's not old, and he's not in bad shape really, considering his father was dead by this age, likewise his eldest brother, and that of the remaining two, one's on total disability with rotted hip joints, holed up a block off North Halsted, petrified of every footfall on the stairs. No, Nick's healthy except for minor complaints, his burning stomach, for instance, which hopefully *is* minor, subsides for days at a time, better if he doesn't constantly baste it with coffee, Tabasco, red wine, sweet Italian sausage . . . hard not to, though. Yet, arguably, he's in better fettle than he'd ever have predicted in that dark span after losing Grace, when day after day he could read it in the girls, *The old guy's in a permanent tailspin,* their efforts to revive him well-meant but dispiriting all the same. And maybe saying he's tired isn't accurate, anyway. Maybe, as Alt has suggested, it's that his heart has gone out of preserving the Vagabond. Why he's resisted Helen wanting to reupholster the booths, why the sight of the loosened tiles in the entryway curdles something in him.

A remark he makes to Billy Krona in jest: *Gimme a new set a problems, huh Bill?*

And Billy: *Coming right up, Mister S.*

Nick looks across the crumb-specked damask at Alt. "I don't care much for that lawyer of yours," he says.

Alt nods, sacrifices Fred Terrell with a flick of two fingers.

Nick says, "You know the Vagabond's sort of a landmark. People would miss it."

"I dare say," Alt says. "But they'd adjust."

Nick expects Alt to raise the example of the Downtowner, long-time Sperry drinking establishment that sold in the mid-fifties, and eventually closed for good. Mourned in the abstract. People went to the Stockman's, to Kid Billy's, to the Pine. But Alt lets it lie.

"You don't mind my asking," Nick goes on, "what would you do without my lot?"

"Of course, I'd have to make other arrangements."

Nick leans forward on his elbows. "And what would those be exactly?"

Alt smiles again. "I don't think we need to get into all that," he says.

"But the point is," Nick says, "you'd rather go along with the plans you already got."

"That's so," Alt says. "I'll give you that, Nick. I very much would."

"Well, then."

Alt leans back to allow the waitress Silvia to bus away the remaining china. She pauses over Nick, says, "Sure I can't get you a splash of coffee?"

Nick tells her a splash of coffee would be fine, thank you. Watches the light play weakly through the glass pot as she pours.

"You know," Nick says after a moment, "I'd half-expected a visit from the fire marshall. That kind of a thing."

Alt doesn't bother to act offended. He says, "Nick, we're just a couple of businessmen, aren't we?"

It occurs to Nick to invoke Grace's name at this table. He could say it was a joint effort from the start, kids or no kids, Grace the soul of the place, strength to his weakness. He could say that and not be far off, but he balks at it, using her as leverage. Or is it that he can't bear the prospect of seeing Alt's lip curl at such a tactic, however momentarily?

"Yeah," Nick says. "A couple businessmen."

Alt turns to his son-in-law, asks him if he'd mind running back to the store and telling Marjorie he'll be another few minutes yet.

No, Luther wouldn't mind.

The two men watch him go. His cantilevered walk, the shirttail showing below his jacket.

When, a while later, Nick and G. K. Alt step into the lobby,

Nick takes this opportunity to buy a White Owl at the counter so as to spare himself Alt's company on the walk back to Second Street, at the same time acknowledging a horrendous cramping in his gut, almost a dizzy sick feeling, his pulse starting to hammer in his temples. He stands gazing at the sluggish traffic, ignoring his change on the prickled rubber mat, finally murmurs thanks, though by now the cashier has moved off. He makes his way down the marble stairs to the hotel's lower level. Best thing about the hotel, the old GENTS in the cellar, frosted glass, black and white diamond pattern of tiles, puts him in mind of the big city. Raised platform for the three pissers, fine old round-shouldered porcelain fixtures, vague smell of coconut. Stall doors louvered. He's barely ensconced, braces yanked down, when his bowels let go in a torrent. The relief's immediate, staggering. He rests his head in his palms, panting, his wits gradually rejoining him.

Overhead, water coursing through the pipes, the wheeze of floorboards. Must be directly under the kitchen, he thinks, cleanup duty. Thump of a compressor. He can no longer avoid asking himself what Grace would have to say about this business with Alt. Gross betrayal, desertion? Ah, but Christ, what's the use in that? In truth, she's gotten harder to hear, the voice itself. A terrible goddamn thing to admit. If she ever seems to speak to him, it's only words she actually said, so dated now. You can't make a religion out of looking back, holding on for dear life. The opposite is also true. He gives himself another few minutes, praying no one will venture in.

No one does.

Silent Movie

Something Whitey said at work one day: "Fog so goddamn thick you don't know if it's a bridge you're walking, or the plank."

Ardent laughter all around.

Fog of your own making, Mark thinks now, driving toward Linny, sooty dusk, late February. He slams the door of the Chevrolet and it's all he can do not to run.

The house smells like cloves, old varnish, tea bags, brandy, Noxzema.

He watches Linny peel off her shirt and shampoo her hair under the kitchen faucet. Her blind grope for the towel, her head-cocked stance, drying.

"And what are *you* staring at?"

Mark grinning from the table, foot waggling on his knee.

While she's in the other room, he swings the icebox door open, stares in. Nothing much. Cottage cheese, a few lank carrots. What's she live on? He gazes around the kitchen, watches the slow drip of the tap. On the sill over the sink, there's the chunk of quartz he found by the Sibleys' garage and brought her, not last time but the time before. Already a history. He picks it up, notes the spot without dust.

Then Mark locating a nipple through Linny's camisole. Marveling, eyes closed. Where Olivia's brassieres are thick-ribbed, grayish from the hard water. Leave grooves on her shoulders, the skin rubbery.

He's no good with endearments. It's odd enough to be saying *Linny* the way he says it now, purged of indifference. Sparingly he does it, as if the spell will wear off. Where she's flagrant about his name. And calls him *sweetpea, shugah,* teasing after the fashion of torch singers, movie women. Calls him *love. Reach me the water, love.*

Like glints of light on him, these words.

But no demands from Linny. No *Tell me you love me, Mark.* No *What would you do for me?* Their absence is disorienting, dizzying.

He hates to seem greedy, but he wants to know about her, wants it all. Fourteen, fifteen years since he first laid eyes on her, and, truthfully, what does he know? In bed, their heads touching, he asks who the first one was.

She says she's not telling.

"Oh, come on."

"I was thirteen."

Mark up on one elbow. *"Thirteen?"*

"Twelve, then. A child prodigy."

"I was being serious."

"You're always serious, Mark," she says, and he expects her to add, "That's one thing I like about you."

Instead, she says, "Okay, who was *your* first, Mark?"

How deeply did she mean to sting him? He can't say. So he backs off: no talking about lovers. But his curiosity's riled. Who was it before him, who was the last to know her before she came home? He's not a jealous man, Mark, or never thought he was, but he's strangely jealous now, of the hours spent with Linny, of knowledge denied him.

A little later, he asks, as he asked once before, fleetingly, why they need no protection.

"I don't get pregnant," Linny says flatly. "Isn't that handy?"

Mark tries to read her face but the room's grown too dark. "It's night already," he says finally, as if dumbfounded by the flow of time.

Olivia and the kids are at a potluck with the Watnes from

up the road and their two boys. A Covenant Church function, everybody piling into Sonja's station wagon, Mark excused as usual. But it'll break up soon, maybe already has.

He strokes her lightly, asks, "Why me?"

"Act of nature," Linny says.

"No, it wasn't."

"Am I the predator, then?"

Nothing to say to that.

"You wanted me," Linny says.

"Yes."

"And you still want me."

"Yes."

"This very minute?"

"God, I can't."

"Coward."

Already teasing again, incorrigible.

"Things can't keep on like this," Mark says, though he'd meant to say no such thing.

Linny's voice, quick, untroubled, "Sure they can."

Mark shakes his head . . . it feels like a gourd full of sand. He removes his hand from her haunch, leaves her in bed, begins to dress.

"You like the light on?" he asks.

Linny says no.

"Anything else I can do for you?"

"I guess not."

When he arrives home, he finds his own house dark, only the floodlight on the garage burning. The yard looks god-awful, mangelike swatches of bare ground, whitish dog turds, trash blown down from the road. But not tonight's problem, he thinks, not this week's. It's above freezing, the eaves weeping. Inside, he's greeted by air that's nearly as cold, can't be much over forty. So the pilot light is out again. And it couldn't be less handy to get at. Their house sits on a cement slab, but there's a compartment beneath the kitchen floor for the furnace. Olivia calls it the *dungeon*. What a harebrained setup: You have to move the table and pull up the heavy trapdoor, brace it with a two-by-four, have to first locate a flashlight, which isn't in the junk drawer and not on the workbench and not under Davey's bed, where once before he tracked it down, so he abandons that scheme, runs an extension cord from the plug-in on the range, uses an old shadeless wobble-necked table lamp his grandmother long ago donated to the cause. He shuts off the valve and waits for the gas to dissipate. Propane's heavier than air . . . Ike's told about it pooling in cellars, blowing at the first spark. He thinks of the elevator fire again, wiring they're saying now. He squats. Maybe three minutes have passed. He sniffs, smells only scaling concrete, waits another minute, thinks of Linny climbing out of bed, walking to the bathroom barefoot, pictures himself pressing her against the sink from behind, the thick nap of her robe, the cleft . . . he cancels that vision almost instantaneously, roots in his pocket for matches, *A-1 Vacuum, South Sperry Blvd.*, opens the valve, lights, can't quite see where the damned jet is, though last time, right before Christmas, he'd gotten it lit without incident, flashlight anchored in his mouth. Now he shuts the valve before more gas escapes, noses the bare-bulbed lamp closer, studies the configuration of tubing and heat exchangers, sees where his mistake was, and that very instant the exposed cowling of the bulb socket touches the furnace's steel housing. Then a pungent spasm of crackling white light, and he's sitting back in the pitch dark as if sucker punched, thinking, What if I'd had my *hand* on the goddamn thing? A total accident he didn't. *Local Moron Fried in Dungeon*. In a moment, he remembers that the same fuse handles the kitchen and the light on the garage wall over the fusebox.

Now voices, the *whang* of the vestibule door, scuffing boots.

Instinctively, Mark lurches to the opening in the floor, ready to intercept a tumbling body. Hears Olivia snapping the switch up and down. He hollers, "Stay back."

"Mark? Where are you? What's going—?"

"I've got the trap*door* open," he says. "Everybody just freeze."

Amazingly, they do. He can hear Amelia snuffling, the squeak of her snowsuit as Olivia adjusts her grip.

Later that night, when the chill's off the house, and the girl's put down to sleep, Mark asks Olivia, "Why couldn't I find the flashlight? Didn't I just put new batteries in it?"

"We had to bring it to the church," his son informs him.

"You did? Are they running out of light down there?"

But Davey's serious, his face quietly aflame. "You know how there's a stage," he says. "Well, they turned out the big lights and we had to wave our flashlights back and forth. It was supposed to look like a silent movie."

"Really?" Mark says. "Did it?"

"Uh huh."

He doesn't inquire if his son's ever *seen* a silent movie. How would he have? Instead, Mark asks what it was about.

"Bible stories," Olivia answers.

"Jesus riding on a donkey," the boy says.

"How'd they do the donkey?"

"You could tell it was two grown-ups inside," Davey says.

"But it was a pretty good show anyway?"

"Yup."

"Fred was one of the men," Olivia says.

Mark lets it go.

But later, in bed, he can't resist saying, "I don't have to ask which end of the donkey Fred was."

Not a murmur from Olivia.

After a long while, she says, "You never used to hate people."

"Well, I don't *hate* him," Mark says.

"At least he was there," Olivia says.

"Liv, if you wanted me there, you should've said something. Because what you did say was, 'I can just take the kids.' "

"Wherever we are, that's where you don't want to be."

"That's pure crap," Mark says, but doesn't care for how testy his voice sounds. More benevolently, he says, "Really, I think you're buying trouble."

She doesn't respond, remains quiet so long Mark supposes she's drifted off. Such long days these are, his own barely recognizable. Linny steals into his head again. He remembers holding her foot while they sat at the table. Cool as soapstone, half-moon nails. Olivia's foot not on Olivia.

"Does this winter seem endless to you?" Olivia asks, startling him.

"I guess you could say that."

"I don't remember ever feeling this way."

Mark doesn't remind her about the winter before Davey was born. If she's forgotten, more power to her. "It's just a mood," he says.

"Moods don't count?"

"I meant it'll pass."

"I hope *yours* does."

Mark takes no issue with that.

Olivia's weight shifts, the springs echo. He wonders if she's making a move toward him. Down in his pajama bottoms his equipment still has that slanky, ropy feeling of having been put to recent use. What if he can't respond? *What if he can?* One sister's bed to another's, sounds like the start of a seedy old joke.

But Olivia has no designs on him, she's only nestling in, assuming her sleep position, vanishing, leaving behind this rising and falling mound in the blankets. He feels a twinge of life, gives himself a hard squeeze, lets go. The other day he heard her tell Davey to quit playing with himself, and Mark said, "Liv, he can't help it if that's how long his arm is." Olivia threw him one of those looks. "What if I went around kneading my jugs?" *Be my guest.* Of course, he didn't say that. No point in arguing certain things, though he sure doesn't want Davey thinking his body's dirty, there's too much of that attitude as it is. One burden his grandmother never piled on him, and thanks be to her. She'd seen enough by then, he guesses. Buried a husband, a son. Aaron Singer, Morgan Singer. Mark's said to favor the grandfather, broad shoulders, forehead like a mixing bowl, bright sandy locks. He was Canadian-born, a school teacher . . . Mark's life overlapped with his but a few months. It must have been Morgan who was the aberration, and wouldn't your heart crash to watch a son like that take shape? What's in the blood, what's not, Mark wonders. He thinks of Davey's little walnutlike scrotum.

He gives himself ten minutes to fall asleep, then ten more. He listens over Olivia. Long rasps of breath, like pulls from a draw shave. He climbs out of bed, empties his bladder, wanders the house as if new rooms will miraculously present themselves. For a few moments, he stands at the south window, looking toward the creek. There's a thick moonless sky, he can't see a thing. The furnace clicks on . . . he almost hates to stick his foot in front of the register, but the air pours out warm, steadfast, scented with dust.

Something's Gonna Get You

21 February 1961. Postlunch lull. Helen asks Stella Baucus to work the afternoon for her. A brief negotiation—today switched for Friday—then she drives home, changes into jeans, cap, canvas jacket. It's been warm this past week, *unseasonable* the radio says. Rainy, water standing on ice, grass showing through like an old pelt. Drips running down the power lines, letting go. In the Skonnards' yard, a deer's leg surfacing: thigh bone, rosy knee, part of the femur.

She wheels her bike from the shed where it's leaned unridden since November. Down the length of McLaren Road, a frizz of spray in the fenders. How good it feels to lean into the pedals, that clenching in her calves. She shifts into low alongside the masonry supply, waits to cross the highway. A logging truck rumbles by, leaves the momentary scent of shredded bark, diesel.

Cemeteries are always on high ground, she thinks. Off the flood plain. Cemeteries and hospitals. She pumps up the long hill, standing for the last fifty yards, traces the outer loop, a mile altogether. Here's the white marble of the veterans monument, Korea at the bottom right, eleven names . . . Bobby Tonjum of Olivia's class, before this remembered as the boy who threw the javelin that struck Lyle Camfry, Lyle surviving but never right afterward. Better he should be killed, people said, but who's to judge? Around to the right, Babyland. Weatherblanched palm fronds, a plastic pinwheel whirring. On other occasions, Helen's left the bike on its kickstand and walked quietly among them. *Lamb. Smallest angel.* Hard not to feel cursed, she thinks. Would you want to fill your womb right away again . . . an act of defiance? In the old days, Nick has told her, they'd burden a later child with the dead one's name. Something barbaric and touching about that. Prowling a junk shop Helen once happened on a cache of photographs: children in coffins, pine boxes propped against chairs, girls with hands folded over hearts, the older boys in stern black suits. Before sulfa, penicillin. She can appreciate the urge to make such a picture, but why this archive, fifty or more, mounted on stiff cardboard, tied with twine, unless it's like her own notebook of clippings from the *Evening Record*? Four healthy girls for Grace, though. No stillbirths, no horrid miscarried fetuses to the best of Helen's knowledge. "Aren't I blessed," their mother often said, but in an offhand, distracted way. Must have had more to do with her temperament than any fierce sense of being singled out. In any case, Helen thinks, it's just human nature, you never feel good luck as keenly as bad.

She pedals on.

Old granite, lichen like rust, some green the color of copper patina. You can't truthfully say the sun's trying to break through, but it's a bright glare, with a semblance of shadow puddling behind the stones.

Here, in one secluded corner, a spit of ground occupied by the House of Cripps. Brick and scaled-down Doric columns, barred windows. Home to Charles and Margaret, spinster daughter Belle. Banking money in those days, mostly real estate now, except for Connie Cripps who still runs the Cripps Bank. Helen recollects walking here, one of the summers they had the tent worms, hearing them spatter from the cottonwoods as if it were hailing out of a blue sky, seeing them stand upright writhing on the grass blades, nauseating things. Today she gives Crippsville barely a glance, climbs the slope beneath the water tank, skirts the vacant hillside. Only a little encroachment along the bottom, chunks of discolored sod.

Coasting now, no warmth in the wind on her cheeks . . . unseasonal maybe but no smell of earth, no buds, not even the pungency of leaf mash on the crumbled blacktop. Then the inner loops. Box elders, birch, gnarls of lilac, one stone in the shape of a stump. Modest obelisks, *Stoick, Wicks, McCutcheon*, sets of beseeching hands, open patches where the markers are flush to the ground, flu epidemic of 1917–18 . . . and finally across into Section G. A small stone with polished face, water dully silver in the bottom curve of the letters:

GRACE F. STAVROS
6 March 1903   21 February 1947

Helen scans the hilltop, confirms that she's alone. She stands at Grace's feet, hands balled in the jacket pocket, no speech coming to mind, the whole business an empty exercise quite possibly, but she hasn't skipped since she was sixteen and able to drive Nick's car. It's often shitty cold this day, wind blasting out of British Columbia, snow wells around the larger stones, but the road always plowed, the hill sanded. Nor has she mentioned these expeditions to Nick or the sisters, wanting no public spectacle. Nick won't come himself. Once he snapped at Olivia, *I'm not going near that hellish place, you understand me,* jolted her into a white-lipped silence. So no one marks the day aloud . . . none of them hot on ritual anyway. Maybe if you were religious, but they gave up church years ago, all except Olivia. Nick turned against it on principle, obscure personal reasons dating back to his big family in Chicago, the heavy dark suits of his uncles, fear-mongering old aunts. Even Grace the Episcopalian lost interest. She was so put out with the priest at the end, a limpid, slope-shouldered man, Father Gleason, who took it as personal failure and wouldn't give up on her, Grace lapsing almost into giddiness with the morphine, making Linny bend close, *Can't you tell him I don't want any? That pest. Can't you send him packing?* And didn't Linny love that story, their mother's final slaphappiness. Helen wasn't present at the very end, nor any of the sisters. Four o'clock in the morning. Spindly Stella Baucus attends that Holy Roller church out beyond the viaduct, squat windowless building, tells Helen that Christians die in joy and comfort. Always in the paper: . . . *summoned by her loving Savior . . . received into the arms of*— There's no reasoning with Stella. Thin little lips, cross bouncing against her bony chest. Still, she did switch afternoons. Do unto others.

A glint of white, gulls taking to the air. The landfill and the cemetery, always congregations of gulls, raucous, today just wing beats, receding. Helen shifts her weight, thinks of Grace Stavros in her box, says once, *Oh, Momma,* one soft exhalation, not talking to her because that's stupid, but even so, what a powerful wish, to burrow into the bedclothes, into Grace's abundant powdery smell, her book sliding thump to the rug, *Good night, good night, let me* sleep *now, honey* . . . so early to bed, not even dark if it was summer, because she'd be up in the small hours to bake for the Vagabond. Selfish to believe my claim's special, Helen thinks, sin of pride. Except love's never evenhanded, goes where it goes, fills whatever hollow. The last daughter most precious for being last, or maybe not, maybe Grace was tired from the weight of it by then? And something else she said in the hospital, *You should have all been boys,* Nick telling her for Christ's sake, don't talk like that, but it's only true, can't get the tumor if you don't have the ovary. Must be on all their minds, but they never bring it up. She can just hear Linny, though: *Sweetie,* something's *gonna get you. Count on it.*

Over her shoulder now, the putter of a muffler going bad, tires rolling on grit. She stands frozen. *Hunk* of the door, squishing steps.

"It *is* you," Olivia says.

"Caught in the act."

"You should've told me. You didn't have to ride your bike."

"No, I wanted to, it's so warm," Helen says, though by now she's cooled off, almost chilled.

Olivia squats, deposits a fistful of white carnations in a wire holder to the left of *Grace F. Stavros.*

"Where's the kids?" Helen asks.

"I don't like to drag them up here," Olivia says, gives Helen an odd, possibly chastizing look. You never know which Olivia you're going to get these days. The friendly, devoted sister, or the one who's testy, whose concerns are of a higher order than yours.

"I'll let you be," Helen says.

But no, that's not what Olivia wants, either. She looks terrified at the idea of being left alone. And you can't help noticing that she's bundled up in their mother's mouton coat with the wide cuffs. Nick's gift to Grace one Christmas. What an indulgence, what a object of contention among the sisters later.

"I used to think she was watching me all the time," Olivia says.

Helen answers, "I know." Sometimes Olivia sounds like she's reciting from a dog-eared page of her autobiography, as Linny once remarked.

But today she goes on, "I'd be with Mark, and I could sense her in the bedroom with us, it was em*barr*assing. And if I didn't happen to feel like, you know, I could hear her, *You'd better give him what he wants, Olivia.* Other times, I'd be just . . . well, once it was carrying the laundry up those stairs at Ash Street, and I heard her right behind my shoulder, *You're doing fine, honey, you're doing a good job . . .*"

Olivia ducks her head, squinting, burying her hands in the fleecy sleeves. "But now, nothing. I feel like she's turned away."

Helen says, "I don't think you need to feel that way."

"It's not a matter of choice."

"Oh, Liv," Helen says, checks herself before she sounds truly out of patience. There's no competing with Olivia on the subject of their mother. Best to stay out of the road. But she can't resist adding, "I don't think she's turned away from you. That's silly."

Olivia shakes her head, as if Helen, who doesn't pray, holds the opinions of an amateur. But Helen won't rise to the bait. Instead, she asks how Amelia's been sleeping.

Olivia seems irritated by this detour. "I've stopped putting her back to bed," she says. "If she wants to sleep on the floor she can. Some mornings I find her in the hallway outside our door. Blanket all wadded up."

"That's something," Helen says.

Olivia nods, passes up this second chance to treat Helen as a know-nothing.

A moment later, Helen notices that her sister's crying, soundlessly. She feels around in her jacket for a Kleenex, but there's only an old movie stub and a Chap Stick. "Come on, Liv," she says softly.

"I don't know why I do this to myself," Olivia says. "I shouldn't come up here."

Don't then, Helen thinks, but there's no point in saying that. Anyway, it's not the cemetery. Whatever's eating Olivia, she brought it with her.

"Drop the kids off for a night," Helen offers. "You and Mark can do something."

"There's nothing *to* do."

"I mean it," Helen says.

And so do I, Olivia's face says.

Helen gives up, shrugs.

At last, Olivia collects herself, bends and touches the stone, returns to the Chevrolet. Helen hears it clunk into drive, waits until the brakelights have disappeared, then another few moments, thinks, *Beats me, Momma,* before turning away, climbing atop the bicycle. She digs into the pedals, builds a head of steam and tears down the long wet hill, too fast to stop if she had to, but God it feels *good.* She sails through the open gate, feet in the air, coasts under the colonnade of pines, and heads home, trying to remember if there's anything to make for supper. There's venison but she forgot to put it out to thaw. The whole idea of cooking irritates her suddenly. She can't fix her thoughts on it, wouldn't mind living on apple slices and peanut butter toast for a while if it weren't for Nick, who requires actual meals.

She waits at the highway. The traffic's heavier now. She decides to cut through town, rides past Jimmy's Machine, where Nick brought her once, she was maybe thirteen. She remembers the greasy dirt floor, the raised bin of coals, Jimmy Teal beating an edge onto a length of iron bar, a leathery *whack* where you'd expect it to ring. She remembers the metal's violent plunge into water, and begging Nick not to leave yet, finally being allowed to swing the hammer herself, two-handed, the men in good humor, their laughter not mean. The tall gray-planked doors are padlocked this afternoon . . . there's no sign they've been open all winter. Jimmy was old even then. She rides past the Esquire Motel with its corny pink neon *Yessiree* . . . past the A & W, past Marv's Mobil, the coin laundry, someone honking at her, she can't see who, riding straight down Montana Street into the sun, dull-gleaming like phosphorus . . . unseasonable, but still a wintry light.

It's a shame Celia's so far out of town, for Helen wouldn't mind a dose of Celia about now. Funny how Helen feels like the irreverent, impatient one around Olivia, but next to Celia so simple and guileless. She wouldn't mind them curling up at opposite ends of the big couch and splitting a bottle of wine, Celia filling the ashtray on her chest. Helen's not much of a drinker, but once in a while she craves that dreamy lethargy, that brake on her energy, and no one's better to drink with than Celia. She can be an itch, Celia, a shameless self-promoter, but what a gift for generosity, for fun. Even this new Celia that Thomas has called forth still knows how to throw her head back and hoot, so it's too bad she's not around, when Helen could use a good laugh.

Left onto Dakota, down First Avenue past the P.O., resisting the temptation to check on the Vagabond, a few headlights appearing now though not yet streetlights, her fingers going numb on the grips, but she's sweating inside her shirt, has her second wind, glides under the bare elms, the horse chestnuts, the catalpas with their obscenely rattling seeds.

Before long she's into Grover's Addition, down to the cul-de-sac, banging across the ruts and through the hedge to the Ochs house. Looks lifeless from the front, but a wan light spills out the back, dispersing in the air above the marsh. Linny's car, the black little Morris, sits in the half-thawed grass, amid an array of earlier tire prints. Helen stands the bike against the shrubs and peers through the back porch windows, learns nothing, steps in through the debris of water-spotted cartons and paint cans and garden stakes, tries the handle, pokes her head into the kitchen, calls out, "Lin, you home?"

It seems she isn't.

Helen scans the counters for something to write with, already assembling a message for her sister, better be something clever, too. She's standing pen in mouth when the bedroom door yawns open.

"Oh," Helen says, "I'm sorry, I thought—"

Linny squinting as if she's stumbled into a bank of klieg lights. All she has on is a man's shirt, old flannel tartan, maybe one of Wendy's father's. Nothing below, her long storky legs white as drinking straws. "Well, sweet Christ," she says.

Helen says again she's sorry, didn't mean to intrude or anything, and only now does it occur to her that perhaps Linny's not alone, that in another instant some man will appear in the doorway, likewise stunned and proud of himself. It's all she can do not to gape.

Linny has a long swill of water at the sink, ignites the range under the tea kettle before turning back to Helen, says, "As somebody brilliant once said, if you're going to take a nap you might as well get in bed."

Throws Helen a look that says, *That's my story and I'm sticking to it.*

Helen nods. Now would be the time to make her getaway, but instead she peels off the jacket, tosses it willfully, says, "You don't have a beer or anything do you, Lin?"

So it comes to pass that it's *Linny* she lounges on the sofa with, toe to toe, Labatt's for herself, Linny working on a smoky bottle of Christian Brothers. She's so thirsty, dehydrated, the first beer vanishes in a few long gulps, then a second, delicious relief. Linny's punched on an enormous tape recorder and the room is washed with blues songs. Billie Holiday, Linny says. It's just a name to Helen, a wire-service squib from the *Evening Record* of a year or two ago: Cirrhosis from alcohol, though she'd been a dope user as well . . . the nurses found fifty-dollar bills taped to her legs. Helen remembers these things. Linny sings a line now and then, droopy-eyed. "Oh honey, you never heard such man trouble," she says to make Helen laugh.

It's gotten dark, windy enough that the storm windows rattle in their sockets. "I should call Dad," Helen says, but feels too contented to move.

So Linny arches back over the sofa, hauls the phone into her lap, dials the house on McLaren Road. When Nick finally answers, she drops into a ridiculous baritone, says, "This Mr. Nick Stavros?"

Nick's voice like a kazoo.

"Mr. Stavros," she says, "we've got your youngest over here and she'd like me to inform you she hasn't fallen off the face of the planet."

Nick at some length now, then Linny slipping back into Linny, "Relax, Dad—" Rolling eyes at Helen. "Just a little meeting of the Ladies' Drinking Society."

Once they've pacified Nick, Linny swings through the kitchen and brings her sister back another beer, slides the dewy bottle across Helen's cheek before surrendering it.

Helen takes a long stinging swallow. "You know what today is?" she asks.

"Could it be a Tuesday?"

Helen smiles, says, "Lucky guess."

She had no intention of getting into how she'd spent the afternoon, no desire to hear Linny's take on this sentimental errand of hers, yet she can't resist describing Olivia standing over the gravestone in the gray mouton.

"Our keeper of the flame," Linny says.

How tempting it is to side with Linny.

"What do you think's going on with Liv?" Helen says after a while.

Indifferently, Linny asks, "Is something?"

Helen lets it drop. Always sparks between those two, she thinks. The far poles of the family psyche.

And now the phone rings. Won't be Nick, not his way to call right back. Helen watches Linny cast a cool eye at it, letting it trill away, ten, twelve, fourteen times. *So persistent.*

"I can never do that," Helen says, hears how damn earnest she sounds, even drunk.

"You ought to try it sometime," Linny says. "Good for the soul."

But this is not just innate contrariness on Linny's part, Helen understands suddenly. Whoever's on the phone is whoever vacated the bedroom.

Plus, when she can't stand it another instant and goes off to pee, the seat's up.

Sending You a Message

Never has Celia been locked in such proximity to one man. Sticky overheated short-lived closeness, yes, an abundance of that, but she could always retreat, recoup, recalculate. Now they're seldom apart, she and Thomas, even on his buying trips, the estate sales and out-of-town auctions. He wants her with him, has spent too much of his recent life eating alone, reading in a chair. And when he's home, he's home, out in one of the two shops, or in the showroom with customers, and certain of these he ushers in to meet her. "My wife Celia," he says with pleasure. Thomas has put her to work, too—for instance, he's teaching her to hand cane chairs. Fussiest job she's ever tried. He's given her six black walnut dinner chairs to practice on. Blossom and leaves carved into the back piece, dingy brocade tacked artlessly over the worn-out cane seat. Up and down, side to side, two passes on the diagonal until a row of octagons appears . . . it's wicked getting the tension right, the old wood cracks easily, bruises if she's not careful, and if the strip of cane snaps, it all has to come out. And yet, strange to say, she likes the work immensely. It quells her thoughts. A year ago, could she have imagined this? Not for a second.

Elinor and Thomas never lived in this house together,

nonetheless Celia can't avoid feeling like an imposter sometimes, a squatter. Needs reassurances. "So what do you
think?" she asks across the worktable. "Think we got a future
here, To-mas?"

"How's that?" he says, feigning absorption.

"You and me?"

A calm, appraising look, glasses low on his nose. "Yes, I'm
sure of it," he says. *And it's not bullshitting.* It's what he
believes. Amazing that Celia Balfour is the object of this confidence, amazing that he can bring himself to say it aloud.

Or maybe he thinks he's used up his bad luck. Imagine that.

She has an unquenchable desire to please him. Holds up
clothes, this skirt or *this* skirt? Which lipstick?

"That one, what's that one called?"

"Um, Night on Earth."

He knows he has to choose, chooses.

Is he the scrappiest lover she's ever had? No fair asking, the
man's fifty-two. Does he surprise her? His staying power, that's
nice, his attention to detail, his lack of squeamishness. But
worse surprises, odd tastes coming to light now that the
hoopla's over? Part of her remains vigilant, she can't avoid it.
Have they worked out how to talk about his dead wife?
Whether pictures of her will be on display permanently, how
often Thomas can say, "Elie used to—" or, "One time we
were—" before Celia has a right to feel squeezed? But what he
says is only conversational, nothing dark and intimate, and
while Celia's curiosity is awful, she knows she's better off igno-
rant of certain things. Scrupulously, Thomas avoids compar-
ing the two of them. Every month or so, she'll see him on the
phone and know from the jut of his neck he's chatting with Elinor's mother, who lives in Baltimore. Celia swings the kitchen
door closed, grants him his privacy.

One afternoon, the first week of March, she's loitering in
the shop door, indulging in a quiet smoke, when a picture of

her youngest sister flashes to mind for no obvious reason: Helen holding out a softball mitt, two-handed the way she used to, as if waiting under a pop fly, mouth open. Vivid color, surreal slanty light like before a thunderstorm . . . nothing she remembers specifically, but Helen was always flinging a ball at the shed roof, half the shingles have cracked and kited off in the weather. Not two minutes later, she spots Nick's old Ford truck bumping down the lane and Helen's at the wheel.

"Hey, girl," Celia says. "I was just thinking about you. No fooling."

"That's because I was *sending you a message*," Helen says, sliding out, not quite smiling. A reference to the time Olivia made everyone try to send her their thoughts. She recorded the data in a ledger book kept wedged under her mattress.

A Mexican sombrero.

A man juggling oranges.

The three of hearts.

All one winter, Olivia relentless, undeterred by the spotty results. Until the night Linny sent her the "two snakes fucking" message. Linny was in the bedroom with Celia, Olivia down at the kitchen table as always, lights out for better concentration. Olivia charged the stairs, "That's not *funny*, Linny—"

Linny trying to make her say it out loud, "C'mon, what'd you see?"

Olivia red-faced, knocking at her with one fist. So much for that project.

Today, this moist, fragrant afternoon, Helen looks great, Celia thinks, legs hard in the jeans, gait firm and springy. It's time to start paying a little more attention to Helen, that's for sure.

Celia gives her sister a squeeze, leads her into the shop to show off her artistry, makes Helen bounce her hand on the chair seat. "Tight as a tennis racket."

"You did that?"

"Don't act so dumbfounded."

The other shed is heated by an electric blower, wall-mounted, but this one has two barrel stoves. It smells of larch, of resin, naval jelly, of the glue pots, the burlap and old horse-hair stuffing. Amazing the comfort it gives. It's tempting to subject Helen to the complete tour, to name off the various hinges, the wood joints . . . she has to remind herself this stuff's fascinating only to *her*. Fascinating because of *Thomas*.

Celia asks instead what she owes the honor of this visit to.

"I don't need a reason, do I?"

But Helen's got *something* cooking, that's obvious. "Coffee?" Celia asks.

"I don't mean to interrupt—"

"It's okay, Thomas is always good for some."

In the kitchen, Helen asks, almost casually, "You talked to Lin lately?"

"I don't know," Celia answers, "it's been a couple weeks. How come?"

"I think she's seeing someone."

"Yeah? Good for old Linny."

Helen nods noncommittally, gets to her feet, plants herself at the plate glass window. "I don't believe your view," she says. Beyond the mudflats, the lake wears a light chop today. Way out, there's a thin black line of ducks, mergansers or coots.

"You know what," Celia says, coming up beside her. "I never spent ten seconds looking at a bird before we moved here."

Helen turns abruptly, gives her a long, calculating stare, says, "You're not pregnant yet, are you?"

Smiling, surprised at Helen's bluntness, Celia says, "No, ma'am. Do I look it?"

"I just thought you might be," Helen says.

"It's not for lack of effort," Celia says, wishing to coax a smile out of her sister. In fact, she and Thomas *have* been trying diligently. Her period's due at week's end, and she's hoping, feels she should know, and doesn't, which is irksome, and therefore she won't let herself think about it, or not much.

"So what'd you get out of Linny?" she asks.

"Nothing."

"Well, that's about right."

She checks the bread box, locates half a package of Lorna Doones, slides them onto a plate. "And what of your own illustrious love life?"

Helen shrugs, her usual response.

Celia's about to press her—*her* usual response—but Thomas swings into the kitchen now and she throws her head back to accept an upside-down kiss. If Helen weren't here he'd cop a feel.

"Thought I recognized the truck," he says to Helen, straightening. "How's by you?"

Helen says she's all right.

"Staying for supper?" he asks.

"Not tonight."

A look of genuine disappointment. "Well, don't be a stranger."

He fills a mug at the stove, tells Celia, "I'm going to run that lowboy up to the Marshalls, shouldn't be any later than five-thirty. If Mrs. Healey calls, tell her I'm still waiting for the globe. I'll call her in the morning, okay? You need anything?"

"Just you," Celia says.

And when Thomas has departed, she shakes her head at herself, says, "Aren't I just sickening?"

But Helen blurts out, "Ceel, I think it's Mark."

"What's Mark?"

"Linny."

Celia takes a moment to screw this into focus, says, "Oh now, gimme a break."

Helen knuckles a hand against her cheekbone, looks off miserably.

"Okay, tell me where you got that idea."

"No place in particular," Helen says. "It just occurred to me. But now I can't stop believing it."

"You didn't *see* anything?"

Helen shakes her head.

Yet it certainly is strange to see Helen upset, brooding. Not her style at all. "Listen," Celia says, "I don't think you need to get your bowels in an uproar." She folds a leg under herself, leans close enough to touch Helen on the flannel sleeve. "Linny's not that mean. C'mon." She pooches her lips for effect, says, "She might *think* about it for half a second, she might flirt. That's if Mark was her *type,* which, believe me, he doesn't begin to be. You know how she goes for those wasted artsy-fartsy guys."

Helen says, "Maybe she's sick of that kind."

"Uh huh. And maybe the sky's going to rain pearls."

For a long time, no response from Helen. Eventually, she says, "Liv's miserable."

"She kind of has a talent for that."

"This is different."

"Well, hon, I'll give her a call if you want."

"But you can't say anything."

No, Celia promises, she won't say anything.

Celia makes a brief stab at getting Helen to change her mind about supper. A pan of lasagna's thawing, there's loads, but she finds she's just as happy when her sister says again she really can't, she's been letting Nick down a lot lately, it seems he's going through one of those periods when he needs her around. So Celia walks her outside, arm around her shoulder. She considers telling Helen about that funny waiting-for-the-ball-to-fall vision she'd had, but can't see the point in it now.

She says finally, "Don't let your thoughts run away with you, okay?"

"You're a great one to talk."

"Oh, I know. But I mean it."

Helen nods, rakes back her hair violently as if she agrees, but sometimes even Helen's hard to read. Celia stands in the wet gravel, watching until the truck has disappeared into the willows.

For a man who's going to spend his evening doing taxes, Thomas is amazingly chipper at the dinner table. Celia listens, watches, eats hungrily. If she *is* pregnant, she thinks for the umpteenth time, the child will have more of a grandfather in Thomas. And what about *her*, crawling into bed with an old man. Weird to contemplate, even now Thomas's calves are baby-soft, milky, the skin by his ears like crepe, but weirder still is that none of this fazes her.

Amazing that Celia Balfour looks her life in the eye and says, *So be it.*

Cleaning up, she can hear the *crank, crank* of the adding machine in the den where Thomas is working at the card table. She'd love to join him, stretch out on the sofa bed, but refrains. You don't want to suffocate a man like Thomas. She folds the dishrag, droops it over the neck of the faucet, and before she can talk herself out of it, lights a Parliament and dials Olivia's, anticipates her voice.

But Mark answers. The TV's going in the background, inane theme music. "Just a second," he says, and she hears him ask Davey to turn it down. "Liv's on laundry duty," he says.

"That's all right. Actually, it was you I wanted."

"Really? What for?"

"Just wanted to see how you were getting along."

"I'm okay," Mark says. "I'll be ready for some decent weather."

"Amen to that," Celia says, jerks the cord loose from the drawer pull it's caught on. "So Liv kind of in a funk?"

Audible sigh from Mark's end. "I guess that's one way of saying it."

"What's going on, Mark?"

"I don't know. Nothing."

"It's not you, is it?"

"It's not me what?"

"That's messing Liv up."

"Ceel, this is a big subject. Olivia—"

"You know how I feel about my sisters, Mark. I can't stand the thought of anything happening to one of them."

"You want me to have her call you?"

Celia runs water over the end of her smoke and pitches it into the garbage. "What I want's for you to reassure me," she says. "Can't you do that?"

Mark's slow to answer, and what he says wouldn't float a shadow.

Celia waits a long while on the other end, says finally, "You be good to her."

No anger, no resentment at having his private life pawed into. Mark tries again, says, "It's not like I don't love her, Ceel."

"Boy, you better," Celia says, that old tough-girl sound in her voice, and so Mark laughs, in relief it must be, and Celia joins him, despite herself.

Much later that night, she wakes from a ragged, crowded dream, sweaty, twisted in her nightgown. The sausage in the lasagna, so salty she's retained water, and now it wants out, though a few minutes pass before she can pull herself away from Thomas. He's such a boyish sleeper, gives off the faint smell of almonds, a tiny hum that sounds like *uh-huh, uh-huh*. Sometimes she runs her finger over the big vein snaking up his temple, feels the slow bump of blood, prays only that it continue.

She swings her legs out, stubs her feet into slippers, scuffs down the hallway, stops under the attic fan, hearing a few random tings on the steel roof. Thinks pleasurably, *Rain*, realizes when the noise keeps building that, in fact, it's hailstones, listens as they pound down in a clattering torrent.

The Moment-to-Moment

It's a late spring, but finally there comes a dawn with fading stars, an expanse of empty sky. A morning when Mark can ride to work with the window open a crack. In March, they'd had a week when Norman Sibley's nine switchbacks were impassable, rain atop breakup . . . one of Poverman's trucks sailed off and mired to its wheel wells, but a grader's been brought in, the road scraped down to a firmer gravel, and by now the ground is more or less dry underfoot, the air sweet and rank, peppered with birdsong. There's dog fennel erupting along the ditches, salmonberry, skunk cabbage. The Sibleys themselves have been absent for several weeks, which improves Ike's mood, not to mention Whitey's. There's fussy shit left to do indoors, plus the exterior siding and trim work, but instead they've moved on to the garage. More heavy timbers, a funny break near the bottom of the roof line, seven-foot eaves. "Looks like a friggin' pagoda," Whitey says. The apartment upstairs has twin bedrooms, an airy sitting room, dormers looking onto the steep grassy drop of the hillside, the valley.

For days, in off moments, Mark stewed about Celia's phone call. Wondered if it truly meant she sensed what was what. Olivia says the sisters track one another with sister radar, and maybe they can . . . what does Mark know about that, a man, an only child? But from what he can observe, they're blind to each other, or plain *wrong,* part of the time, so who can say? Nonetheless, he's been unsettled, felt giddy and doomed, has waited for another fishing expedition from Celia, *expected* it. But a week passed, another, a third. He saw Thomas Balfour downtown, and Thomas inquired after his well-being, and Olivia's, the kids' . . . the two men waiting out a brief downpour. "All fine," Mark said, detecting no special scrutiny from his brother-in-law. So he writes off his edginess to the guilt that murmurs at him, spits in his ear, *Mark, what the fuck?*

Linny never talks about them being found out. Taboo subject. Nor will Mark force her . . . he's not about to display that weakness to her. The few times he's brought up the future, even indirectly, she's thrown him that sidelong look, which a moment later will deteriorate into letdown, into frank disappointment. So he's taught himself to let it go. If they have any future, it will catch them without a story. The thing is, he can't imagine not having Linny now.

One afternoon, then, Mark passes before the empty window hole on the upper story of the garage, pauses in the breeze it offers, the kind of moment you'd pull out a smoke if you smoked, otherwise just stop and get your bearings, when he happens to notice his sister-in-law Helen conversing with one of the stone masons far across the lot. The two of them turn and look his direction, the way people suddenly turn and stare at you in a dream. He gets an immediate plunging sensation in his gut. If something had happened to one of the kids they wouldn't send Helen, would they? Would her gait be so steady, or is she only being deliberate, keeping cool? He casts a look at Roddy, whose cheek is engorged with chew, then at Ike's bearish mound of shoulder, decides whatever Helen's errand, he doesn't want to hear about it in front of them, and so hustles to the ladder and climbs down, catching a sliver in the meat of his hand, but never mind that.

"Something wrong?" he asks, intercepting her.

"I don't know," Helen says. "Is there?"

The day may be springlike, but there's a chill rising off the floor slab. "Let's get out where it's warm," Mark says, edging her into the sunlight.

Helen's in an old canvas shirt and jeans and a pair of swamp boots, her hair swept back in a blue plastic clip. No makeup, a severe look, but handsome. He almost wraps a friendly arm around her.

"What's up, Helen?"

Now it's Helen who hesitates, who suddenly seems to believe she can pass her presence off as a social call.

"Imagine living like this," she says, her eyes on the sprawling backside of the Sibley house.

"The other half," Mark says. "The other tenth of one percent."

"They must have a big pack of kids."

"I don't think so," Mark says. "Two, I think, and they're older. In college?" On the blueprint are bedrooms marked *Lucien* and *Allison,* but until this moment Mark hasn't considered the formality of it, hasn't contemplated the rooms standing empty.

He pulls back so he can see Helen face-to-face, asks, "You want to see inside? The grand tour?"

"No thanks."

"It's no trouble."

She shakes her head. And so, as they stand in the loose gravel, neither of them talking, it dawns on Mark that it's forthright, practical Helen who knows. He feels a rush of pity for her. Coming all the way up here, then not able to get a start on it. He's always been fond of Helen, remembers her as a twelve year old with bangs, bike-chain grease on her cheek. Strange, but he always thought if he was like one of the Stavros girls, it was Helen. Not that he can make this any easier for her.

He senses Roddy's leer burning into him, turns and whips a look back. No one's there. Now he *does* touch Helen, lightly, urges her to walk with him.

She gives in.

Down Sibley's road, the two of them, looking out at the day. A frail green on the valley floor, shadows of lumpy fairweather clouds passing soundlessly over the uneven ground.

Mark doesn't know until the last second whether he'll lie or not when the allegation comes.

Still walking, Helen says, "You know why I came here."

He makes her say it aloud. In reply, he laughs goodnaturedly, acts flattered, dumbstruck. And, inside, he *is* dumbstruck, all right . . . not so much appalled at himself as curious to learn that he's reached another new stage.

He can't tell immediately if Helen buys it. She won't come back at you like Celia, just walks on, arms crossed, watching her feet.

Of course, you can protest too much. So he adds simply, "You know I'd never do that to Liv."

They stop at the next turn, stand breathing deep breaths.

"Helen, I need to get back," he says. "You know how it is."

She pats a moist temple, says nothing. They hike back up the road to where she's left the truck. Mark grabs the door for her, can't help admiring the muscular way she pulls herself in by the wheel. He offers a brotherly smile.

She says something in return, but behind him one of the cement mixers comes to life, drowning it out.

"I'm sorry, what?"

Helen leans toward him, says, "I said, if it's true you have to quit it."

Which stuns Mark. Shouldn't, but it does.

Then she's gone. And where does the rest of the day disappear to? Down the sinkhole.

Quarter to six, Whitey lets him out at the end of his drive. He drops his toolbox and apron on the bench in the garage, enters through the kitchen. Olivia has Amelia up on the counter, wiping a purple stain from her face. "There isn't any beer, is there?" he asks.

"I didn't get to the store," Olivia says flatly, unapologetically.

Mark leans in and kisses his daughter and hoists her down to the floor.

"I'll run and get some," he says.

"Take the list," she says. "And put down hamburger buns and Vaseline."

"That sounds appetizing."

A ghost of a smile from Olivia. "Write it down, will you?"

Marks assures her he'll remember. He digs out his wallet, looks in. Three ones, wilted, damp. "You got any money, Liv?" he asks.

Checkbook's in her purse, she nods to where it's hanging off one of the chairs.

Mark loiters at the dinette, flipping through the register, sees that Olivia has failed to write down a couple of checks, decides not to make an issue of it just now, though why in God's name she can't just write the checks down like an ordinary person is beyond him. He runs some mental subtraction, guesses he'll be okay if he watches it. Payday's day after tomorrow.

At the door, he tells her he won't be long.

Daylight savings now, evening light to squander, people out mowing, walking uptown in thin jackets.

The last place on earth he should go is Linny's, what if

Helen's actually *watching* the place. But that's crazy, isn't it? You can't give in to thoughts like that.

Store first or after?

After, if you want the beer cold. He heads toward Grover's Addition, only has a minute, no time for anything, but it's imperative that he see her. Touch base, at least. A quick word. He pilots the Chevrolet through the break in the hedge, getting that rush that starts in the groin, like sparks showering into his legs, up his back where it's sweating against the seat, and he's still half-giggling over the Vaseline sandwich.

But, Christ, the Minor's not there. Just simply, no matter how long he stares at the oil-spotted grass, not where he had it pictured. *Where is she?* He climbs out, takes eight or ten long strides toward the back door, changes his mind, stops cold, tries to think, all that energy in his limbs suddenly useless, toxic.

Back on Paxson Road, he sits outside with one of the blessed beers, waiting for the coals to heat. No matter where he moves, the stink of lighter fluid seems to follow him, and it's not that warm out, really. He crams the fingers of his free hand under his armpit. He can just about see his breath. Down at the edge of the lawn, under the crab apple, the picnic table's still covered with a blue tarp, weighted with stones. One of these days he'll have to peel it off, get ready for summer.

Olivia slips out through the sliding door with the hamburg patties. "You want two?" she asks him. "I made you two."

Mark nods. He hears the flare as, one after another, they hit the grill.

"How was your day?" she asks. "Was it okay?"

"Yeah, fine."

"You look tired."

"No," he says, "just, I don't know—"

"I'll be glad when you're done with that house," Olivia says.

"They'll just be another one."

"I only meant—"

But Mark says, "I didn't mean to jump on you." He stands. "Can I get you a beer?"

She hesitates, thinks about it, looks at him, says all right.

Inside, he pulls out two more Lucky Lagers, flips the caps, not his favorite beer, but they were on special. He starts back, stops and pours Olivia's into a glass and brings it to her, slips it into her hand, hears her nearly inaudible thanks.

No, the thing is, he doesn't think about the future much at all these days. His grandmother: *The older I get the more I just live in the moment-to-moment, it's the only way that makes any sense to me now. I can't explain it, Mark.* It's not exactly wisdom in his case, though, just the way he's become since Linny. But he was a champion planner when he and Olivia were first in love, was he not? Couldn't stand it until they were married and he was working . . . felt like he was coming out of his skin, saw himself learning what there was to learn, acquiring his skills and winning Ike's favor, having the kids with Olivia, buying a house at some point . . . granted he wouldn't have pictured this exact place, who in their right mind would, but anyway here they are dutifully making payments, and though it's true he doesn't dwell on his father's life twenty-four hours a day, isn't it also true that he's pleased down in his bones that his grandmother can say he's turned out all right, that Morgan Singer was just one unfortunate side trip, not a mutation the family would be saddled with forever? All he'd foreseen, however hazily, has come to pass. And now, as Linny would say, he finds himself out of the foreseeing business. The future turning out not to be a place to show his worth, but a no-man's-land, an expanse of pitted ground to cross until he's with Linny again, and nothing, nothing to speed the crossing.

"Mark?"

He rises and follows Olivia inside, calls the kids to the table, waits staring at the circles of onion.

Davey's hair is sticking out in back as if he's been sleeping on it. He has a paper construction over the ends of his fingers. "Pick a number," he tells Mark.

"Six."

Fingers weaving in and out, four, five, six. "Now pick a color."

"Burnt umber."

"No, a regular color."

"That's the color of the house we're building," Mark says. "Cream and burnt umber. One of the bathrooms is 'seafoam,' another is 'the rosy fingers of dawn.' " But he smiles before Davey can get flustered, says, "Blue."

The boy finally peels back a flap and reads Mark his fortune: *You're a silly goose.*

"I want a different one," Mark says.

"You only get one."

"What about tomorrow?"

"You can have another one tomorrow."

Mark picks up his beer bottle and salutes his son. "Here's to tomorrow, then."

He looks to the opposite end of the table and Olivia lifts her glass as well.

To tomorrow and tomorrow and tomorrow.

That night in bed, Olivia tells him he's a good father, that it's clear he's trying, even if sometimes it seems he's bored with *her,* and leaves no opening for him to say no, he's not bored with her, for Christ's sake, how could she think that, he loves her . . . but shows him *she's* trying, too, finds his hand in the bedclothes and maneuvers it to the bodice of her gown, the myriad buttons unfastened tonight, slides it across her sternum onto the breast, which is filmy with bath oil, still radiating heat, tightens her fingers atop his, and even when his hand begins to work of its own volition, keeps hers there, moving it almost violently.

But later he finds himself thinking about boredom. If ever there was a sin in his grandmother's house, that was it, saying you were bored. Not that she put in that way, invested it with fire and brimstone. She treated it more as an affront to common sense: *If you're bored, do something.* Which is how he learned to play chess, drifting about the stacks of the county library looking at the spines of books, glassy-eyed, November drizzling down the long windows, until he came upon Kepler's *Basics of Chess* and pulled it down, frayed yellow cover, he can see it perfectly.

Which is why his grandmother would, on occasion, stick the CLOSED sign in the front window and load them into her boat of a sedan, no destination in mind. They'd wind up in junk shops or cafes in other towns, his grandmother ordering a big platter of chicken livers and making him try one, which is how he discovered *that* taste. Even now he craves it sometimes. Olivia screws her face up in disgust, so he fries them for himself when no one's around. And once he and his grandmother drove as far as Adriane Springs and she talked Mark into the mudbaths, so there they were, two heads floating in the fine silty broth, camas fields undulating and sulky blue under the overcast, mist becoming rain finally, splattering craters into the mud, slow-motion, comical, intensely fascinating to old Audrey Singer in her black bathing cap, and Mark thinks now, if this worked for her, more power to her, Jesus Christ.

Olivia stirs, licks her lips in her sleep, settles again.

Puny-sounding word, bored, boredom. . . . *even if you're bored with me, Mark.* Can't begin to describe the sensation that blindsides him sometimes, crumples his knees, *This is my life and no other.* Why doesn't love dispel it? Why only excitement?

No answer for that. For anything.

Vagabond

One July day, the summer after Grace's death, Nick was picking his way through the red willow along the river, getting some air, stretching his legs, a late afternoon, the light coming off the shallows in fiery spangles. He was hot and his head ached. He'd done nothing but run the cafe for months, had barely been outdoors, and was only taking this walk now because he'd promised Olivia he would. He crossed under the Old Steel Bridge, stopped a minute to watch some boys jumping. They were a little older than Helen, thirteen or fourteen, tanned a rich caramel, two of them. The other boy was in long pants rolled to the shins, his torso gangling, milky. It seemed late in the summer for jumping, but Nick gathered that a deeper channel lay out between the pylons. He watched the boys hang from the struts, watched them wave and horse around and finally let go. Three miraculous seconds in the air, then the tenderfooted hike across the rocks and up through the brambles and back across the splintery bridge planks. That's about how things work, Nick thought. Half a dozen jumps he watched. Then he saw the white-skinned boy dangle outside the railing, dodging his hands back and forth to avoid having them pounded by the other two. Next thing, the boy was tumbling over backward. His shoulders curled and smacked the water.

Nick waited for him to surface. Saw nothing but the oily dimples on the river, spinning away.

The boy, it turned out, was Aaron Cripps, one of the banker Connie Cripps's kids. The other two were riffraff he'd been forbidden to associate with. Nick woke from his stupor, shucked off his boots, surmised where the current had taken the boy and swam there. The water was astonishingly cold. He caught sight of an arm, waving tendrillike. He reached down, and hauled him up. The boy began to cough and flail, so the neck hadn't broken, Nick thought. No iron lung for him. It came to pass that the Cripps family wanted to honor Nick's heroism publicly. One evening that August, Nick was obliged to walk out across the rodeo grounds in a dress shirt and stand on a plywood platform facing the bleachers and accept a token of the Cripps's largesse. By far the worst of it was bending his head to the microphone, and hearing his words boom from the loudspeakers. Deeply mortifying. In the car on the way home, he whispered into his oldest daughter's ear, "If I'd known about that part I would've let the little bastard float away." Thank God for Linny who loved Nick's dark jokes.

Anything smacking of ceremony and Nick balks. Why it should be like that, he's at a loss to explain. He remembers giving Olivia away, the church full of well-wishers, a May afternoon, unseasonable, the heat concentrated and unstirring, the reek of gardenias nearly suffocating. Managing all that without Grace. Two of his sisters had come out on the train for the event . . . Nick hadn't been back to Chicago in some time, so add in a little undercurrent of reproof. The house on McLaren Road was aswarm with women. Olivia was on another planet. The planet beyond the planet she was usually on, according to Linny. Mark's grandmother had sewn Olivia's dress, and there were endless fittings, but it was a nice dress, Nick thought, eyelets across the front and sleeves that hung loose like a kimono's. And then the long walk up the carpet to Mark Singer, who managed, in his good clothes, to look nearly old enough to be getting married. A proud moment, you'd think, and Nick *was* proud, this was Olivia, after all, the one who idolized him, who could worry herself sick over him. At the same time, the ritual of it, the way he was all fathers, seemed to cut off his air.

And he feels anything but ceremonious at present, but he can't put this off any longer, succumbs to the logic of getting today's lousy business done in one fell swoop. He asks Helen and the other waitress, Connie Bell, and the salad girl, Rochelle Henke, to stay when they close at half-past three, and he's phoned the others, asked if they wouldn't mind coming in for a minute, won't take long. Stella Baucus, Billy Krona, Olivia, Linny, Rochelle's mother who's been baking pies for the Vagabond here lately, and even Beryl Sykes, who worked for Nick and Grace years ago, and still believes Nick will call on her to take a shift if he's stuck, even old Beryl with her face powder and wattles and croaking laugh. Only Celia is missing—off at a sale in Great Falls with Thomas—but it can't be helped. Nick hasn't called a meeting like this in ages, and though he's trying to keep an even keel, as Grace would say, it's obvious the way he's grumping around, adamantly waiting until everyone's present, that he's got something out of the ordinary to say. Not even Helen can shake him loose. Finally, it's just Linny they're waiting for, then she comes traipsing in through the back, rayon blouse rippling as she walks. She slides her sunglasses onto her bristly head, tosses Nick one of her sly smiles, asks, "What're we celebrating?"

It's been almost two months since his confab with Alt. He's thought about taking Helen aside, confiding, but couldn't face it. Every day it gets worse. He's let her go through the charade of ordering months' worth of syrup, malt mix, Borax, pie cherries. It's a slap in the face, he knows that, knows too that Helen, though youngest, is the one most attached to the

Vagabond. But at no time has he considered undoing his agreement with Alt, and for all he knows, he may not be *able* to back out of it now. What he finds himself wishing, fervidly, is to reclaim some of the decisiveness he had in his thirties, even his forties. It must have worn through, the way his teeth have, down through the enamel, into the pulp.

He reaches up and yanks off the ceiling fan. Except for the coolers' low hum, it's exceptionally quiet in the cafe. He backs against the counter, fingers the chrome edging, nine faces trained on him. "Well, this is how it is," he starts, sallies ahead with his news: Building's been sold, Vagabond's going out of business.

An ugly silence then, Connie Bell the first to respond. She asks when. Pretty, pale blonde girl, hard to overstate the lift Nick gets seeing her every morning. Her husband's an earnest-looking kid who works with the Mahughs at Equity Supply . . . something wrong with one of his legs, doesn't bend.

"Couple weeks," he says. "Not much time, I realize." He palpates his whiskery cheek. "I don't expect this thrills any of you. Doesn't thrill me having to say it."

Picking his words, he tells about Garvin Alt, the expansion of the furniture company. Nick's antipathy for Alt is no secret, so there *is* explaining to be done. He hesitates, squinting, says finally, "You have to do things when it comes time," which is certainly a mealy-sounding way to put it, but suddenly, as if shamed, he's unsure how willing he is to get into it with them.

Old Beryl shakes her head, the way she would at an obituary in the paper.

Helen won't even meet his eyes.

Nick looks from Connie to wispy Rochelle to Stella, who no doubt thinks this is a test devised by her Savior, lets his gaze rest a second on Billy Krona, feels genuinely bad for him, kid like that, says, "I'll make some calls for all of you, see what I can do. And you'll be getting a check when the dust settles."

He wipes at his face. "There's something else I need to ask you, too," he says. "I don't want you saying anything to the customers. I'd rather if we didn't make any announcement."

"We're just going to slip away in the night. That your big plan?"

This from Olivia, her voice raw, affronted.

Nick's caught offguard. Sarcasm's the last thing you expect from Olivia.

Support arrives from an odd quarter. Linny slides off the table she's been lounging on, wheels around to face Olivia. "Don't give him a bad time, Liv."

Pulling rank.

"I can't believe you wouldn't discuss this with the rest of us," Olivia says. "And I don't see why we can't just *move* the cafe."

"Maybe he doesn't care to make the Vagabond a vagabond," Linny says. "Maybe he wants to make a vagabond of himself."

"Is *that* it?" Olivia snaps. "You're going somewhere?"

"Liv, it was just a decision I had to make," Nick says. He gives her a look that says he's finished dissecting it in public.

Olivia's nowhere near ready to let him off the hook, but she's getting no help from anyone, not even Helen.

"I'm sure this is hard enough without you making it worse," Linny says.

"I'm just sick," Olivia says.

Nick looks to Linny, *Don't say anything cruel,* and Linny merely turns away.

In a few minutes, it's over, this moment he's dreaded, and the cafe has emptied. Nick douses the lights, checks the front door, though he's already checked it once, ditto the stoves, heads down the back hall, believing at least one of this crowd will be waiting to waylay him outside, but he finds the alley deserted.

He drives home the longest way he can think of, rolls into McLaren Road, creeps past his neighbors' houses. The Skonnards' plums have exploded into blossom. A nice evening, warm at last, and his chore accomplished, but the relief he'd tricked himself into expecting has failed to show. His stomach's burning. He'd guessed Helen wouldn't be here, that she'd steer clear of him for a time, and why not? But the truck's in its usual berth by the shed. Nick parks, shuts off the engine, takes a cigar from the glove box, pats his pockets for a match. Then slumps back in the seat, stares, returns the cigar to its package, and goes inside.

The kitchen light is on, the newspaper lying on the oilcloth, still folded. Nick pokes his head into the living room. No sign of Helen. In seclusion upstairs, he imagines. He opens the icebox, pulls out a Ballantine Ale, uncaps it. Always seems like a wonderful idea, drizzle cold anaesthetic down his throat. Immediate peace. Twenty minutes later it's worse. He knows that, does it anyway. What he really needs is food—he's had nothing but a sweet roll since morning, orts of Jack cheese and whatnot. He steps back out to the front room, listens to the house, hears water running in the pipes, a door latching.

Half an hour later, he climbs the staircase, carrying a tray, stops outside Helen's room, asks her to open up. After a bit, she does.

"Brought you a sandwich," he says.

Helen looks from his face to the china plate and back again, nods. She's changed into sweatshirt and dungarees, ratty slippers. She peels back the top flap of rye bread. Fried liverwurst, a private craving of Nick's that Helen shares, both of them subject to derision when the house was full of people. A slice of raw onion, a skim of German mustard, two wedges of pickle, a handful of Fritos. "Thanks," she says.

Nick lets her eat, stands regarding the backyard. The light's at a low slant, and the west side of everything looks like gold leaf. "I went about this all wrong, where you're concerned," he says finally.

"But that doesn't mean you're changing your mind."

"No."

A while later, he says, "I thought it would be you got mad at me. I never dreamed it would be your sister."

Helen shrugs, as if to say, *You never know.*

"Mind if I—" he says, easing his body onto the edge of her mattress.

Helen reclines against the headboard, cross-legged, hands cupping the two walnut finials.

"I don't know about Olivia," Nick ventures. "Seems like something's wrong there."

Helen nods.

"Well, is there?"

"She's not very happy, Dad."

"I can see that," Nick says. "But what is it?"

"I don't know," Helen says.

"You don't have any idea?"

Helen looks at him. "You know how it is with her," she says. "It comes and goes."

"She's not pregnant again?"

"Not that I'm aware of," Helen says.

Nick rubs his hand on the ribs of the bedspread. "Well," he says at last, "what about you?"

"I'm not pregnant either," Helen says. "That I'm aware of."

Nick says, "I hope to Christ not. I meant about the other."

"About the other," Helen says. "I don't know. I thought we'd keep doing it a lot longer." She bends and slides her plate back onto the tray and clears the hair from her face. "But now, I don't know. I'm not crushed or anything. *That's* what's so surprising. I'm just—"

"I know," Nick says. He stands, checks the yard again. Nothing has changed but the light.

"What I wanted to explain back there," he says. "It occurred to me I didn't have to fight the man. I mean, I was ready to, Helen, I was going to tell the son of a bitch, 'Over my breathless body.' But I didn't. I saw it a different way all of a sudden. That he was cutting me loose."

"*Us.*"

Nick sighs.

"That's what Olivia's afraid of," Helen says.

"What?"

"People getting cut loose."

Nick nods, though only partially getting her drift. He waits for her to go on. She doesn't.

He's beat, he realizes. Footsore, almost swooning with fatigue. He pictures himself careening over backward onto his own bed, swallowed by the comforter. But if he succumbs at this hour, he'll only wake at two, two-thirty, and nothing's worse. So when Helen gets up, stretching, and says she's going outside, going for a walk, asks if he wants to come, Nick surprises himself, says, "Sure, okay."

Up McLaren Road to where it dead-ends, and down a gravel lane beside the Murkett's horse pasture, then single file along a ditch running high this evening, splashing loudly at the head gate. Helen in the lead, encountering eddies of cool air, pockets of fragrance. They emerge onto Cavandish, walk along the crumbled blacktop, father and daughter.

Bang-up Job

One afternoon, Mark asks Whitey to drop him at the City Service station. He calls Olivia from the pay phone outside, plugging his other ear with a finger. Gonna be late, he says, maybe an hour, go ahead and feed the kids. He has to help Whitey haul a water heater out of his cellar. Full of sediment, weighs a ton.

"Can't it *wait*, Mark?"

Since Nick's pronouncement, a week ago, Olivia's been edgy, watchful, keeps challenging Mark, asks why Nick would do such a thing, as if Mark understands and won't say, as if they're in collusion. It does seem odd his father-in-law would jettison the cafe so abruptly, odd he consulted no one. Still, you sink your life into a place you're entitled, aren't you? And maybe it wasn't so abrupt after all, maybe the branch had been cracking for years. Mark swears he's as disturbed as anyone. Let's not forget the hours he logged there himself. Let's not forget how the Vagabond drew him in, how it virtually delivered him into Olivia's arms, so it's not like he has no *stake* in this, but he can't say he sees anything ominous and sinister behind the sale, the demolition. It's just the way things work out. Olivia looks at him as if he's speaking Mongolian.

Into the phone, he answers, "I'll be back as soon as I can," and hangs up.

He gets a 7UP from the machine, drinks it in three long swallows, slides the bottle into the wire rack. He picks his way though the cruddy lot behind the station, out onto Three Mile. Old cottonwoods tower over the road, not yet in full leaf, some of their limbs brought down by the wind of two nights ago, crushed to pulp under tires. Sperry's begun to spill out this end of town, four new streets bulldozed into a field he can remember rippling with clover. Anita, Betty, Cheri, Donna. He pictures an envelope, *25 Donna Street,* shakes his head. Finds himself back to that thought he had the other night, *Finish one house, there's always another.* He's been with Ike Conlon since 1952, and how many have they built? He's lost track. Sometimes he'll cruise by a place and get a blast of memory . . . the afternoon it was so hot the truck from Poverman's blew a tire while they were all standing around, he can even remember the cooped-up smell of the air, everyone watching the rim settle into the mushy tar. Or the time Whitey's girlfriend had the telegram delivered to the worksite, or the afternoon they puked up bad well water, all but Mark who'd been put off by the stink of the hose. He remembers the layout of certain houses, pictures them with only the stud walls in place so he can float between rooms at will, and some houses naturally stick in the mind, the place on Valentine with the turrets, or the ex-mayor's, which sports a wall of glass blocks either side of an Italian slate fireplace. But whole expanses of these last few years he can't remember at all. He guesses this doesn't make him so different from the next person. Except Olivia . . . her memory is ferocious. The collars on dresses she wore in fourth grade, which year which sister had chicken pox. She rides him for not trying. *You'd remember things if you worked at it.* Maybe so, maybe he should. But where would you be if you remembered every worm that squiggled out after the rain?

He walks on.

Still, it's unsettling, that this moment he's living—the bars of light and shade on the blacktop, the ditch water splashing recklessly along at his right—will leave no mark. Might as well not have lived it. What a thought. He probably won't even remember thinking it.

At last, he hears the Morris, its spartan old engine banging away, hears it slow and crunch along behind him. He walks on as if oblivious, ogling the sheeplike clouds, hears Linny goose the accelerator, clutch out, picks up his pace, lets his arms swing, pretends to whistle. It's delicious. But when he halts suddenly, she lets the car bump into the backs of his legs.

"How're you going to explain running me over?" he says once he's inside.

Linny leans over and puts her lips to his cheek and he's instantly aroused. *"Mmmm,"* she says, "you're a sweaty boy today."

Mark smiles, says nothing, watches her bare legs flash in and out of the sun as she drives. She downshifts onto a gravel road, rattles across Church Creek on a log bridge, ignores a pellet-shot PRIVATE sign, and takes them through a stand of aspen into the remains of an orchard.

Apples, the few not dead in blossom.

Linny climbs out, leaving the door open, sits on the hood.

Mark stands in front of her, asks, "Isn't that *hot?*"

"No, it's fine. Feels lovely."

He nods, looking down at her. Wonders, in passing, if this is the high point of his life.

"You're not tired of me yet?" Linny asks.

He doesn't answer.

"It's that bad, is it?"

She draws him closer with her ankles, reaches, pats him through his jeans. "Would you happen to know if this belt unbuckles?" she asks.

Later, surprising himself, Mark tells her, "That was the last time."

An abject, cast-off look from Linny. "Was it really?"

Mark palms the sweat off his forehead, looks at it as if it will be some bright hue.

"You weren't going to tell me that, were you?" she says.

He shakes his head.

"I told you you were tired of me."

He touches her leg, rubs the flesh just inside the knee. She allows this. "No," he says, "it's all the rest of it."

She rises off her elbows. "Never decide anything right after you get laid. Your judgment's clouded."

"My judgment's clouded all right."

"Sweetie," Linny says, "I never asked you to choose."

"I know you didn't, but that doesn't mean I don't have to."

Linny slides off onto the ground, takes his arm momentarily as she snugs the strap of her sandal.

Kisses him again. That strange wallop of intimacy, never fails to catch him unprepared.

Climbing into the Morris, he gets a whiff of smoke and old leather, of the car's foreignness. Scraps of thought hound him, *You've never been anywhere—* He turns away before he's swamped by an uncontainable longing.

Linny drives them back across town helter-skelter, fails even to slow at the place he asks to be let out. She ignores his objections, takes him straight down his own driveway, jumps out and strides into the house. Announces to Olivia, "Look at the sad case I found trudging along the road."

Scrambling, Mark adds, "Whitey was in a yank, I had him drop me at the turn."

His words barely register with Olivia, whose eyes are on her sister.

Linny shrugs. "All right, all right," she says. "I'm very sorry about the other day. I just thought you ought to leave Dad alone."

You *never* hear Linny apologize, so Olivia weighs this for its true meaning. Lifts her chin, presents a not very convincing lie of her own, "If it's sold, it's sold. I don't care. It's out of my hands."

Mark looks back and forth between them, his heart bounding like a spaniel.

Linny slips away to the dinette where Davey sits rimming out the last of his pudding. "How's about a smooch for your old aunt," she says. The boy happily tips his head back and presents his lips.

"*Very* nice," Linny says. "And where's the sleepy-time gal?"

"B.R.," Davey says, pointing down the hall.

"I ate with the kids," Olivia tells Mark.

"I told you not to wait," he answers.

She looks at him, turns to her sister, asks, "Can I get you anything? Sun tea?"

Linny smiles, in no hurry whatsoever. "That would be lovely."

Watching Linny drink, a picture appears briefly in Mark's mind: the clearing in the orchard, drifting with pollen. But, strangely, it's a bird's-eye view. He sees his own milky buttocks, furiously busy.

"What's funny?" Olivia says.

Mark buries his face in his hands, shakes his head hopelessly.

"No, *what?*"

"Something at work," he says, and has to quickly dredge up Whitey's story from the other day, about the man who was having trouble with his septic system, a place he'd just bought. When they dug the yard up, it wasn't a concrete tank down there but an old Cadillac. He steals Whitey's exact words: *Somebody'd rolled up the windows, flipped it on its back and run a pipe into the goddamn thing.*

A perfunctory smile from Olivia. "You guys and your bathroom humor," she says.

Two-handed, Linny fills the tall glass again, overfills it, has to lean in and sip before it spills, lifts up and thumbs the excess from her lip.

I'm lost, Mark thinks.

Next morning, he's awake with the sparrows. Another high, fathomless sky. Ike and Whitey have been summoned to do the walk-through with Norman Sibley, and you can bet there'll be a list as long as your arm. Both arms. Still, after months, only a few days remain. Ike's been acting like it's a load off, everyone is, but the next job is nothing, a boxy two-bedroom place like the ones he passed yesterday on the girls' name streets. And more in the pipeline. Can't say out loud you're going to miss the Sibleys'. It's just work. Drive away the last time, that's it. Picture coming back, say a year from now, landscaping all in, pond teeming with goldfish, how awkward that would be. *Just wanted to see how your house was doing.*

Get a hold of yourself, Mark.

All morning, he's up and down the ladder, nailing fascia on the southern exposure. He peels off his shirt finally, first time this spring. The sun bakes his shoulders, gives that sweet, incandescent feeling, but as soon as he moves around the corner the air's too cool. He fights it awhile, then slips the shirt back on. This is only May, after all.

As it happens, he remembers plenty from the day before: Steel drums in the lot behind City Service, blue as pool table chalk. Amelia charging down the hall just as Linny was about to go, stubbing her toe horribly on the cast-iron door stop. Killing the wasp on Davey's window screen later, squeezing it between a couple of Kleenexes. All of it useless, or else essential. When what he *should* be trying to remember is how it felt to wait for Linny in a slow fever, to know all day he'd call Olivia and bullshit her. What his exact frame of mind was. Because isn't it astonishing, when he steps back from himself? How he still thinks he's a decent guy. How he clings to the very idea of decency, as if that was all the armor he'd need to take with him into the world.

He hears his name.

It's a woman's voice, floating. A moment of vertigo before he pins it down as Gloria Sibley, her head out one of the dormers. Red-sandy coils of hair falling, clutched back.

"Mark?"

Mr. Sibley wants everyone to convene in the kitchen, has a few words he'd like to say.

Mark climbs down.

As it turns out, Norman Sibley's in a fine humor today, expansive, benevolent. In fact, there are bottles of champagne nestled in crushed ice, a stack of Dixie cups with floral print.

"You gentlemen did a bang-up job," he begins.

Ike's not wild about the idea of drinking on the job, but how can you refuse? He hoists his cup in Sibley's direction, says, speaking for everyone, it was a real piece of work, all right.

Even Roddy gets his, and you can see Ike's quick glare, *One's all you're getting. Don't test me.* Roddy sipping with enormous delicacy, ambassador from some upstart republic.

"I hope I haven't been too big an SOB to work for," Norm Sibley says with a festive laugh, replenishing cups. "As Gloria often reminds me, I can be a grade-A pain in the hind end, but you want things done right you have to see to them, you have to tend to your knitting. Isn't that right, Ike?"

Ike says it is.

Mark's had champagne maybe four or five times in his life, the last being Celia's wedding, only nine months ago though it feels like eons. He remembers the ranks of rented glasses on the damask, Helen and Olivia in their wispy blue-green dresses, everyone clammy in the close heat, except Thomas, who seemed to be bathed by a private breeze, and now Mark recalls the toast Thomas offered Linny at her homecoming, how it broke the ice, wonders where you acquire such a talent.

He drinks.

"But seriously," Sibley goes on, "this was our dream, coming here, putting up this place. We're damned grateful for the work you all did. I mean that, we both do."

"Oh, yes," Gloria Sibley says, at his side. Denim shirt with embroidery, shorts, lowcut white socks that leave her ankle bones exposed. Slender legs with fine eruptions of vein, the color of grape juice.

Sibley pauses, looks at everybody in turn, Ike and Whitey, Roddy, Goudy the paint contractor, Rota the mason, Mark. "A moment like this," he says, "it's too damn easy to let it get away from you." He brandishes the bottle again, and Mark accepts another cupful, downs this in a single effervescent gulp that seems to explode in his throat.

"Attaboy," Sibley says, gives his shoulder a chuck, moves on.

Even Whitey, his back against the pristine countertops, seems to have called a strategic truce with the ruling class. He tosses back small fistfuls of peanuts, shakes his head in apparent earnestness at whatever Gloria Sibley is confiding in him, her voice so little Mark can't hear it at all.

He waits for her to come give him a special thanks, and when, after a fair interval, she fails to, he removes himself from the party, scuffs out into the big room, and down the long wing, keeping to the brown paper runner, breathes in the new carpet smell, the lingering smells of gypsum dust, muriatic acid, Dutch Boy.

He takes to the ladder again, crooks his arm around the next-to-top rung and stares out at the valley of his birth. Tries to imagine seeing it with fresh eyes, rushing to it with a child-like relief. But it's hopeless, there's no relief for him. The air seems thin, empty. The farthest leaves look to be etched with a fine tool. It's closer to home where the murk lies.

Yes, he's done a bang-up job.

The Stavros Girls
Stick Together

True to whatever stony bargain her father had struck with himself, Nick gave no warning to the Vagabond's loyal clientele. He went so far as to plant himself in the kitchen doorway and tell his old friend Albert Sowerwine he was a fool if he believed every scrap of nonsense that blew into his ear, then wrapped a hearty arm around the man's shoulder and strolled him toward the till, and later gave everyone the third degree trying to pin the leak down, deciding finally that it must have come from Alt's end. So the afternoon of the twenty-sixth, Friday, Helen extinguishes the neon at the usual hour, locks the door without fanfare. It's just herself and Nick and Linny. She asks if he wants her to stick a sign up, and Nick indicates no, he'll take care of it. He sits at the counter with a square of posterboard and a marking pen a few minutes before squeaking out:

THE VAGABOND HAS CLOSED

THANK YOU

Nick and Grace Stavros
Evangeline
Celia
Olivia
Helen

He blows on it, walks it up front, and Scotch-tapes it to the glass. That's it. No valediction. Retrieves his jacket, his cap, departs.

If he stops for a drink, if he confides in someone beyond the family, Helen never learns of it.

"I feel like I ought to sweep up or something," she says once he's gone. "Stupid."

Her eldest sister is at the counter, smoking, elbows splayed. "If it was me," Linny says, "I believe I'd buy a keg and throw the fucking doors open."

Helen looks at her, looks away.

In a moment, she flaps open one of the double lids to the ice-cream freezers, stares in. The Vagabond's down to vanilla and pistachio. For three days, she's been saying, "Sorry, out of chocolate, out of maple nut, no, I'm sorry—" She hauls up the tub of pistachio, fishes two long spoons from the drainer. "Can't stand to waste stuff," she offers, aware of how lame it sounds, but so what.

"This looks radio*active,*" Linny says, though pretty soon she picks up the second spoon and reaches in.

And so they eat, and nobody eats ice cream as languidly, with as much sly pleasure as Linny Stavros.

After a time, she asks Helen what she's going to do, what her plans are.

"No plans," Helen answers.

"*No plans,*" Linny mocks, though lightly, benevolently. "You could go to college," she says.

Helen shakes her head.

"Think about it?" Linny says. "One of us brains ought to. You still could."

But Helen's in no mood to talk about herself. "What about *you,*" she says, "what do you have in—?"

Linny sets the spoon down, dropping it the last inch. "Well, kiddo," she says.

"Don't *kiddo* me, okay, Linny?" Helen says, and waits until Linny's eyes have lighted on hers.

"All right. Fair's fair."

Who knows what fair means to Linny?

"Lin," Helen says, vaulting off into what feels like empty space, "Olivia can't find out."

To her credit, Linny makes no more than a moment's show of incomprehension. Just flares her eyes, rolls her lip, as if this calls for a whole new appreciation of Helen.

"I mean it. This would ruin her. And don't say she's already ruined."

All this long, difficult day, Helen's shied from wanting to know how Linny will explain herself, but when it comes right down to it, she has to hear. And don't think she can't outwait Linny no matter how snaky she cares to get.

Linny launches into her roundabout answer, but Helen cuts in, takes her sister's cool shaft of forearm between her fingers, says, "Just tell me that Olivia's not ever going to know."

"Well, *I'm* not telling her."

"You don't think she knows already?"

"Are you kidding?" Linny extracts her arm, roots in her pocket for her lighter, clacks it open and fires up another Winston. "It's almost funny," she says. "Olivia, the queen of prognosticators."

In some black sense, it *is* funny. Not that you can acknowledge it. Even Linny shakes her head after a second, says, "Oh, man."

"She's keeping herself from knowing," Helen says. "I mean that it's *anyone*."

Linny offers no commentary on this insight.

Helen backs off, lifts herself atop the freezer, tilts her head at the indolent swirl of the ceiling fan, and can't help thinking *last few revolutions*—

"What is it between you and Liv?" she asks.

Linny doesn't bother denying this, either, though the public line has always been that the Stavros girls stick together, their grievances shallow, as short-lived as mayflies. "I don't know," she says. "It's always been so damned easy to get her goat."

"It's not her goat you got this time."

Linny laughs, backhands smoke away from her eyes, says, "That's sweet."

Helen holds herself still, waits.

"Liv's such a good girl," Linny says, and Helen hears an echo of Nick on his sisters, *good Christian women* . . .

"Is that why?" Helen asks.

"Kiddo," Linny says. She winces, shrugs it away, says, "Look, I'm sorry you got dragged into this. I don't know how you did, but I'm sorry. Honestly."

"It's not that," Helen says. "It's not me I'm worried about."

A shadow crosses the front glass, stops, someone reading Nick's sign, then vigorously trying the locked latch. Both sisters look up, look away simultaneously.

Helen says, "I mean, you're not in love with Mark."

"Oh, hon," Linny answers, right on the edge of pity.

"Whatever you want to call it, then," Helen presses on, and if she's irredeemably naive, so be it.

After a moment, Linny says, "I thought Mark could use a little cheering up. Okay?"

Cheering up? There's something so odd, so skewed about the sound of that. Doesn't begin to be the whole truth, but neither is it untrue. Pure Linny.

"Doing your good deed," Helen says.

A smile from Linny that disturbs only the left eye. "Wasn't entirely selfless," she says.

Helen tests the idea of Mark as needy, downhearted, can't see it. She's always liked him, thought him nice to look at, kind of sleepy-eyed, neat and agile through the waist and hips, and isn't put off by him the way she's put off by so many grown men, but can't see *wanting* him, not that way.

Not that much.

"I just can't believe he went for it," Helen says.

Linny nods, *World's full of surprises.*

She catches Helen's eye again, and says, "Actually, he was quite eager."

In that one word, Helen hears the rush of sexual energy, Mark's release, feels her own face burn, though she had no intention of letting Linny get to her.

Linny shakes her head, smiles, stretches. She's always doing that, arching her back, making her bones crack as if she's been sitting cramped for years. She swivels off the stool, comes around the counter to Helen.

"Time to clear out," she says, offers a hand.

What can Helen do but take it?

She casts a look around at the cafe. Feels ashamed to leave it in disarray, confusion.

Then again, Linny's right: Time to go.

Not a Bad-Looking Day

The first Sunday in June, and not a bad-looking day. Mark dawdles in the clover-choked backyard with Amelia. When his wife and son return from church, he follows Olivia into the bedroom, watches as she unrolls her stockings, lets the dress fall. He asks how the service was. "Fine," Olivia says, as if more would be lost on him. But it's too sweet a day to make an issue of anything, and so he manages to talk her into an outing, a drive to the lake. The Vagabond's finally empty, stripped to the bone. The wreckers arrive in the morning. The last thing on earth Olivia needs is to hang around the house and stew on that.

"You want me to call Fred and Sonja?" she asks.

"I thought just the four of us," Mark says cheerfully. He's not sure if this is the right answer, but it appears to be.

"We going to swim?" Davey asks.

The lake's at full pool by now, still icy with runoff, but there's a pebble-bottomed shallows near the boat landing, and he's hoping the recent days of sun have made it tolerable. "If you're up to it," Mark offers. "Take your flippers."

Olivia's wearing a white smock top, a rounded straw hat with clumps of shiny plaster cherries. He can't bear the smock, but he imagines it feels good, old and loose, so he says nothing. In the car, Amelia stands on the floor behind Olivia and grabs her about the neck. Olivia asks her to please quit it, and she does for a mile or so. It occurs to Mark, pulling off the main road, that they didn't come here at all last summer. The last time, Amelia was toddling around in diapers, napping in a blanket tent Olivia contrived.

Mark totes the cooler down a gravel trail to the water, makes a second trip for the charcoal, the inner tube they probably won't need.

Olivia floats a table cloth over the picnic table, pats it out, says, "It *is* a pretty day," her voice so surprised that Mark stops what he's doing and looks around. A high gauze of cloud is beginning to overtake the sky, but the sunlight is plentiful, dreamy.

"Let's try to enjoy it, then," Mark says, right away regrets the bite he detects in his own voice.

Davey wants Mark to take him to the rock ledges at the far end of the park.

Olivia darkens, says, "No horsing around." And to Mark, "See that he stays back from the edge."

Mark lifts a hand. No problem.

Up the path they go, to a grassy promontory and onto the outcrop where there's a tumbled-down stone cabin people call the Hermitage. About as big inside as an old Packard.

Mark explains what a hermit is.

"Not a line of work many people are called to," he says, and has to laugh at the tone he adopts with Davey so often. "To tell you the truth," he says, "most people like living around other people. They get tired of talking to themselves. Most people get married and have kids. Otherwise, where would we come from?"

Davey gives this a moment's concentration, nods at Mark.

As the boy plays, Mark sits cross-legged on the lichen-blistered shale, studies the lake. He can see the two close-by islands, a third receding into the soft glare. There are a few aluminum boats glinting dully, sailboats moving without apparent purpose.

Beyond the stone hut, the rocks drop away sharply in random terraces. Later in the year, you see the occasional diver perched here, catching his breath, building his nerve. Once, just after the war, so Mark must have been sixteen or seventeen, he saw a woman down on one of the secluded lower ledges. A woman in her thirties, shirtless. Lounging, hands behind her head, slatted rib cage, white goose-bumped globes taking the sun. Every time he's been here since he looks, finds the rocks vacant, feels let down. Even today he looks, thinks isn't it stupid the way you can't let go of things?

When Davey tires of the cabin, he edges closer to the drop-off, but Mark's watching, and the boy's cautious, stares down at the waves in awe, steps back.

Mark opens a beer when he starts the coals, drinks another as they whiten. Olivia has assigned Davey the job of finding as many different pinecones as he can, perfect specimens. Mark rips into the potato chips. They're the cheap kind, excessively oily, but he can't help himself. He catches Olivia staring, and finally she says, "It's just that's all there are, if you want any with lunch."

Mark says nothing, rests his forehead on the tablecloth, hears water slishing on the beach stones, the ratchet of a boat winch, Olivia's ministrations at the far end of the table, the can opener on the baked beans. When he raises up, she's staring off, scanning the woods.

"He wouldn't go back up to those rocks, would he?" she asks. Takes a few steps, calls, *"Davey?"*

Mark climbs to his feet, notes Amelia on her blanket, looks down along the length of the picnic area for the red-striped shirt and Yankees cap. Not all the sites are full this afternoon, but still there are moving bodies, clumps of laurel and juniper shivering in the splotchy light. "I'm sure he's right around," Mark says, and yells out his son's name somewhat louder.

He sets off in the direction of the stone cabin, walking at a decent clip, asks a group at another table sheepishly, "You didn't see a first-grader?"

"Carrying something in his hat?" one of the women in the party says. Thrusts her chin toward the hill, the rocks.

Mark thanks her, breaks into a trot. It's not that he's worried—Davey isn't a reckless kid, not like the Watnes' older boy who's always crashing around, in fact he seems if anything *too* careful, at least physically, hangs back. But you get a sudden panic when they drop from sight, no question about it. He passes the outhouse on the way, canted, shingle-covered thing, calls out, "Davey" on the off chance he's inside, hears nothing, runs up the path to the overlook, where now a young couple in sunglasses have laid out a checkered blanket. Mark reluctantly asks if anyone's come past, a boy about this high? They shake heads in unison, but Mark guesses they wouldn't notice if King Kong sauntered by, so he makes his way to the Hermitage. No sign of Davey there. He pauses, heart now authentically hammering, forces himself to the lip of the rock, peers over. In soft blue water below, a barkless log, banging back and forth with the waves.

Underbrush, stray evergreens grow in the thin soil back

from the ledges and Mark inspects that area quickly. Beyond, the park ends in a wire fence and battery of KEEP OUT signs. He heads back toward Olivia, convinced that by now Davey's returned on his own. As he reaches the cars and boat trailers, he sees a burst of red at their table, and relief splashes through him, sets his scalp tingling. He slows down, already starting to chide Olivia for letting her imagination run wild, has to quickly remind himself that he'd vowed to keep the day upbeat no matter what. But when he draws nearer he can see that, in fact, it's somebody else's child, the shirt a Nebraska sweatshirt with the arms torn off.

"You don't have him?" Olivia asks, which she can clearly see for herself.

"I didn't see any other kid," the boy repeats for Mark's benefit.

"Where *is* he, Mark?" Olivia says, and Mark very nearly says, *I wasn't the one sent him off somewhere.*

"Okay," he says. "Let's just . . . have you looked—" But there really isn't any other place *to* look. And how far can she get with Amelia in tow?

The boy who isn't Davey stands gape-mouthed, looking implicated. "You want me to see if he went up the road?" he asks, and Mark nods impatiently, watches him lope away. He turns back to his wife, says, "Let's just stay cool, huh?"

Though *he's* the one, can barely breathe.

There's nothing to do but hike back to the rocks a third time, and he does, but can't help feeling that everyone's eyes are on him now, as if he's loosed a toxic cloud among them. Up the path by the outhouse, and again, hopelessly inquires if his son's inside. This time the door cracks, swings open, and there's Davey.

"Am I glad to see you," Mark bursts out.

But the boy's face is in misery.

"You been in here the whole time? What *is* it?"

It turns out he's had an accident. Didn't want to use the out-house in the first place—this early in the year it's not so foul-smelling, but it's a skatey old place, full of silverfish and who knows what. When you think about it, what an act of faith to expose your bottom like that . . . Mark can't say as he blames him.

"Well, let's start with your jeans. Are they okay?" And the jeans appear only slightly stained. "Give them to me," he says. Waiting, he peeks over his shoulder, but the day is going on its course without him. He rubs the denim on clean gravel, holds the pants to the light, gives another quick rub, returns them. "Now the underwear," he says. The boy balks, finally indicates a shadowy wad on the floor. Mark picks them up and drops them straightaway into the hole.

Tells Davey, "Nobody's the wiser."

Davey's not so sure you can get out of trouble that pain-lessly, but Mark says, no it's okay, just hustle and get the pants on and let's go, aren't you hungry?

Mark lays a hand on his son's damp neck, squires him back to civilization, Davey carrying the hatful of pinecones crooked in his arm.

Before Olivia can commandeer the moment, Mark says, "Here we are. Everything's fine, false alarm. He was just up in the woods doing what he was told, must not have heard us calling."

He extracts a beer from the cooler, a grape drink for Davey, smiles extravagantly.

So finally, lunch. The coals are past their prime and the meat takes forever to cook, but no one complains. Even Amelia, though late for her nap, seems on her best behavior. Olivia starts picking up, and Mark knows the next thing she's going to say is she wants to leave. The whole idea was to get away, the four of them, and if they drive home now, well, it's a little early, seems an admission of defeat. So he says, "You want to go sit on the dock, I'll stay here and watch things."

Olivia studies him, cranes her neck at the sky, which has become a flat glare, says all right. She yanks the smock up over her head. Underneath, she's wearing a tank suit he doesn't immediately recognize. It's white, abundantly filled with her.

Mark watches her walk down the slats, her bottom undulating. She sits, staring out. The water's like tinfoil. Amelia fusses on the blanket briefly, then falls heavily asleep, arms over her head as if surrendering. Davey has parked himself on the grassy bank, his flippered feet in three inches of water. Mark nurses what he realizes is his fourth can of beer, feels an overwhelming lethargy steal over him, not so much fatigue as paralysis.

Driving home, he casts sidelong glimpses at his wife, but she's impossible to read. The day, which he'd had such hopes for, is getting away from him, and not just the business with Davey, which was nothing, after all.

At the stop sign where the road divides, he says, "You want to swing by Ceel's?" He looks back at the kids for support.

No, Olivia says, she doesn't feel like it.

Mark shrugs good-naturedly, turns right instead, the long way, which skirts the blue-green foothills. What's the hurry to get home, where there's only Sunday night to face, the car to unload, another small meal to fix and clean up after, tomorrow's lunch? He crosses the bridge, stops at a filling station and buys everybody Creamsicles.

It's light far past the kids' bedtimes now, but once Amelia is finally down, and Davey at least bathed and happily in his loft, Olivia seeks Mark out where he's making a halfhearted inspection of the classifieds, stands square in front of him and says, "I didn't like the way you covered up for him."

The beer and sun, or maybe just the accumulated confusion of these last weeks, whatever, Mark's fuzzy, fighting off a low-grade headache. "Let's skip it," he says.

"Yes, let's just let everything go."

Mark sighs. "He didn't *do* anything, Olivia. I just thought, why blow it up?"

"You were worried, too."

Mark admits he was.

"But you two stood there and acted like I was some foolish woman who needed pacifying. I didn't like it. You two boys."

"I'm sorry, then," Mark says without conviction.

She says, "If something happened to either of them, Mark."

"You think I don't feel the same way?" Mark says, though really he's not up to this, should heed his own advice and let it go.

"I don't think you do," Olivia says. "I don't think it's the same, no."

"Well, that's stupid. Forgive me for saying so."

He stands, goes into the kitchen, and once there makes a token inspection of the icebox, comes away empty-handed, though he feels dehydrated, shaky.

She hasn't followed him, so he's obliged to go back to her. From the set of her shoulders, he imagines she's crying, and he's never keen on wading into the middle of that. Still, he'd like her to know that all he'd wanted was for them to have a good day.

But she's not crying, only watching the violet evening without expression.

"If you want to go out somewhere," she says, "go ahead."

"I'm not *going* anywhere," Mark answers. Though, instantly, an awful restlessness wells up in him. He fights it, tries to stanch it like a bodily fluid.

"Why do you have to be like that?" he says.

Olivia ignores this. She's going to bed, she announces, but makes no move toward their bedroom.

And Mark will wonder from this point on why in the name of all that's sensible he didn't simply answer, "All right, I'll be in in a second."

Said it hundreds of times, why not once more?

Instead of: "It's like you're trying to be unlovable, Liv. It's like you're really working at it."

That round, unabashed face he chose from all faces, doesn't honor him with so much as a blink, until she says at last, "I've given you everything, Mark. If that's not enough, then I don't know what."

"*There*. It's that sound right there," Mark says. "I don't know why you do that."

When she doesn't respond, he goes on, "There's not a man alive who can stand that sound."

"You say such awful things about me."

"It's just—" Mark says. But it occurs to him that he *is* saying awful things about her, so he stops.

In the lull that follows, he remembers that skinned log bobbing in the water, his vertigo, feels it anew, a yawning, sickening rush. How differently this day might've come out.

"*Liv,*" he says, the anger suddenly dissipated, tenderness sweeping into its place, a hunger to relieve them of this goddamn weight, this weariness.

Olivia's standing with her two fists flat to her collarbone, a gesture peculiar to women, he thinks. He doesn't intrude upon it, only watches, feels his limbs trembling.

"Look, Liv," he says, "there's something else."

And, as if he's doing them all an enormous service, he tells her about Linny.

Alterations

Odd maybe, considering what follows, that Olivia's first response isn't outrage, but a mordant curiosity. She wants to know everything. At first, it seems she can't separate his news from the demise of the cafe, acts as if there's a certain perverse logic operating here: One thing turns on you, why shouldn't all others, in due course, turn as well? Mark cringes at the idea of divulging more of the procedural detail than necessary, yet he has to make her see it has nothing to do with the Vagabond.

So, in answer to her next question, Mark says, "No, it wasn't just one time, but that's not the point, Liv, the point is—"

Except that the point is evaporating like rainwater on hot steel.

"Three or four times, then?" she asks.

Hand to forehead, Mark says more like twelve.

"Twelve," Olivia says, as if weighing the number in her hand, its heft.

And what a temptation for Mark to try to actually count the times.

"At Wendy's this was?"

Mark nods.

"Not in our house?"

"No."

"None of those twelve times."

"I said no."

Then she wants to know when it started.

Mark says, "A while ago."

"All right, was it before or after Melia's birthday?"

Both kids were born in the dead of winter, Amelia on the last day of February, and Mark can't think of it without remembering how certain Olivia was the baby'd come on the anniversary of Grace's death. "I guess before," he says, doesn't like the chickenshit, stonewalling way that sounds. Tells her finally it was New Year's Day.

"While I had the kids out sledding?" she asks instantly, and he has no trouble believing she can reconstruct the day flawlessly.

She looks at him, expression unchanged, asks, "Does she do things I won't do?"

"Liv, it's not like that," he says. Though as soon as he's said it, he realizes his mistake.

Olivia nods, says, "I thought from what you said it was mostly *physical*."

"No, that's true," Mark says. "It was. But it wasn't because I didn't love you, or because you don't—" What's a way to say this? "Because you don't satisfy me."

"But that's what 'satisfy' *means,* Mark. That you don't want anything else."

Mark lets a breath escape, says, "I can't explain it," though this is no refuge. He turns his face to the screen door. Outside, it's almost dark. A few isolated crickets are scratching away in the field grass, foolish things.

"You didn't answer my question," Olivia says behind him. "What she does for you."

Just these words and he starts to have that heavy, jazzed-up sensation in his groin, and fears that Olivia will reach around him and feel.

Though, that's crazy, it's Linny who'd do that.

But, strange to say, he *would* like to tell Olivia. How much fun he's had with her sister. How blessed he felt, even now feels. Every inch of Linny dreamily familiar from knowing

Olivia, a languid, pulled-taffy, blackly comic replica . . . other but not totally other.

When Mark finally turns, he sees that Olivia has eased herself down to her customary seat at the dinette. What can he do but take his?

"You two must have had a riot talking about me."

Mark says nothing. It's only now he realizes how little *was* said about Olivia in those sessions, sees what restraint that took, not a trait you'd ordinarily associate with Linny.

Olivia shakes her head, impassive, neither believing nor disbelieving.

"It's funny, it was like it was happening in another world," Mark says. "I know that's stupid."

Olivia's face says: *You have no idea how stupid.*

After a minute, she says, "You think it didn't have anything to do with me."

Irrationally relieved, Mark's about to jump in and wholeheartedly agree with her, but she presses on, "The truth is it didn't have anything to do with *you.* You couldn't even see that."

Mark should have some snappy answer but does not.

Now she tells him he can't stay in the house.

How can this possibly surprise him? He says, look, he understands how hurt she is, he doesn't blame her, it was reckless, they have a lot to straighten out . . . in a way, he says, he's as baffled as she is, but he wants her to know there was never a question of him *leaving* her, of running off with Linny. He says if she'd like him to sleep in the other room, okay, he understands, he does.

But what she means is, he can't stay in this house *from now on.*

"Liv, we're both exhausted," he offers, though Olivia looks as though she may never shut her eyes again.

She gets to her feet, tells him he has ten minutes.

"Liv," he begins again, "I'm not leaving the house in the middle of the night. That's loony."

But she's gone down the hall, sandals going *pock-a-pock*. He hears the firm snap of the bathroom latch.

He squanders the ten minutes twirling one of his son's pinecones between his fingers.

And another ten, vague scraps of soliloquy passing in and out of his mind.

Then he collects his work clothes from the basket, boots from the hall. He steps down into the smelly garage, scoops up belt and tools, carries this awkward armload to the Chevy and dumps it onto the backseat. Stands in the gravel, elbows on the car roof.

Then he's back inside, athwart the bathroom door, hears the separate strains of sink faucets and shower, senses steam collecting on the opposite side, running down the yellow enamel in rivulets, though perhaps by now the hot water's gone. For a moment, he tests the picture of himself putting his shoulder to the door, the cheap trim shredding, Olivia's arm rising in defense of her face.

Then his headlights sweep down Paxson Road, the bunch grass at the shoulder stirring like undersea foliage. Around the big curve and into town. It's past midnight, Monday now. Some of the downtown bars are open yet, the Pine, Kid Billy's, but the last thing he wants is a drink, or the company of drinkers. He pulls up under a streetlight and checks his billfold. There's the change from buying gas on the way to the lake. He probes the secret compartment with his little finger, finds the backup ten missing, and more or less remembers using it weeks ago, so there he is, five dollars and twenty cents.

At least the tank's full. Nearly full.

He turns down East Sixth, drives past his grandmother's.

Drawn blinds, porch light burning in its conchlike housing. A. SINGER. ALTERATIONS. The spirea needs a trim, but otherwise the place seems to be holding up. He hopes his grandmother is safely asleep within, dreaming of ponies. Old family joke. He has no idea where it came from, perhaps something between herself and his grandfather. Long-ago stuff.

He drives on.

Railroad to Percival to Valley. There's Whitey's boat trailer, tarped, tongue resting on a concrete block. The garage is shut tight, and no light shows in the house. He creeps past, circles back, the Chevy in a low idle. Pictures himself banging on the kitchen door, paper sack of beers clutched to his chest. *Wife threw me out, man, can you believe that?*

And Whitey: *You sorry fuck.* Stubble-faced, grinning, *All right, get your butt in here. It ain't the end of the world.*

Some other Mark, some other Whitey.

Back through the oldest part of town, where the trees meet overhead. A patrol car parked in the church lot. He makes a full stop, signals, turns, drives on.

What if he goes to Linny, middle of the night?

Not a sexual picture now. His hair being stroked in dim light, *Don't say anything, Mark.*

Damn this life.

Shh, now—

He pulls into the blacktop lot behind the Park Inn, extracts one of the dimes, and carries it to the pay phone, which proves to be occupied. Cowboy with a blistered face, arguing with the ground.

And so, inside, where the light's merciless.

"Coffee," Mark says.

"There's one wedge of pie."

"What kind?"

"Lemon."

He shakes his head, rests it on his forearms. A Fats Domino tune wafts from the kitchen, stately in its sadness.

Mark cups his hands against the glass, checks the phone. Still taken.

He sips at his coffee, mouth close to the cup. After a while, the cowboy scuffs in, letting the door bounce, joins two other men in the far booth and nobody speaks to him.

Mark ducks outside, dials the Ochs house, coin poised to drop.

Thirteen, fourteen rings. Might as well be a hundred and fifty.

He drives down Montana as far as Second Street, pulls up opposite the cafe. The slot of potholed ground once belonging to Wilfred Espy is blocked off by a pair of sawhorses tied with red rags. Mark drags them aside, drives in, replaces the barricade, backs the Chevy into a patch of heavy shadow.

It's dropped into the forties, and his jacket's at home on the peg. He shrugs on the work shirt, runs the heater a minute, checks his watch. Not even half-past two. He happens to know that the Vagabond's rear door was taken off in the move and the pins subsequently lost, so tonight it's only resting on the hinges, and he could push it in if he chooses. A last communion in that sanctuary.

Lot of good that would do.

He crawls into the backseat, wads the coveralls under his head and tries to sleep. The upholstery smells of milk and sweat, decomposing vinyl. Once, when they lived on Ash, he spent a few hours in the back of the Dodge, but returned to bed while it was still dark, and he has no memory now of what that was about. He gets out, takes a leak in the cool air, listens to the night, the scattered noises of downtown, climbs back inside.

He dreams not of ponies, but of graphite-colored waves slapping rock, rowboats adrift. When he opens his eyes, the sky is faintly gray.

You Asked for It

Helen wakes in the early dawn, surprised to find she's slept the night through. She dresses, brushes her hair at the mirror, hears it crackle in the dry air. She pauses on the carpet runner and listens at Nick's door, nudges it open, sees the comforter rising and falling, backs out. Yesterday she approached him, "You thinking of going into town in the morning?" as neutral as she could put it, not wanting to set him off, though Nick has contained himself admirably this week. No, he said, he wasn't. Had paperwork to do, the hot-weather plants to install in the garden. "If you want to," he said, tugging one wing of his mustache, "then you be my guest, Helen."

She's almost unbearably alert, perks coffee nonetheless, fills the tartan Thermos, stoppers it. She retrieves her bike from the shed and pumps up the hill, rides through the somnolent shadows of the East Side. A cool morning. June in this corner of the state is often cool, often rainy, though the sky today is a high wash of overcast, the sort that can linger. Down past her mother's old church, past the boarded-up Central School, into downtown, Second Street.

She stashes the Schwinn, climbs the fire escape along the Wren's east wall, up to the landing outside the balcony, where she killed time when she was fourteen, fifteen, sixteen. A view of chimney stacks, drowsily spinning ventilators like rusted king's crowns, tarred roofs with a lawn chair or the odd garment, pigeons swirling into high funnels over downtown, sometimes a crow with its glossy eye, roving. Made the mistake of bringing boys here a couple of times, David Sutherland, Packy O'Keefe, not that they didn't appreciate it, especially Packy, who saw what it meant to her. Not that kissing them was disagreeable, or led to trouble. Strange to think of Packy O'Keefe. She remembers an assembly freshman year, the vice principal trying to hammer the fear of God into them, *I want you all to look around, take a good long look at each other. Two or three of you won't be alive to pick up your diploma, I guarantee it to you* . . . met with grunts and catcalls. But it was true, two weekends before graduation Packy and the da Silva twins and Rochelle Henke's cousin Eric and Marnie Lumquist catapulted off the road above the reservoir. Tequila. Two killed, one paralyzed.

Scissored from the *Evening Record,* pasted in her notebook that no one sees, *Patrick Francis O'Keefe, 18.*

Helen consults her watch. Eight-twenty. Unscrews the Thermos, drinks.

An episode of *You Asked for It,* three or four winters ago, demolition of a Chicago hotel. She called Nick in from the other room. "Yeah, the old Octavian," he said. "My uncle Sil delivered meat there. Gloomy goddamn place."

"You want to see?"

No, Nick didn't care to see. But Helen couldn't take her eyes off it, the camera swooping through the deserted lobby, down into the catacombs, eerie, like a scene from *The Twilight Zone,* the huge drill bits boring holes for the charges, and outside again the crew boss, "If it works right she just falls in on herself." That touch of doubt, whether real or like at the circus where they mistime the first swing purposely, she couldn't say. But then the Octavian blew, slunk to earth in seconds, as if its mortar had vaporized, leaving the brick powerless to stand.

You asked for it.

All that's needed for the Vagabond is one front-end loader and a pair of dump trucks.

At twenty minutes to nine, the bucket engages a pier of bricks at the southwest corner, the tires skip in the gravel, a clot of diesel smoke rises, disperses. The wall's ivy has been shorn to the height of a man's shins. And the canvas awning, unbolted and eased down onto the sidewalk, the two gray-painted benches that stood in its shade likewise carted off, the plate glass unglazed and tapped from its moorings in green-tinged sheets before it could draw fire. Not a building you'd recognize now. Another push from the bucket, a chunk of brickwork tumbles out, producing a tremor Helen feels in the iron slats where she perches.

At nine-thirty, Alt arrives. Walks like a pug, Nick always said. He stands with another man, pointing, leaning forward to spit. The other man nods. A couple, three times, she sees him eye the sidewalk, up and down, looking for Stavroses, even checks behind him furtively, though not high enough to notice her. He stays as long as it takes to fill the two trucks once, and when the second one has bumped over the curb onto Second Street, he steps through the dust to have a word with the wrecking man, who reduces his machine to an idle and listens impassively, and then Alt departs and does not return.

Who else gets in on this action?

Stray gawkers. Three boys on bikes. Augustus France with his grimy paper pouch, his grizzled clown hair. Miscellany of old patrons whose eating foibles are as familiar to Helen as any landmark. Briefly, the west wall missing, it's like looking into a diorama, the Vagabond's insides on display. There's Nick scooting eggs onto a platter, willowy Grace Stavros with fingers laced under one of her girl-swollen bellies, Linny in a cloud of flour. There's Celia waggling imaginary maracas overhead, Olivia waiting for her boyfriend with nervous squints toward the front glass. And Helen herself, there she is, hand on the light switch, inspecting the premises to her satisfaction. Another few bites and the cantilevered roof sags, flaps down like a slow black wing, and that's that.

It's history, as Linny would say.

A little past noon, the machine goes abruptly silent. Helen

scrabbles from her roost, walks the alley to Montana Street and across to the News Agency. Orders a grilled cheese, a chocolate milk, watches a high school girl thumbing paperbacks on the swivel stands, thinks of Olivia and her bags of books with their falling-apart covers, remembers Celia saying, *All we ever see is the top of your head.* And Olivia, *Well, is the part straight?* She eats in a rush. She's never been that hot on the News Agency, too much light and clatter, and the grill's right behind the counter, imagine working all day with people staring at your backside. She pushes the plate away, wants something to rid her mouth of the aftertaste, maybe some Junior Mints, but she can't decide, can't bother with it, flees to the bathroom instead, then out through the alley door, eyes to the ground, before any busybody can snag her, *I see where you're out of business . . .*

Before anyone can ask, *So what now, Helen?*

With time short, Nick had made no arrangement to sell the fixtures, except the radiators, and the two upright coolers, relatively new. So the morning of the twenty-ninth, he and Mark and Helen, and two high school boys, along with Thomas Balfour, loaded out whatever was deemed salvageable, ferrying it on flat-bed trailers to one of Thomas's sheds, where now it reposes under tarps. Booths, cartons of flatware and china and fluted soda glasses, two cast-iron ranges, the several clocks, the old NCR register, and all the rest. *The Vagabond,* the painting, was brought home to McLaren Road, where it spent one night leaning atop the mantelpiece. The next evening Helen found it wedged into the closet beneath the stairs.

Ought to have been no surprise, but still a shock how ravaged things looked. Scoured, disinfected how many thousand times on the outer surfaces, but down between they were filthy, scummy, the bottom of the cases boot-strafed, gouged, the varnish pitted and sticky. There was Thomas working right along

with Nick, keeping an eye on him, in Helen's opinion, saying it
was fine old stuff for the most part, just required a little
reclaiming. No big deal. Some of it they just left. For instance,
the stools with their shot bearings. And the cellar, what a rat's
nest that was. Legless chairs, wood-slotted cases of ancient
soda bottles, a sink and horrific upended commode, a hat tree
bearing a pair of suspenders Nick briefly fingered and let fall,
lamp hoods and swan's neck conduit, a tall wavy-veneered cabinet with glass pulls that dated from Cecil Jordan's time, demi-
johns, pails and headless mopsticks, bags of rock salt that had
wicked up moisture and moldered, Ball jars of rusted dirt-
furred brads and screws and lock hardware, others quarter-full
of dark lacquer stiffened to rosin.

Nick leaned against one of the floor jacks. It was shimmed
top and bottom with two-by-sixes. He ran a gloved hand on it.
"I ought to just whack this out of here," he said.

Footsteps overhead, scuffing.

"Well, now," Thomas said in brotherly fashion, "don't do
that."

When the men climbed the stairs, taking little with them,
Helen remained.

She opened the cupboard. There was a short black apron
with scalloping along the bottom, silky, not nearly so moth-
eaten as she'd expected. She held it to her waist a moment, pictured a woman wearing this and nothing else. She folded it
away, left it. But what else might she find . . . and why had she
never looked here before?

Not long after Helen's back at her post, Celia appears
below, Celia and Thomas. Jeans rolled midcalf, fuchsia scarf.
She couldn't stay away, had to see for her own self. She, too,
casts a look around for family, takes Thomas's arm, speaks
into his ear. Thomas's shoulders rise and fall.

Maybe she's saying, *I wonder where everybody is.*

The mood she's in, Helen feels no burning obligation to make her presence known, to scurry down and join them just now. Hand it to Celia, though, she lasts the better part of an hour, Thomas standing patiently by.

The last twenty feet of the west wall topple in, leaving the white-washed baking room knee deep in brick. Then the alley wall comes forward, slumps. Helen rocks minutely, arms around her knees, anticipating which bite of rubble will be next, finds herself in tune with the shovel man, begins to admire his dexterity, pictures herself conversing with him, *How long'd it take to get this good? All my life. Well, you* are *good.* Won't let him say, *It's just a job, sweetheart.* Watches as he begins to peel back the single thickness of sloppily mortared brick that separates the cafe and the wall of Alt's storeroom, gently positioning the tines and retracting, bringing down one course at a time.

Just as well that Nick's not here.

Or Olivia.

As recently as this morning, though, Helen would've bet that Linny'd show before day's end. Arrive for a last cool-eyed assessment, a final word. Now, as the flat light begins to thin, as only the debris-clogged cellar hole of the Vagabond remains, she sees how wrong she was. Knows with a deep, instinctive clarity that Linny is already miles from here, untrackable in the greater world. And despite all the harsh, confounding thoughts she entertained about her sister these last weeks, her absence comes like a kick to the gut.

THREE

SUMMER 1961

New Foundation

A mist falling, Whitey squats atop the northwest corner of the new foundation, pinions the tape end with his boot, hands Mark the spool. Mark walks it to the opposite corner, stretches the yellow cloth tight, calls out, "Fifty-one, six, plus a little." Then the other diagonal. "Fifty-foot, even."

"Those sons of bitches," Ike says. "Try it again."

They try it again, though they were right the first time.

"Those rat-hearted sons of bitches," Ike says, clamps the sheaf of plans under his armpit. He checks the sky, which is virtually the same color as this errant concrete, looks back again, wiping his cheek, says, "You don't need the tape, you can see it with your goddamn eye."

Mark starts laying out the sill plates. It's a matter of cheating one end in, the other out, but there's a limit to how much you can correct because the siding needs to hang down. He can't think when they've had one this bad.

"You look perky today," Whitey says. "Sleep in your vehicle, did you?"

This being Wednesday, Mark's spent the last *three* nights in the Chevrolet. Still, the remark blindsides him. "That bad?" he asks neutrally.

Whitey says he's seen fresher-looking roadkill.

"You're a good one to talk," Mark says, but he'd rather drop it.

Whitey goes off shaking his head. Lunchtime yesterday, Mark drove back into town and visited the savings bank, half-expecting to find himself locked out of his account, but no. He withdrew a twenty, then, on second thought, another twenty. He stopped by Cahill Drug and bought a toothbrush. After work, he drove out Highway 2 for something to do, got as far as the canyon before turning around. A glowery evening. He wasn't hungry, but made himself pull in at a diner called Stell's where nobody knew him. A club sandwich folded into wax paper, a chocolate milk. He took them outside and set them on the seat of the car and drove again. He located a gravelly, poplar-edged clearing along the river, nosed up to where he could watch the deadfall hurtling by. Toward dark, he fished a package of matches from the glove box and made a smoky fire and sat beside it until it went to coals. Sometime later, another car crunched into the clearing, only the parking lights on. Then the brakelights flared, illuminating the scabby under-brush, and Mark thought he could hear the driver go, *Shit, shit*. A boy's voice. The car began to creep backward, jostling through the holes. Thereafter Mark was undisturbed.

This morning, he woke under the flutter of new leaves, stiff-necked and chilly, but lucid, which he took to be no small piece of luck. It occurred to him that today would be the day to return home. As the morning progresses, this intimation slowly blooms, starts to dazzle him. Early afternoon, the mist lets up. He and Roddy sail sheets of plywood across the floor joists, kick them into place, nail them off in a barrage of hammer blows, and now there's a glare on the tools, on the wood itself, so bright his eyes ache from squinting, but in his present frame of mind, this break in the sky seems auspicious, a gift.

Toward quitting time, Pettinato, the concrete contractor,

shows up, shambles across the soft dirt from a new-looking three-quarter-ton Ford.

Ike brightens, puts a finger to his lips, tells Pettinato, "Don't say nothing." He takes him by the coat sleeve and leads him around, citing chapter and verse. Dares him to say the goddamn thing's square.

Pettinato nods. "I give this one to Leonard," he says. "We been backed up." He shakes his head, aggrieved. "It's a piece of crap."

He and Ike exchange a look. Leonard is to Pettinato as Roddy is to Ike. Only more so.

"What you want me to do, Ike?" he says. "You want me to repour?"

"You don't have to repour it, for Chrissake, we've got the goddamn deck on now."

"No, I will," Pettinato says. "You shouldn't have to put up with crap like this."

Ike sighs, adjusts his footing.

"I mean it. I'll repour the son of a bitch. Say the word."

Mark's on his haunches by the nail keg, already hearing this exchange transfigured into a tale of Whitey's, *He's got Ike begging him not to do the frigging job over* . . . grinning despite himself.

God, it's a relief to let down for a second.

Later, as he walks to the Chevrolet, a dark green convertible pulls noisily in, blocking him. Two girls in scarves, honking, waving for Roddy.

Roddy saunters over, plants his inane face inches from the driver's, toys with a wisp of yellow hair that's escaped the head wrap. The second girl climbs over into the rear seat.

Mark stands waiting, a portrait of patience.

"Singer," Roddy says, straightening. "Want to go for a little ride?"

"No, thanks," Mark says.

"I'll let you sit back here with me," the second girl says, patting the vinyl.

"That's okay."

Roddy strolls around to the passenger side and slides in. "Last chance, bud," he says.

"Have to be another time."

Roddy hangs his head at the depth of Mark's foolishness. The convertible lurches backward across the rutted dirt and for a few moments Mark can hear their voices as they speed away.

Yet even this exchange raises his spirits, confirms his convictions about the day, so that his only immediate worry as he drives, elbow out the window, is whether to return home empty-handed, or bearing a peace offering. He sees himself clutching a great wad of roses, but instantly cringes at the transparency of the gesture. He stops at the filling station on the upper end of Commerce, locks himself in the men's room, cleans his face and arms with wet paper towels, rolls off the stained T-shirt and replaces it with the flannel, still reasonably presentable, folds back the cuffs, twice, three times, steps outside into the hazy sun.

Nor will he march into the house with any prepared speech. If he's meant to be redeemed, the words will just have to be there. But maybe he'll start by saying he's sorry to have stranded her without the Chevy. Most likely, Helen will have lent her the truck. What will Olivia have told her . . . *Mark had to take the car?* She can throw walls up even to the sisters, especially now, he imagines, for she'd want the trouble contained. Or, *It's at the shop again . . .* no problem having that believed. Sometimes Mark wishes he had that old Dodge back. Stodgy he thought at the time, but *built*. Classy upholstery, Bakelite knobs that never broke off, probably the best car he'll ever own, he thinks with a shudder.

But there's no sign of the truck in the gravel drive of the

house on Paxson Road. No toys in the yard. The breezeway
door is locked. He cups his hand against the glass, peers in, jig-
gles the knob . . . usually does the trick, but not this evening.
He circles around back to the sliding door, and that, too, is
secured. So he uses his key and in he goes through the front
door, the door for salesmen and missionaries, calls out, "Hey,
it's me," though it's plain he's alone.

Tracks of the Electrolux showing in the carpet, the brown
nap standing in peaks. Countertops swabbed off, cleared of
debris. The same industry evident in the bathroom and
Amelia's room. Back in the kitchen, he opens the icebox, finds
it obscenely barren, reeking of ammonia. So he has misread
the day from its very beginnings.

He lets his clothes drop in a heap and steps into the shower,
uses bar soap on his hair, runs the jets on his neck, which is
knotting up again. Then, above the rush of water, he thinks he
hears the telephone, cranks the faucets, and it *is* the phone,
but, having dripped his way into the bedroom, he's too late. He
towels off, collapses naked on the bedspread, and after a time,
it occurs to him to check the top drawer of his bureau. There,
untouched, are the balled white socks, the odd coins and
receipts and rolled-up tubes of foot salve. He lies back down.
When the phone rings again he answers at once, heedlessly,
says, "This is Mark." There follows an interval cavernous
enough for him to anticipate each of the Stavros girls' voices in
turn.

It's none of them. Instead, his grandmother asking for
Olivia.

"She and the kids are out," Mark manages.

Mrs. Singer's dry cough. "She mentioned running me up to
Stillwater tomorrow."

"I'm sorry, I just got in," Mark says. "I believe she's over at
her dad's."

"Well, you have her call me."

"All right. But she might be late."

Another sizable pause. Mark thinks his grandmother's about to ask how he is, and he's ready to insist, "I'm *fine, Gram*," already hoping he doesn't sound too defensive. Ready to say, "Just got spring fever," for she used to tease him about that.

But Audrey Singer says, "I don't like to drive on the highway if I can help it."

Mark says he could take her.

"You'll be *working*. Don't be silly."

"We're not that busy," he lies.

"For pity's sake, Mark, it was mostly for Olivia. I've got plenty to do here."

"Then maybe you should put it off for another day," he says.

"Yes, all right."

That decided, Mrs. Singer rings off rather brusquely. Indomitable talker in the flesh, she's all business on the phone. It often seems he fails to engage her fully, yet tonight he's relieved.

Dodged a bullet.

In fresh clothes at last, he locates a can of pork and beans on the lazy Susan, heats it, walks the saucepan outside, touring the Singer homestead, as if his leave of absence will show it off in a miraculous new light. In fact, it's the silence that gets to him. It seeps out of things.

Olivia and the kids probably *are* at McLaren Road. Where else would she be? What's she told people . . . Nick? Not the unvarnished truth, you can count on that.

Overhead, a contrail drifting into ragged tufts, a military craft halfway to Great Falls by now.

Mark goes back inside, runs soapy water in the pan, turns on the transistor radio atop the icebox, listens to the national news as if it concerns him intensely, though ten minutes later he can't imagine why.

It's after nine o'clock when he presents himself at the Stavros house, not walking in as he's accustomed to, but waiting on the back stoop amid the swirling millers. The same radio station is thumping away somewhere within, so maybe he'll need to knock again, but first he takes a step back to look up at the windows, and finally notices Nick standing a few feet off in the grass.

"She doesn't want to see you," Nick says.

But there's no fury in the voice, only fatigue, unless he misreads that, too. Mark offers a fractional smile, says, "I guess that's so."

"Then why don't you let her alone."

Mark says, "It's not going to do anybody any good her hiding out over here."

Nick nods. Could mean anything.

"Just let her know I'm out here, would you do that for me?"

"I'll tell her," Nick says. "But you'll be standing here until you grow moss."

He climbs past Mark, pauses in the vestibule to clean his boots, enters the kitchen without looking back.

Mark eases himself onto the pebbly concrete, watches the yard darken, the fence posts flatten into silhouettes. The breeze stirs, brings a smell of damp bark, mulch. Someone lowers the radio. A light comes on upstairs, Celia's old room. It spills through the birches onto the shed roof, goes out.

There's a thing to do here, Mark thinks. Maybe it's charging inside and gathering her up. *Enough, we're all going home now. You, me, the kids.*

Something out of a movie.

Then again, this may call for a heroic act of patience. Not budging all night from these steps. *See, I'm still here, Liv.*

Doesn't have his watch on him, but it can't be quarter-past ten.

Jesus Christ.

What he'd love to do is dial up Linny and take a sounding from her, and isn't *that* a laugh.

Been nine days since he's seen her, Linny.

He stands, stretches, jangles the coins in his pockets a moment, sits back down.

Or make as if he has better things to do with his time. *You think I'm waiting around forever to talk to you, you're out of your gourd. Hear me, Olivia?* From the grass, hollering up, getting his feet wet.

Different movie.

The kitchen door rattles open behind him, then the vestibule door, and one of the Stavros cats bolts past him into the puddle of shadow under the barberry. Then a pair of sneakers on the top step, two dungareed legs folding, settling in beside him.

Helen.

"You need a jacket?" she asks.

Mark says he's fine.

Helen hugs her own bare arms, volunteers nothing. Eventually, Mark has to ask, "What's she *doing* in there?"

"She went to bed an hour ago."

Mark nods.

"She said anything?"

"Not to me."

After a while, Mark says, "Well, I guess I'll go home, then."

Helen says she thinks that's a good idea. She gets to her feet, waits for him to follow suit, but Mark can't seem to tear himself away, from the house itself, can't bear it somehow. Nor admit he doesn't know what in the world to do.

Her knee against his back, soft persistent nudge, and he gives in.

When they're eye-to-eye again, Helen says, "For what it's worth, I don't hate you, Mark. I love both of them myself."

He has this urge to take her by the sleeve, to kiss her cheek. Of course, he doesn't.

The Half of It

Helen's been playing catch with Davey in that weedy slot of backyard between the shed and the garden fence, getting him to throw the right way, stepping, using the whole body. Nick hears her encouragements, *Yes,* much *better. Now put some zing on it, okay, kiddo?* The ball's one she found in the vestibule, wrapped with electrical tape. Crossing the grass, he sees her send him in to wash up, and Davey displays his black palm for his grandfather with guilty pleasure. "Use that Lava soap in the downstairs," Nick says, kneads the boy's damp shoulder, but as soon as he's gone, Helen collars Nick, tells him for the third or fourth time the house needs painting, she's sick of looking at the grimy scales curling off the eaves, makes him arch his neck and stare where she points.

"Ah, it's worse in back here," Nick says. "Nobody sees it."

"*I* see it," Helen says.

"I'm not up to it," Nick says, continues walking toward the shed. He's got his outboard motor torn apart on the bench, the carburetor soaking in gasoline. Hasn't worked on it in a week, but they leave him alone out in the shed. There's an old love seat, a coffee can full of sand and cigar butts.

"I was going to do it," Helen says. "It's not like I'm doing anything else."

He hears the part she holds back, *As long as I'm out of work. As long as you*— Nick waves over his shoulder without turning. He's not having his daughter paint his house, that's all there is to that.

"Don't run off," she says.

So he stops, says, "Maybe I'll just ditch the house, too."

Hardly a rise out of Helen. "Don't say what you don't mean," she tells him soberly, then proceeds indoors herself, having a fine instinct for how far Nick can be pushed, and when.

Jesus but he loves her. Loves all his girls.

He sequesters himself in the shed, smokes, tries to see himself trolling the river, that shaded stretch below Graves Landing: retired man in a wooden boat. A hatch of glittering flies, the low glide of an osprey. But it's a picture he's spoiled by calling on too often, too wantonly. Only aggravates him now, makes his legs prickle.

He hears a knock and calls out, "I'm busy, Helen."

But no, it's Olivia.

Nick sits up, waves his hand through the cigar smoke that hangs in the air like bug bomb.

"We're eating," she says, standing before him, dishtowel on her shoulder.

If Helen and Celia understand what this deal's all about, they're not saying, and there's no badgering anything concrete out of Olivia.

It tests his imagination to picture Mark violent. You never know, though. Grace had a friend married to the mildest guy— Nick used to get tomato plants from him, those Tiny Tims. He always thought the wife was a little off, outgoing one time, reclusive the next, or simply absent . . . until Grace finally explained it, asked, exasperated, why he didn't see things with his own eyes. Even in his own family, though, if he's honest, he remembers his aunt Evangeline had lost a baby that way—her husband had taken a fit, people said, by which they must have meant he'd been blind raging drunk. He'd kicked her down a flight of stairs. Yet, there he was at family dinners, Nick's

Uncle Tull, black humorless eyes, too close together like a bear's, and nobody objected to his presence, not publicly. He'd been let go from a decent job on the railroad, then a lesser one at the Fulton Street market. Always getting screwed by the big boys, that was Tull.

First time Nick took the meaning of *Shit rolls downhill.*

But the thought of your own daughter pummeled, turns your stomach. He remembers Grace in the early days, Chicago, "You'll never lay a hand on me, will you," not a question. Nick tried to make a joke of it, "I'll lay a hand on you, all right," rubbed her breast, which was exquisite to the touch, Grace going on, ". . . or any of our children." Children-to-be. Nick had yet to think out any philosophy of childrearing, but realized instantly that he agreed with his whole heart. None of that spare-the-rod, spoil-the-child crap, out of the Dark Ages.

No, it's true you never know, but in his gut Nick doesn't believe Mark capable of that sharp, convulsive anger. If anything, his son-in-law's fuse is too damn long. Ah, Nick wants to shake him sometimes, *Wake up, huh? This is your life here.* No, if it's meanness, some gross affront, it's another kind. Or it's something else entirely. Almost nauseates Nick to speculate. All she'll say is the marriage is over. Olivia's pronouncements you take with a grain of salt, you wait and see what surfaces, but this time Nick's not so sure you don't just take her at her word.

One thing Nick *does* know: She hasn't forgiven him for the cafe, and maybe she won't. So he knows this, too: Whatever misadventure forced her back here outweighs her anger at him, makes her swallow it down. The day of her arrival, some weeks ago, he watched slackmouthed as Helen led the kids upstairs with their things, and was reduced to asking Olivia what it was she needed from him.

"A place to stay," she said.

"Always," Nick replied. "You know that." Figuratively, he'd meant it.

Looking up from the love seat now, Nick's inclined to ask, "We making any progress, Olivia?"

Her gaze stops him. That wary, furious look, which has come to seem indelible.

He sticks out his hand, lets her yank him to his feet, peels a couple of antacids from the roll on the bench, says, "I don't want you to think I'm not on your side, Liv, not for one second, but he's got a right to see his kids."

Impassive, Olivia answers, "Helen's going to take them over."

"When? Tonight?"

She nods.

"He's giving you some money, is he?" Nick asks. He already knows the answer, for Helen's been slipping her sister cash for days. Olivia hasn't spoken to Mark about it, because she hasn't spoken to him at all.

"I'm getting a job," she says.

"Oh, yeah? What doing?"

Whatever's out there.

"And the kids?"

"Helen's available."

Nick shakes his head. "I hate to see all this," he says. Instinctively, he takes a step toward her, pulls her against his chest, and what a pleasure to hold his daughter, to feel the resistance give way, the flesh pillow momentarily against his. The sweaty, salty smell of her scalp as he breathes.

From outside then, Amelia's shrill, pleading voice, "Momma, where *are* you?"

He can feel the shiver it shoots through Olivia, lets go.

"You coming?" she asks him.

"Yuh, sure," Nick says. "Just be a second here."

The slap and bounce of the shed door, almost weightless. Nick leans against the bench, listening to the flies in the rafters, thinks to look down, eventually, to see if his cigar's out.

A flowered cloth's been laid on the picnic table. There's a blue bowl of potato salad, steam rising from a second dish. Beer in a tall glass waiting at his place. Could be heaven if you didn't know better.

Once they've eaten, a meal mercifully free of spills and dangerous silences, Olivia produces cut-up fruit and whipped cream, doles out token helpings for the kids, the plan being that Mark's taking them for cones.

Nick has migrated from the bench to the canvas sling chair adjacent, is sitting back in the mottled shadow, top pants button undone, hoping to give the impression of a man minding his own business. He keeps an eye loosely on Olivia, monitors what she says to the kids as they prepare to leave, but it's a disappointment. Only, "You be very good, both of you." And, to Helen, "Tell him nine o'clock, no later." The true instructions must've been imparted earlier, in private. He studies her, sees her turn to stacking plates before the truck clears the driveway.

Nick grunts to his feet, follows Olivia into the house with an armload.

When it was just himself and Helen, they traded off on the kitchen work. But every night now, Olivia insists on taking charge, shuns help. She's defrosted the freezer, scoured behind the long row of canisters, winnowed the junk drawer, wrapped the tip of a paring knife in a rag and gone after the counter moldings with a vengeance. If Helen takes this as a rebuke, she doesn't let on.

Nick sets his things in the sink, collapses at the enamel table, says, "Why don't you let that wait, huh Liv? It's stifling in here for Christ's sake."

But if she doesn't do the dishes now, what else is she going to do?

After a while, Nick says, "I hate to be mercenary about this, Olivia, but he owes you part of his paycheck. If you won't talk to him, I guess it falls to me."

Nick waits a second, says, "Livia?"

"I don't want you having anything to do with him."

"Do we need to have a lawyer?" Nick says. "Is that where we are?"

In his mind's eye, a glimpse of the lawyer Samuels, profuse brows, cheeks puffing out like a blowfish, Samuels nodding in frank admiration of the sum Nick had coaxed from Garvin Alt. A nice moment, to be sure, but it, too, is losing its glow.

"Yes, Dad," Olivia says, as if, through all this, Nick's been woefully inattentive.

"Well, then."

Olivia palms the sweat off her forehead, wipes it gracelessly on the apron.

"You know what I feel like, Liv?" Nick says. "If it's any satisfaction, I'm starting to feel like selling the cafe was a bum idea."

She offers a look over her shoulder, but it doesn't extend far enough around to reach him.

"It's like I pulled the pin out and everything's come apart."

He's nuts if he thinks Olivia's going to say, "Oh, don't be that way, it's not *your* fault."

He remembers Helen, outside, "Don't say what you don't mean." That lick of chagrin every time one of his girls lectures him, worse when they're right. But how do you know what you *do* mean until you hear how it sounds in the light of day? He'd fully expected a bout of remorse, but not *this*—he doesn't even know what to call it, this taint on everything, the way his well-being, too, had once seemed general, when he was a man under the dome of heaven, as Grace said, two-thirds in jest. He doesn't see how there's any legitimate link between his own failings and Mark's—whatever these turn out to be—but around Olivia you wouldn't bet against it.

He sighs, stands, plants himself in line with the screen door where there's a dribble of air. "What do you think's become of your big sister, anyway?" he asks by way of changing the subject.

Olivia cranks off the faucet. "I wouldn't know," she says.

Nick nods. "I ought to be adjusted to her comings and goings by this late date," he says. "But I have to admit I thought she'd call. I honestly did."

Olivia gives the remainder of the whipped cream a scowl, as if it's turned in this short time, plunges the bowl into the suds.

"You think she's back there in California?"

When Olivia declines to honor this with a reply, Nick says, "Well, Lin could stand our company for just so long. At least some things are etched in stone."

A few more days will drag by before Helen breaks down and tells Nick the whole story, or as much of it as *she* knows. He'll wonder why in God's name he didn't see it for himself. Since when has he been blind to Linny? When has he ever failed to notice the red flags snapping in the breeze? Goes to show where Nick's been these months, down in his own thoughts, down in the catacombs. And once the extent of Linny's perfidy is clear to him, the stunning casualness of it, Nick will recall this precise moment in the sweltering, airless kitchen. He'll marvel at Olivia's restraint, which is epic. She's not even trembling, only sponging grease from the walls of the old porcelain sink with the same unnerving concentration every act of hers seems to require these days. Think of it: not going after him in a fury, *For Christ's sake, will you shut up about* Linny—

But, for now, in his ignorance, Nick soldiers on, says, "She's something, your sister."

And misses his wayward firstborn with a sudden blistering pang, wonders how on earth he'll bear another protracted absence.

He looks up just in time to see Olivia vacating the room.

Later he's out watering, happens to notice it's nine o'clock, then ten after, can't help noticing, too, how wound up he feels, that clenching, constricting in the lower abdomen, as if he might be pressed into action tonight.

He crimps off the hose, listens a moment for the truck, and, blessedly, there it comes, and there's Davey standing up in the back, one hand slapping at the low-hanging leaves.

If there's a debriefing, it too takes place behind closed doors. So Nick waylays his youngest, inquires how things seemed over at Paxson Road.

"All right, considering," Helen says. She plucks a folded check from her breast pocket, says, "This is for her."

"How much?"

"Hundred."

Nick nods. "It come with any message?"

No message, Helen says.

After a minute, Nick asks if she really told Olivia she'd watch the kids.

"I don't mind," Helen says.

"Well, you're being damned generous, Helen," Nick says, "but the thing is, Olivia has got to—"

It's been quiet upstairs for some minutes, and now Olivia appears again, barefoot, wearing an old summer gown of Grace's. Where's she unearthed *that*? The thin cotton is sticking where her skin's clammy. She picks it away impatiently, informs Nick she's going to bed, her voice flat as brown paper. Helen takes this opportunity to slip off.

"You don't want a drink of something?" Nick asks. "I could put some water on."

No, nothing.

"Why don't you have a seat."

"I'm going up to bed, Dad."

"Why don't you tell me what's going on, Liv. What would be so wrong with that?"

No, she can't, she won't.

"Okay, all right," Nick says, lets his hands slap against his pant legs. "Tell me something else, then."

"What?"

"Oh, I don't care. Just sit for a minute, huh? Humor me. Tell me something I don't know already."

"I have to go," Olivia says.

"You sleeping okay? You're not lying awake up there? I hate to think of that."

She's sleeping fine, she says.

"Well, that's something," Nick says, sits himself at last, feels like he weighs three hundred pounds.

"Good night," Olivia says, clutches the neck of the gown before turning.

He remembers that gesture from Grace, the forearm keeping her from bobbing around loose.

"Good night," he calls through the doorway.

He waits at the table awhile, smoothing down his mustache. *Swear to God, Grace,* he thinks. *You got out early. You honestly did.*

Of course, Nick doesn't know the half of it yet.

Bird's-eye Maple

High summer in the valley.

Long evenings and not much in them.

One night Mark takes a spade to the bare spots in the grass, busts out the shards of clay, rakes in peat, broadcasts seed from his hand, sets up a sprinkler, watches its two upraised arms hurl spray in the coppery light. No telling how long he'll stay in this house, but you might as well do what needs doing, where's the harm in that?

Occasionally, the Watnes drive past. The boxy, wood-sided station wagon. Fred, Sonja, Scotty, Little Fred. They look at him as if he's a stone post left by an earlier civilization.

By now, Mark's been informed that Linny Stavros is no longer staying at the house in Grover's Addition. When, finally, he drove through the gap in the caragana, he found not Linny but Wendy Ochs. She happened to be walking the side yard, arms folded at the waist, looked so unsteady Mark very nearly backtracked without approaching. Or not unsteady exactly, but inward, perplexed by the bony roots of the spruce, the grass clippings stuck to her shoe. She repeated his name, but he couldn't tell if she remembered him. For his part, he'd never have recognized her. No makeup, her hair plain brown and gummy-looking, the skin around her eyes no thicker than a dried flower petal, faintly bluish.

He asked if Linny had left a message for him.

"Not that I'm aware of. No, I don't think so, I would have seen something like that."

"Well, do you know where I can . . . did she give you an address?"

"Nope, nope," Wendy said. "No address, no phone. Nada."

"But did she *say* something?"

"Oh, I haven't talked to her."

"Since she left."

"Not at all, no. Not for ages."

Could this be right? Because Linny had given the impression that she and Wendy Ochs were the closest of confidantes, that in fact Wendy had happily conspired with them from afar.

Mark's heart sank.

He managed to extract the solemn promise that she'd call the minute she had any news. He left unconvinced, sorry he'd come.

Was he the absolute last to know Linny'd skipped town?

These days, his phone seldom rings, but one night Thomas Balfour calls, asks how he's getting along, invites him down to the house above the lake.

Supper tomorrow, if he's free.

Undoubtedly, a scheme Celia's put him up to. Mark can't face getting the third degree from her. Don't think I can make it, he tells Thomas, then braces himself.

But Thomas says, peaceably, "That's a shame. Another time, then?"

"Sure, why not."

He feels authentically lousy afterward. Almost bad enough to call Thomas back.

At work, the word's gotten around. Nothing *Mark's* said, for goddamn sure. What exactly do they know? That he and Olivia are on the outs, living apart, probably that's the extent of it. He catches Ike giving him glints of disapproval, shrugs them off, though the last thing Mark wants is to be on the wrong side of Ike. Makes him queasy to think of the others talking about him when he's not there, but he shows nothing, refuses the bait. He oversleeps one morning, wakes in full sun, stuporous, his throat clotted with panic. Later, Roddy prods him, "Nobody to boot you out of bed, huh?" but he doesn't flare, only straps on his belt and says, "Good to see you, too." But as the week grinds along, he finds himself thinking about Thomas's overture again, wishing the two of them could hook up without having Celia to contend with. Feels reasonably confident he's blown his one shot.

It turns out he's wrong.

Friday night, Thomas calls again, tells Mark he has a load to pick up in Mullan's Crossing, says he realizes Mark's probably working tomorrow, making hay while the sun shines and all that, but on the off chance he isn't—

"Tell you the truth," Mark says, "I was thinking about taking the day off."

So late morning finds them on the West Fork road in Thomas's panel truck, BALFOUR ANTIQUE AND APPRAISAL, scrolly gold on green. The road surface alternates, a mile or two of blacktop, eight or ten of dirt, already washboarded, the powder spuming behind them in a choking fog, though Thomas can't be going over thirty. Now and then a mailbox, a sliver of ranch among the cottonwoods, and across the river the mountains of the national park. Blades of rock, snowfields burning like arc lights. Another forty miles, they'd cross into Canada. It's been years since Mark's been up here, not since before Amelia's birth.

It's hard to hear in the truck so they barely speak. A Chesterfield rides between the fingers of Thomas's right hand. He brings it to his mouth infrequently, acts surprised to find how good it tastes. They pass Cole's Meadow and Thomas says, almost shouting, "The bootleggers used to land their planes in there."

Mark nods, thinks, *Bootleggers. Another world—*

Mullan's Crossing consists of a tall-fronted mercantile, one spindly gasoline pump, a squat log-walled saloon called

Reuben's. Thomas lets out the clutch, rolls to a stop. At a plank table under a shaggy willow, there's a man somewhat older than Thomas. He glances up from the paper he's reading. Thomas shuts off the ignition. "Reuben Leveque," he tells Mark, "Mayor of the West Fork."

Though his face is long and sad and generally unwell-looking, the mayor of the West Fork lights up at the sight of Thomas Balfour.

Thomas shakes his hand, introduces Mark as his brother-in-law. "I'm *married* again," he says.

"I don't believe it," the mayor of the West Fork says hugely, the ghost of French-Canadian forbears in his voice, *daunt*.

"No, it's true," Thomas says, tells him Celia's a godsend, a ball of fire, asks if Reuben remembers the Vagabond in Sperry, down on Second Street? Anyway, she's Nick Stavros's daughter.

Adds, "Mark's married to one of her sisters, Olivia."

The mayor of the West Fork insists on a round of beers, three beaded tallboys borne outside, forearm against his belly. A salute to Thomas's good fortune, and then as if some communication has passed between them, invisible to Mark, the mayor of the West Fork clasps Thomas on the sleeve and disappears around the back.

"Hell of a fine day, isn't it?" Thomas says.

Mark has to agree. The light underneath the willow is green-gold, elusive as the light on a streambed. He asks how Thomas knows Reuben.

"Elinor and I used to drive up here," Thomas says, and Mark instantly regrets his curiosity.

Thomas seems not to mind. "She hadn't been in the West long," he says. "She found all this *fascinating*. Our little road trips." He smiles at Mark. "She grew up in the city of Baltimore," he says, asks if Mark's ever happened to see a picture of her.

No, Mark says, never has.

"We were college sweethearts," Thomas says. "Million years ago."

Mark nods, upends his bottle. "So where's our load of furniture?" he asks finally.

Thomas dismisses this with a vague riffling of his fingers, as if to say, *Everything in due time.* Mark feels lightly chastised.

After a moment, Thomas catches his eye. "I wanted to ask you how things stood," he says.

"With Liv?" Mark answers. "I haven't talked to her since that night, not once. She's got herself barricaded in over there."

"That's what I hear."

A magpie slants in to inspect a patch of dark ground out front of the mercantile, waddles around it, head bobbing, takes flight again, raising dust.

"What do you think's going to happen?" Thomas asks.

"Well, I don't know. I'm kind of numb, to tell you the honest truth."

"What would you *like* to happen? Maybe you don't know that either."

Mark can't think of a way to answer this.

After a bit, he says, "I suppose you know the whole thing."

"I know what Ceel knows," Thomas says.

"Liv's talked to her?"

"I believe most of it's come by way of Helen."

Yet another thing Mark regrets, the way Helen got caught in the middle.

"There's not a lot I can do if she won't talk to me," he says.

Thomas nods.

"What would *you* do?"

"It doesn't much matter what I'd do," Thomas says, though without rancor.

Mark looks off, fighting the tightening in his chest. He sees the mayor of the West Fork, apron-clad, approaching with

sandwiches. Slabs of cheddar and side meat on hard rolls ooz-
ing mustard. Quartered dills. Two more beers.

Thomas thanks him extravagantly.

The mayor of the West Fork raises a palm. No, the pleasure
is his.

Though he hadn't been aware of being hungry, Mark tears
into the food, feels his eyes water at the salty bacon, the German mustard routering out his sinuses.

"Whoo," Thomas says, one hand going to the table edge for
support.

The mayor nods in grave sympathy, hears the *thuck, thuck*
of truck doors over his shoulder, goes off to attend the two
men shambling toward the boardwalk.

Once he's done eating, and has sat staring for a time, Mark
says, "I don't know if she's trying to show me something, or if
she means never to lay eyes on me again." He picks at the
corner of his mouth with a thumbnail. "If it's the second, it
doesn't seem that reasonable."

"No, it doesn't," Thomas says. "But you almost have to
admire it."

Mark lifts his face, about to ask, Whose side are you on?
Instead, he considers Thomas's remark a moment, the proposition that Olivia's adamance could inspire awe, remembers
with a twinge the icy set of her lips the last time he was permitted to see them. Remembers Linny asking, years ago, "Isn't
that part of what attracted you?"

But there's something else he'd like to put to Thomas, a
question that's slowly taken shape these past minutes: Does
Thomas think he'd be so delighted with Celia if it weren't for
losing his first wife.

Or this: Would he still love her now, Elinor?

He doesn't know Thomas well enough to ask. Very much
wishes he did, though.

Mark shoves back from the table, gets to his feet. Can't sit any longer, he knows *that* much.

Thomas tells him to hang on a second, ducks into Reuben's and returns with a little brass key on a stick. Then the two of them file down a footpath behind the saloon, past a boarded-over privy where someone's written *Full Up* in blue crayon, back to a cabin with a blinding tin roof.

Thomas works the lock. Inside it's all storage, the air swirling up rank with their footsteps, dry rot and newsprint shredded to lace, mouse droppings like a scatter of wild rice. The first breath leaves them woozy.

Slow motion, ceremoniously, Thomas draws the sheet from a dresser in the center of the floor. Beveled oval mirror supported by two serpentine arms, three banks of drawers with curved fronts, cut glass pulls. The wood blond, mottled with fudge-colored whorls.

"Bird's-eye maple," Thomas explains. "Don't see it that often, not here. Grows in the Upper Penninsula of Michigan, they slice it off in sheets with a kind of guillotine." He runs a finger over the veneer. "Isn't this lovely?"

Mark gives it a touch. Buttery. Would've walked right past it in a room, but now that he has it pointed out, he has to agree. It *is,* lovely.

Thomas indicates the rectangle of slightly lighter wood. "Dresser scarf," he says.

"What's he doing getting rid of it?" Mark asks.

"I'll tell you what," Thomas says. "I don't ask, as a rule." He kicks a wedge under the door. "People are funny about these old pieces. They hang on to them for years, wouldn't think of parting with them, then they look up one day and think, *Christ Almighty, all this old stuff!* Suddenly they can't stand it until they're out from under the weight. But even when they explain themselves, there's more to the story, that's what I find. In Reuben's case, I think there's been a family squabble of some sort."

He turns back to Mark, says, "I'm just glad he didn't leave it out in the snow. Now I'm going to bring the truck. Why don't you slip the drawers out for me."

"This all we're taking?" Mark asks.

Thomas nods. "Just the one piece."

As he watches the truck bump across the grass, it occurs to Mark that Thomas and Reuben could have managed fine without him.

One dresser.

It turns out to be about four inches too tall with the mirror on. Thomas patiently unscrews the brackets, wraps it in a quilted moving blanket, secures it with twine.

Now that Thomas is all business, Mark's reluctant to head back. He leans against the warm hood hoping Thomas might squander a little more of his day here.

"Ceel doesn't know where Linny is, does she?" Mark asks.

"I don't believe so."

"It's not like I have anything more to say to her. It's just—"

"Not being able to," Thomas says. "In case you did."

Mark nods.

In a minute, he asks, "What's Ceel have to say about her? Linny."

A small smile from Thomas, a long pull on the Chesterfield.

"Because," Mark goes on, "Olivia's convinced it was all between the two of them, had nothing to do with me."

"And what do you think?"

Mark shakes his head. "I hate to think she was fooling with me."

"Maybe a little of both," Thomas says. "Were you fooling with her?"

Mark checks the sky for inspiration, peers sidelong at Thomas, closes his eyes.

Late afternoon, Thomas crunches down the driveway of the house on Paxson Road, lets the engine idle, and thanks Mark for his help. Privately, Mark offers his own thanks, that Thomas has maintained this fiction. Still, there's the long evening ahead, and he stalls.

"Can I ask you something," he says, and doesn't wait for Thomas's okay, but pushes on, tells him about reading Davey the train book that night last fall, early winter, suddenly seeing the image of Thomas so clearly in his mind's eye: the trestle spanning a huge ravine, rain whipping down bitterly. He hears himself asking if Thomas ever visited the spot of the accident.

"I did," Thomas says, and pauses so long Mark thinks this is the kind of curt answer he deserves for butting in where he doesn't belong.

Then Thomas says, "It wasn't until the following summer, though. And you couldn't call it a ravine, it was just rolling hills and the river. By that time the bridge had been rebuilt, of course. The tracks didn't follow the road, so I had to walk in, a mile or two. Other people had been there before me—there were bunches of flowers, a Saint Christopher medal, folded-up notes anchored with rocks or nailed into the new wood. The river was low by then, a dreary brown. The night of the accident it had been just below flood stage—a barge had gotten loose and rammed one of the bridge supports. The trains didn't pitch off any great distance, so much as roll sideways and flip over. All the Pullman cars, filling up with water, black as the inside of God's brain.

"But there *I* was, a day like today. The goldenrod was out, acres of it, purple martins swooping by my head. A sharp smell of creosote. I just stood and stared and it all seemed terribly unreal, unbelievable."

He turns to Mark on the seat. "What are you, about thirty? I was a little older, thirty-seven. I thought I'd feel something being there. I don't mean this to sound mystical, but I thought I'd feel closer to her somehow, or enjoy some feeling of release, or at least under*stand* it better, but none of that happened. I thought, Well, all right, now I've seen where she died, then I walked the mile or two back to the car. I stayed that night in some little town and the next day I drove up to Cleveland and got a hotel room.

"I started to think about the notes people had left on the trestle. I hadn't let myself read them, but I mean the fact they'd been left, the idea of sitting down and writing a letter to your dead loved one and toting it out there. It seemed like an incredible act of faith. So I sat in the room for some time marveling at these people I'd never seen, never would see, and got to berating myself terribly because I had no such faith myself.

"The window was open and it was the hour the lights were coming on and there was a lull in the street noise. A transitional hour, is what I mean to say, so it's possible I was susceptible to thoughts like that . . . melancholy. I'd been more or less poisoned with recriminations all that year, anyway. I'd insisted she go on the trip in the first place—her mother was scheduled to have one of her cataracts operated on, and I thought Elinor ought to be there. And I won't say we'd been fighting, but things were unsettled between us, which I'm sure had to do with her not being able to have a baby—ever since I'd gotten back from the army we'd been trying valiantly, but no luck. I suppose each of us secretly blamed the other. We were still hopeful, but we'd begun to feel kind of duped, I guess, too, or tainted. So there was that. I thought about what I'd stick in a letter—I actually got out a sheet of the hotel stationery—and it was mainly a list of things I was sorry about. Well, what a *miserable* exercise. I pictured Elinor reading it, and I couldn't see her getting the least bit of joy from it.

"In any case, the longer I sat, the more those letters bothered me. I started to change my mind about the whole operation. They began to seem pathetic. *Nobody was going to read them*. They'd be rained on, the ink would run, the paper would go to mush and wind up in the river, and none of it would have made one whit of difference to anyone but the writers. You'd have to be seriously deluded, I thought. I swore I wouldn't be that way, Mark. I won't say I felt enormously better, but it gave me a little charge, and that was the frame of mind I was in when I fled my room that night. Hard-nosed, like I wasn't going to get taken in by any nonsense.

"So I walked away from the hotel. It was dark now, but the pavement was still soft from the heat, and tires of the cabs were making that molasses sound. I walked and walked. Finally I decided I needed a drink, but more than that, I wanted to be around other people. I stopped in a chophouse . . . there was a combo playing in the other room, piano, bass, drummer, two or three couples dancing, nothing out of the ordinary, except a mood was in the air. I don't know what, if anything, it had to do with it, but this was the year the Indians had a team—Boudreau, Bob Feller, Lemon, they actually beat Boston in the series that fall. In any case, I had my drink, then I ordered a big steak and wolfed that down, and boy it tasted good. You know how once in a while a taste hits you just right? You can't explain it?"

"Sure," Mark says.

Thomas nods, says, "Well, so the later it got, the more the place filled, and this wasn't a weekend, just a Thursday night in July. A horn player got up with the band, and he was good, or at least everyone thought so, and it was wall-to-wall on the dance floor then, the women with their bare shoulders, their jewelry, the men in their shirtsleeves, sweating. You'd catch someone's eye for a second. As I said, earlier, when I'd left the hotel, I'd been in this hard-edged mood, quite scornful, convinced I was only seeing things realistically, and congratulating myself for it, as if it were a major turning point. The walking had started to take it out of me, though. What a long, difficult day. Think of it. I was drained, and one thing I was drained of was the urge to understand everything. No, that's wrong, I did want to understand, I *still* do, but I found I didn't need to pass judgment on every single thing. If people wanted to talk to the dead as if they were paying rapt attention, then it was all right with me."

Thomas pauses. "I'd gotten to a third place in my thinking in just that short time," he says, still amazed, Mark can see. "I felt like a guest in the world."

Neither speaks then.

Finally, Mark says, "I thought you were going to tell me about one of the women with the bare shoulders."

Thomas smiles. "Hey, I told you I was *drained*," he says. He gives Mark a soft cuff on the leg, thanks him again, tells him to take care.

Mark says he will.

This day's been such a relief that Mark is back in the house for some time before it sinks in that Thomas hasn't given him much to go on with respect to Olivia. Nothing you could call a plan, really. He stands outside the breezeway, watching the crickets spring off the hardpan. The valley's baked all afternoon, pure August heat though it's still July. He bends and cranks on the hose . . . futile time to be growing grass, probably, but what the hell.

When it's mostly dark, he lies on the bed, uncovered, waiting.

Never slept alone so many nights since he was a boy. And the sleep that comes is poor, sleep like a leaky boat. He wakes with sweat in his hair, the room close, airless. Olivia could never have the fan on—blocked the sound from the kids' rooms, panicked her. Now, though it makes no sense, he can't either.

He runs a damp cloth up and down his limbs, walks into the moonlit yard in his undershorts. There's a faint jostling of leaves in the crab apple, the top-heavy bob of Olivia's holly-hocks. It's no mystery how he's come to be here, his shadow slate black, as gangly limbed as a figure on a cave wall. And yet, in these early hours of the morning, his life does seem starkly unfamiliar, detached from him and worthy of wonder . . . it's as if, awake like this, he's about to wake into another state, but can't quite, can't quite.

Outnumbered

"I'm hitting the deep freeze," Celia says.

Late afternoon, she's lathered with sweat, burs stuck to her socks. Been down to the mudflats with Rudolfo, one of the black Labs. She's all for the heat, the heavy sun baking her skin, but wouldn't a shower feel sweet, carry her beyond that slump in the day, so she unbuttons her shirt in the kitchen, hands it to Thomas, says, "You wouldn't like to bring me a cup of coffee in a minute, would you?"

The air conditioner affixed to the bedroom window is the legacy of Thomas's Aunt Caro. His father's sister, a business-woman—real estate, antiques. Never married, though there had been liaisons, as Thomas put it. Some fierce rapport had existed between her and Thomas. Hanging in the sunny kitchen is a watercolor of Aunt Caro, pale and freckled with a bloom of carnation red for the mouth, snappy thirties dress of black crepe, puff sleeves. She'd spent her last year in bed here, listening to opera, lung-scarred, ninety-two pounds.

Thomas and his two dead women.

Celia feels anything-but. She's determined to stay healthy, strong. Love's made her wobbly in the past, but no more. Not this girl.

She steps into the wall of cold air—well, seventy degrees, maybe, but delicious, like pure ozone. She peels out of the rest of her things and loiters under the needling shower, shaves passably, squeezes the water from her hair and returns to the bedroom without toweling off, stands with her backside to the airflow, watching her skin set up, the bronzed and the not-bronzed. Which is where Thomas finds her. Which is where she intended Thomas to find her.

The better part of an hour later, decked out in fresh cotton, she leans over Thomas, says, "Oh, don't wake up, sweetie," but he's partially resurrected, one blue eye regarding her.

"Where you off to?"

"Got to run over to my dad's. There's a nice salad in the icebox if you can't wait. Black olives and all that. I love you."

And so when Celia Balfour arrives at McLaren Road, Celia piloting the T-bird, top down, a rhythm going in her head, *doo, doop-a, do-doop,* her mood is deeply ensconced, no *tristesse* for her.

Not even Olivia's a match for it.

Up into the vinegar-smelling kitchen, screen door patting behind her. Forthright squeeze for Nick, a smack on his chapped old lips. She was never dead center of Nick's universe—never so intricately vexing as Linny, as adoring as Olivia, as uncomplaining and gal Fridayish as Helen—but it hardly matters anymore. Her skirmishes with Nick are past history, and, lately, hours of contemplating Thomas have lent her a new appreciation for the stages of man, a free-flowing charity.

Letting go of Nick's arm, she can't resist a little bump of her chest against his, loves to fluster him . . . *Jesus, don't do* that, *Celia—*

She turns to Olivia, says, "Hon, you look so blasted hot," and before Liv can throw up a roadblock, tells her she's come on an errand of mercy.

"I can't bear any more pep talks," Olivia says.

"No, no pep talks, we're just going for a ride."

"I don't want to see anybody."

"You don't have to," Celia says. "Just me and Helen, if you can stand it."

And to Nick, preemptively, Celia says, "You don't mind watching the kidskis?"

No way he can refuse.

So they're out on the road then, Olivia shotgun, Helen knees-splayed in the T-bird's cramped backseat. Cripps Drive, Carrier Road, LaBonty, sweeping around a trundling hay-wagon, passing windbreaks, sloughs already mud-banked and choked with water lilies.

"Isn't this car a hoot?" Celia says. Much as she'd love to floor it, she constrains herself, keeps it down to a clip where they can hear one another without hollering.

"This isn't some trick to get me over to Mark's," Olivia says.

"So suspicious."

"You can save the trouble."

"Will you relax, Liv. I meant what I said, I thought you could use some *air.*"

She hardly expects Olivia to open right up. Never was easy. As much as she and Liv clung together in Linny's wake, their natural outlooks were at cross-purposes—Celia's favoring action, improvization . . . Olivia's rumination, a cleaving to principle. And, let's face it, Celia's always had a soft spot for Linny. Isn't it there even now?

Celia glances into the rearview and there's Helen, bristly

bangs standing up like a headdress. She smiles, Helen smiles back, though watchful.

"Tell me this is better than hanging around the fort," Celia says.

"Yes," Olivia says. "I'm sorry."

"What are you sorry for?"

For all this. Being the way I am. Such a pain to everyone.

"Forget it," Celia says.

She pokes in the lighter, smokes with a fine pleasure, watching the hazy rise and fall of the foothills, sneaking looks at Olivia now and then.

Where the road makes a T at Farm-to-Market, she cruises to a stop, idles the engine, says without much premeditation, "Let's drive over there and kick his butt."

No response from Liv.

"Come *on,*" Celia says. "We've got him way outnumbered."

She hesitates just a second, cranks a hard left, back toward town. Drops it in gear.

Olivia explodes across the bucket seat and yanks the wheel from her hands.

In a wild blur, the rear of the T-bird sails out ahead of them, humping over the grassy shoulder, heaving itself down into the borrow pit . . . it bounces to the spring load, grates on the field-stones, comes to rest like a nocked arrow against a length of wire fence.

For a moment, only the tings of the hot undercarriage, Olivia's wrenching breaths.

"Well, that was impressive, Liv," Celia says. "Honest to Pete."

She looks around, takes stock. No banged heads, it appears. Miraculously, Helen hasn't pitched out the back.

But here Olivia breaks into frantic sobs. It's a horrid, braying sound, as if she were actually gagging, choking to death.

"Stick your arms above your head," Helen says from behind.

She reaches over the seat, helps peel Olivia's hands from her face and get them lifted. "That's it, tip your chin up—"

Not a single outburst before this, as far as anyone's witnessed. No puffy, Kleenex-roughened eyes.

It takes a minute, longer than you'd think, really, but once Olivia's chest stops jerking, Celia says, "Hey, c'mon—" and pulls her over. Olivia's stiff for a second, but yields, lets her sister work a hand into her hair, cradle the hot streaky face.

"I was just joking with you," Celia says, almost a whisper. "You know that's my way. You know how I am, not the subtlest person in the world."

Celia says, "It's not like I don't take it seriously, Liv."

She bends gingerly and pops the glove box, where Thomas has left a brand-new chamois cloth, never been used. Applies the soft leather to Olivia's cheeks and eyes.

What you have to do, Celia thinks, dabbing away, is see this thing with Mark as Olivia sees it.

Picture a glass globe dropped onto marble.

Olivia finally takes the chamois with her own nail-bitten hands, stares at it, says flatly, "I put everything into Mark."

The Celia of two years ago would've leapt at this, *There's your trouble right there, sister. You don't hold some back, you're begging for it.* She'd have told tales, war stories. But this new Celia, oh, she can see the temptation, she can. Name one thing she'd hold back from Thomas.

"The thought of him touching me again," Olivia says.

Yes, well.

"I feel so fooled, I feel like the biggest laughingstock."

From the backseat, Helen says, "I don't think anybody's laughing, Livvy."

"I can hear her from here," Olivia says. "Can't you?"

Actually, Celia *can.* That wicked, gargled laugh of Linny's, descended straight from Nick Stavros, and who knows which sardonic old forbears owned it before that . . . except what Olivia can't see is, it's aimed at the stars, not at her.

Fat consolation.

Anyway, Celia comes back to what Helen reported to her about the day the Vagabond closed, Linny's *I thought he could use some cheering up* . . . remembers an old boyfriend's pearl of wisdom, *You got a bad spot on your tire, one day you're gonna run over a chicken bone.* And so she says, "Obviously I'm no expert on marriage, Liv, but, I mean, what was going on between you two?"

"Me and *Mark?*"

"If you don't mind my asking."

Of course she minds. Of course she's mortified, her pride corroded, eaten clear through in spots.

"Because, to be honest," Celia continues, "and I know I've been distracted here lately, I admit it, I've been wrapped up in my own stuff, but you and Mark haven't seemed all that great. Or am I inventing it?"

She eyes Helen for confirmation, and Helen nods soberly. Yes, it's true.

"Don't you two gang up on me," Olivia says, wedges herself farther down in the seat, knuckles to her mouth.

But Celia's not having any of that just now. "What about it, Liv?"

"I didn't *drive* him to it, if that's what you're getting at. What a thing to say."

"I'm not," Celia says, though in a way maybe she *is.* "It's just that things can be kind of smooshy, you know what I mean? Complicated? You go through slumps with another person. You want an example, look at the *folks.*" Here she's on serious thin ice with Olivia, but skates forth nonetheless. "You don't think they got on each other's nerves, you don't think they rubbed each other ragged some of the time? Houseful of girls, a business to keep afloat? I know what a saint you think the old man is, but—"

"You're not getting me to believe he played around," Olivia says, as if slapped by a board. "Not if you talk straight through till tomorrow."

Celia smiles at the thought, then moderates this into a guarded frown. "Well, I won't hazard a guess about that," she says. "All I'm trying to tell you is they had their ups and downs, didn't always want the same things at the same times." She swivels on the seat, makes a halfhearted effort to locate the package of Parliaments. She ought to remember how damn taxing a conversation with Olivia can be. "Same thing with Thomas and his first wife," she says. "Not all roses by any means." Here they are, down under the brake pedal. She lights up again, says, "Thomas has a line he quotes, *Everyone knows this triumphant life is periodic*. Don't take this the wrong way, Liv, but it's like you expect too much."

"I expected to be able to trust him," Olivia says, unrepentant. "There's nothing complicated about that."

Celia sighs, looks off.

Oh, man.

All this time, no one's come by. There's just the tasseled fields, the evening turning blue and stretching out, the dizzy traffic of insects.

She asks, "But now what, Liv?"

"I wish you'd all stop interrogating me," Olivia says.

"Nobody's in*terro*gating you," Celia says. "We're just concerned. You know? That's what we're for."

Olivia gives her a long stare, as if to say, *Oh, yes, aren't sisters a blessing . . .*

The kind of shield Linny might throw up. You hate to see it on Olivia.

Now Helen shifts noisily on the white vinyl, slips a hand out and touches Olivia on the neck, rubs. Olivia doesn't shuck it off . . . she exhales in a tired burst, bends her head, rakes the mass of hair up off her damp skin.

After a while, she turns back to Celia, says, "I'm sorry about your car."

Celia waves it away, *No big deal.*

"But don't tell anyone. Promise."

"Me?"

"No, I mean it," Olivia says. Out of fairness, she turns and casts a look back at Helen as well.

"Tell about *what?*" Helen says.

So Celia tries the ignition, and the engine, after some rattling hesitation, catches. If the paint's scratched, if anything's racked-up underneath . . . well, she's resourceful. No big deal. She noses the T-bird up the slope, pauses at the road's edge, tells Olivia, mock-stern, "Hands to yourself now, hon," though, in fact, Olivia's hands are knit firmly together in her lap.

Not Picturing You

Monday, but for the low hum of apprehension he wakes to every morning, Mark's thoughts are near-blank as he steers Conlon Construction's reprobate of a truck along First, his mood upbeat, stubbornly and for no reason. He waits at the light, shudders double-clutching over the heat-ridged blacktop onto Montana, and almost doesn't notice the familiar two-tone black above white of the Stavros Buick, slanting into a spot outside Lindell's, nor quite register the significance of who gets out. Nick and Helen, and clutching her hand, swinging it jerkily as he walks, Mark's firstborn.

Mark squints into his side mirror, loses them in the clutter of sign poles and sun-deviled chrome, catches another split-second view as they disappear through the supermarket's new electric doors.

Just those three, he's sure of it.

And tempting as it is to imagine surprising Davey down one of the aisles, *Well, look who it is . . .* instead he takes himself back to the pay phone alongside the Park Inn.

First time he's heard her voice in seven weeks. He says in a rush, "Liv, this is the last time I'm going to call, don't hang up."

When she hangs up, he thinks: All right, here's the test. He dials again. When she picks up wordlessly on the sixth ring, he lets the dime drop, says, "What I meant was, that was the next-to-last time I'd call."

Did he imagine this would break the ice, inspire a cathartic laugh?

He goes on, without pause, remembering what Thomas said up the West Fork, Thomas's presence in fact hovering benevolently about him, "I know this sounds funny, Liv, but I admire how you're being. Part of me does. Part of me admires the hell out of it."

Olivia doesn't inquire as to the rest of him.

She tells him to save his breath, what he says now doesn't matter.

"No? Why'd you answer, then?"

"To be sure you understand that."

"All right, I do," Mark says too readily. "But why don't I come over to the house for a minute—"

She says if he tries that she won't be there. Asks him not to follow her, not to spy on her.

"Well, I'm not spying, Olivia. But okay, just talk to me for a second? Do you think you could do that? I was wondering what your plans were. You going to stay at your dad's awhile?"

If she answers, he can't quite hear.

"I'm sorry?"

For the time being, she says.

Mark nods, brows bunched, as if she can see him.

He's downwind from the restaurant's kitchen vent, trapped by its fumes, the scorched oil, the dense peppery griddle scrapings. All he's had today is coffee and a jelly doughnut—God, it's putting an edge on him, making him greedy despite what he's telling himself, *Go slow, slow,* camel's nose under the tent, as Audrey Singer might say.

"You upstairs?" he asks.

"Why?"

"I wanted to picture you."

The upstairs phone at McLaren Road sits in a niche at the far end of the hall. The girls used to talk from an old armchair stationed there beside the radiator, the wallpaper gone slick and shadowy from their feet, their flung-back hair. Seemed a fearfully intimate spot the first time he laid eyes on it, years ago . . . Olivia had to tug him away.

"You shouldn't be picturing me anymore," she says.

"I won't then," Mark says.

But what a thing to expect. A stunning demonstration of her thinking.

"I have to go now, Mark."

Water in the background, the *whang* of a pan lid, so she's downstairs after all, and then the line's dead, but back in Ike's truck again, working the balky choke as the noontime traffic blurs by, he thinks, *That wasn't so bad, could have gone worse.*

He lets three days pass. Blistering, cloudless. Waits until the air begins to cool on Thursday evening. When Helen answers, he asks if she'll put her sister on, knowing she will, and that this time Olivia will be upstairs, tucked into that old stuffed chair. Wearing the tan shorts, a blousy top, her thick hair in tortoise-shell barrettes.

"I'm not picturing you," he says.

If she thinks he's trying to joke with her, if it nettles her, there's no sign. She says she wishes they didn't have to discuss this, but can she count on him for a regular check, not just the occasional crumb . . . it's not for her, she's at pains to have him understand, but for Davey and Amelia, who are after all, she says, innocent bystanders. He won't cheat them, won't try to use them as leverage against her, will he?

"That's the last thing on my mind, Olivia."

"You say that now."

In no position to argue on behalf of his constancy, Mark answers simply, "I'll send over what I can, after the payments. If that doesn't work I'll see about selling the house, assuming you don't want it."

No, she doesn't want the house. He guesses he can understand why.

Precious little equity they have in it, in any case.

"I didn't call to talk about that," he says.

"Mark, I can't listen to anything else."

He knows she means it, yet senses in the sudden drop of her voice that maybe she *would* listen, despite herself, if he had something revolutionary to say.

It's a moment that passes.

"Good night, Liv," he says. "Kiss the kids."

He holds the phone in his lap awhile before returning it to the dresser.

He gets to thinking about Thomas Balfour again.

Thomas seated at the desk in his Cleveland hotel room, a page of writing paper under his hand. Mark's knowledge of big-city hotel rooms is largely the product of gangster movies, so the whole scene's abnormally sooty in his mind's eye: pigeons strutting malevolently on the sill, Thomas bent under

a stingy halo of light. But never mind, something's been trou-
bling him about Thomas's account, and it's this: He wouldn't
have kept on apologizing to Elinor very long. In no time, he'd
have been listing off the things he missed about her, rhapsodiz-
ing. Hard not to sound sappy in the process, but Thomas
would've pulled it off. And, anyway, Elinor wouldn't care how
it *sounded,* it wouldn't sound sappy to *her.*

Of course, this is all a fantasy.

But Mark remembers another strange thing Thomas said,
perhaps the strangest: . . . *I'd gotten to a third place in my
thinking.* That he'd talk about his interior life, that he saw his
thoughts progressing, not eddying ad infinitum.

Mark stands, sloughs off his torpor, visits the kitchen and
checks the icebox as if it might hold something he didn't
deposit there himself.

By now, of course, Mark's grandmother knows the story . . .
or the gist of it.

Not who it was.

As keenly as Mark had dreaded disappointing her, he was
that relieved to have it done with. She didn't land on him like a
load of bricks, only nodded in that chronically surprised-but-
unsurprised way of hers and said, "I could tell *something* was
fishy."

She asked was it over, this straying of Mark's?

He said it was.

And the other party, did she live in Sperry? Was this somebody he'd keep bumping into?

No, she'd gone.

But what if she were to show up again?

Mark said he didn't expect to see her.

This wasn't quite the response his grandmother had been
angling for, so Mark said, "I wouldn't be seeing her that way,
even if I did happen to see her."

If this were the cold part of the year, Audrey Singer

would've sent him home with a tub of soup, a platter of sauerbraten, but not in this heat, no. Instead they strolled along the root-heaved sidewalks while she smoked one of her little brown cigars. She'd taken to wearing a pair of boy's high-top sneakers. Support for the ankles.

"I certainly cut a jaunty figure these days, don't I?" she said. She had a loose hold of Mark's arm.

They passed a young girl flinging a baton, picking it up where it careened. Down the block a man in a ribbed undershirt stood musing over the empty engine compartment of a car, as if the motor had vanished while he was inside changing clothes.

"I suspect you picked the wrong person to pull this on," Mark's grandmother said, back to the subject of Olivia.

You could say that.

"Oh, we make such an ordeal of things," she said. "Sometimes I wonder, really."

But what exactly did she wonder?

They walked on.

No, Audrey Singer didn't come down on his head like a ton of bricks, and this was a blessing, all right, but also a disappointment.

Or so he thinks now, drinking ice water at the sink in large, painful gulps.

Then a night passes and it's Friday. Still hot, the talk at lunch about the dry woods, the lightning fires burning north of the border, in British Columbia. The air has a faint sepia tinge, feels oxygen-starved. Nobody wants to do much. Roddy nods off, snores, one palm open in his lap. Whitey lays a mummified dog turd in it. In short, a day materially no different from the day before, except it's a day he's not going to call Olivia.

Then comes Saturday. Ike's promised to take his wife to Lake Genevieve, and Whitey's headed to Missoula, so the crew knocks off early and disperses. Mark cuts across Sperry, takes Railroad past the elevators, the scavenging seagulls, past the site of the Farmer's Union fire, bulldozer cleats in the clay all that's left, past the freight depots, the loading docks with their shredding foot-square timbers, the cherry warehouse. He's always loved Railroad Street. He used to bring Davey here some nights, and they'd walk beside the rail spurs, the boy on his shoulders. He used to point out the gang of mongrel cats lounging under the grain augers, used to show off the open boxcars as if he had something to do with their size, their great weighty presence.

Then he's driving up Second Street. He's avoided it for weeks, but now he learns that Alt has wasted no time. The side-by-side empty lots are gone—Wilfred Espy's, the Vagabond's—replaced by a continuous wall of concrete block, two floors high, broken by rectangles of glassless steel sash, primer red. Mark slides into the NO PARKING opposite the Wren's marquee, sees workmen dodging through the uneven shadows, calculates where the row of booths had stood, the swinging door to the kitchen. He starts to get out, changes his mind.

It dawns on him that courting Olivia the first time was *easy*. Even the word, which was his grandmother's, though she used it lightly, knowing how archaic it sounded to his ears, how he'd think, *Froggie went a-courtin' and he did ride* . . . not even the word rightly applied. Olivia had simply been waiting for him. There must have been a literal first time they saw each other, but Mark can't recall it. They'd gone to different grade schools—Cordelia Walker for Olivia, dungeonlike Cyrus Chittick for Mark, his class the last to sit in its drafts, to trip over its swollen floorboards, the class that escaped annihilation when the boiler blew on a Sunday morning. But by junior high they must have brushed by each other in the corridors, begun to recognize the other. Olivia claimed they'd shared a study hall all one winter and spring, but Mark has no memory of this either. No, it was at the Vagabond they truly met. He'd been coming in for some time, of course, drinking his Cokes, popping ketchupy fries into his mouth one by one, back to the wall, legs out on the seat, but there was a single October afternoon everything changed, when he saw the shiver of astonishment cross Olivia's face: Oh, so it's *you*.

That he remembers.

And how he wasn't the same thereafter. Not that it was any presto, lead-into-gold kind of thing. The change must have been gradual . . . it only *felt* sudden, sudden and irrevocable, as if a new blast of puberty had kicked in, this one ignoring his glands but purging him of a great backlog of fears and boyhood confusions, giving him a reservoir of patience and hope to go along with the urgency of his body, the power to sit and talk and listen hours on end, to see himself in the wildly unlikely role of grown man, lover, citizen, father. From then on it was Mark-and-Olivia. The only question was how long before they'd make it legal and binding.

Saturday night, showered, his hair still wet, he sits on the edge of the bed, and these thoughts return. In the car, they'd struck him as comforting, stabilizing. Compared to the muddy swirl of the recent past, they stayed in focus with little effort. But now his mood has eroded. He thinks, *You can't just burrow in nostalgia, either, that's a trap, too—*

He lies back, breathing slowly, the telephone on his chest. Rising, falling.

And then it rings. He grabs it up in self-defense.

"Oh, good, you're home," Celia says.

"God, you scared me."

"Really? You *ought* to be scared."

Can he face sparring with his sister-in-law? He sticks out an arm, starts to right himself.

Celia goes on without waiting, "Mark, here's what's bothering me. Bad as this is, it's given Olivia the upper hand with Lin. You follow me? After this stunt, Linny'll be driving the low road forever. Liv's going to want to savor it. That's in addition to how proud she is, and all the rest."

Mark lets the logic of this soak in a minute. "I admit they seemed to get to each other," he says. "I just never paid it much attention. Liv's so attached to all of you . . . I don't know, I just thought maybe it's only natural if there's some friction."

He hoists his legs onto the floor, stands barefoot, the bottom half of the phone still squeezed to his rib cage. "I didn't see that there was more to it."

"No shit."

Mark sighs. "So why don't you tell where this all came from?"

"It's not like there was some big *incident,* Mark. Things don't work that way."

He waits for Celia to elaborate, but all she says is, "And even if you dug to the bottom of it, what would you know? A fool's errand, if you ask me. No, I'm just telling you, you gave her something she's not going to want to part with. You two geniuses."

Mark takes a deep breath, squints out the dust-matted window screen, and says finally, "I want you to know, I never meant any harm."

Celia actually bursts into a laugh. Throaty, explosive like Linny, but freer, too. She asks Mark if he has any idea how dumb that sounds, how spectacularly lame.

Strange, one minute he's trying to be his most solemn and true, the next he's laughing right alongside her . . . strange the way relief ambushes him, slaps him off his roost.

"Yeah, I *do* know," he says. "It couldn't matter less what I meant."

"Not from where Olivia's sitting it doesn't," Celia says. "Okay, now how about this one: What if she'd asked you to go with her, Linny?"

"She didn't ask."

"Oh, sweetie, you're such a jerk," she says, exasperated, but sort of teasing . . . Celia who's so accustomed to talking to men. Mark's never sure if she's about to scour him out or what.

"She didn't want me like that," he says. "If she did maybe I'd be gone by now. But she didn't, and I'm not."

"Two things, Mark. First is you're never going to know what Linny wanted. Outside of the obvious. Understand?"

"And the other?"

"The other is: You'd better get good and straight what you'd do."

"I am."

"No, I'm not buying that," Celia says. "Having Linny gone's a luxury. You don't have to see her standing in front of you with her hand open."

"I realize that, but the thing is, Ceel—"

"No, you listen to me, Mark Singer, you went to Linny because Linny's more fun that Olivia. Period. You were *seduced*, Mark. It does happen, and you know why? Because it's *thrilling*. You think I don't *know*? And don't you think I know all about having Linny's light shine on you? Suddenly you think, Man, this house has *a lot* more rooms than I ever imagined . . . oh, but then your regular life seems so cramped, Olivia starts to seem *ordinary*, you're pissed off for no special reason half the time, you can hardly remember what you're doing, can't work up a teaspoonful of enthusiasm. But you're a good boy, you want everyone to still *like* you, you're going to hang in there and make good on your vows, there's the kids to think about . . . you just need a little absolution, and then you're back in business. But here's what I'm telling you, and I hope you can hear because I do love you, Mark, don't ask me why . . . it's just this: *That's not going to be good enough*."

Mark doesn't move, except to open his eyes, which he doesn't remember shutting.

It galls him, shames him, that she's not wrong, shames him that she *sees* him . . . he has the boyish impulse to cover himself, remembers women customers of his grandmother's interrupting him in the bathroom, which wouldn't lock, *Oh, sorry, sorry* . . . and he couldn't remove himself without falling a second time under their gaze. Irrational the hot-faced shame, Mark nothing to them but a boy doing his business. Shames him that he can't say to Celia: "Just leave me alone, you don't know *anything* about me."

And so, as it turns out, Saturday he doesn't call Olivia.

He's back, somehow, to zero.

Stir-crazy

Saturday at 412 McLaren Road.

Helen's stir-crazy from the instant she wakes. It's the heavy air, undeniably smoky now, trapped against the mountains, though why it should make her restless when it swaddles everyone else in lethargy, she can't say. She throws on the jeans she's worn all week, then can't stand them, the way the crotch seems suddenly to bind. She peels them off, kicks them under a chair, walks down the hall to the cedar closet in her underpants, no top, remembering an old striped sundress of Celia's hanging there. Olivia emerges from the bathroom, catches sight of her, asks her to please remember they have a young boy living in the house now. Reflexively, Helen brings a forearm across her chest, says, "Oh, sure, sorry—" But later it irks her, Olivia's tone, the implication. She wishes she'd answered like Celia, *For heaven's sake, two little nipples.* Downstairs, she and Nick exchange looks in the kitchen . . . he's about to get into something with her, maybe it's seeing her in the dress, maybe he's going to say, "What happened to priming the house? You're not bailing out on me now, are you?" No, she's not, but it's too hot today, she needs a breather. She sees Nick willfully shut his mouth. She fills a bowl with cornflakes and carries it outside to the concrete steps, but can barely sit still long enough to eat.

By afternoon, there's nothing to do but drive the kids to the city pool. Olivia changes into her suit, but keeps a shirt draped over it and sits in a spear of shade, though she has Nick's skin, never burns. Helen's is ruddier, capriciously freckled, given to tiny bumps, comes via the Fraleighs, along with the gingery locks, the stare . . . Nick claims she's from a long line of watchers, peepers through knotholes. In any case, *Olivia's* the one with the great skin. Silky, olive-toned, no pits from chicken pox, no acne gouges . . . one vaccination on the left bicep, that's all. It's not so hard to remember sitting in the bathtub with her, Linny rinsing their heads with a tin pitcher.

Amelia waddles into the splash pool, and instantly her feet fly out from under her. Olivia starts to go after her, says to Helen, "Stupid the way it's sloped like that," but Amelia's already upright again, under the fountain's spray, feet planted wide. Helen takes this moment to grab Davey's hand and they jump into the shallow end of the big pool. One bright spot in this current mess, the time she's gotten with him. An appreciative boy, undemanding, maybe too *much* so. He asks only the most reasonable questions: Will he have to go to a different school? Helen answers, "We'll just have to see, honey." Still, he seems to be coming out of himself, yesterday actually told her a joke. "What's *Ha, ha, ha, thud?* A man laughing his head off." Oh, and the black lashes he has, such abundance. What an odd, sweet thing to be Aunt Helen. "C'mere, droopy drawers," she says, and fixes the string on his trunks, reminds him to stay on this side of the retaining wall. Says, "Why don't you go horse around with those other kids," doubtful he will, but when she looks up after taking a lap in the congested waters of the main pool, amazingly, he has.

Helen comes dripping over to her sister, sits cross-legged in the sun.

"I'm never going to get rid of this," Olivia says, slapping at the top of her leg, making it jiggle.

Maybe she means: Nobody will look at me now.

Or: I give up.

But she hardly eats, and some of the weight *has* gone. What hasn't she carries well enough. "You look fine," Helen says. "We can't all look like Audrey Hepburn."

A little later, Helen says, "You were talking about getting a job?"

Monday, Olivia tells her. First of the week she'll start making the rounds.

"Try Daugherty's?"

Olivia rolls her shoulders, nods.

"I was thinking of that myself," Helen says.

Before Olivia can pointedly remind her about the baby-sitting, Helen says, "We'd have to get different shifts." She sinks onto an elbow, says, "I don't know that they're even hiring."

"I thought you were painting the house," Olivia says.

"Well, I am. But that's just . . . I've got to find something to *do*."

On the drive home, Amelia falls asleep in the backseat, that clobbering summer-afternoon sleep. Seems a pity to wake her, but Olivia insists. You pay in the long run, and who's in a better position to judge than Olivia? So Amelia goes squirming into the house on her mother's shoulder, tiny teeth bared in confusion.

Helen pins the wet things to the line, notices her bike leaning against the shed, impulsively hops on and rides down McLaren Road, then left and up the hill, indulges in one of her favorite routes, sailing through the back alleys of the East Side. The Virginia creeper's already brittle on the fences, specked with bugs. And the smells in this heat, moldery clippings and potash, crankcase oil drizzled into the clay, petunias in a hanging basket, a whiff of briquettes, humus. Goose-bumped from the shower, momentarily cool, she'd slipped the sundress over bare skin, maybe to draw a censorious glance from Olivia, it's true . . . now the cotton billows out, the air plays through it as she stands against the pedals . . . her heart pounds, her lungs work in delicious searing bursts, but, apparently, no amount of exercise is going to kill this mood, this stubborn restiveness.

That evening, without making a show of it, Helen hangs around home, convinced this is Mark's night to call again. Olivia won't answer, and Helen prefers Nick not be the one. She sends them outside to play a few hands of cribbage at the picnic table, hears Nick's voice through the screen, *Fifteen two, fifteen four, pair is six, nobs is seven* . . . pictures herself crossing the grass, tapping Olivia, *Phone, Liv,* aiming a look at her . . . pictures herself waiting with Nick, fingering the plastic pegs. But what if Olivia refuses? What if everything comes down to Helen's choice of words . . . and they had better sound offhanded, too, virtually weightless. You can't let Olivia get her back up.

He says he just has some quick thing to ask you . . . why don't you just—?

What if Helen blows it?

But now that the kids are in bed, the light gone, she realizes that he's *not* calling. She feels let down, oddly shaken. She's not on his wavelength, after all.

Nick happens to see her pick the truck keys off the hook, asks where's she going this time of night.

"Nowhere," Helen says. He looks as if he's going to give her a hard time, so she adds, "You want to come? You're invited."

No, he's bushed, the only place he's going is up those golden stairs.

She kisses his forehead, says she won't be late, gets as far as the vestibule, waiting for him to quit the kitchen, then slips back and grabs a quart bottle of Pabst from the icebox.

Another still night in the valley.

But away from the canopy of downtown lights, she can see clouds packed above the mountains to the north and west. She stops in a dirt lane to watch the heat lightning. Listens for the boom, but that would be too much to ask for.

She fits the beer cap to the door latch, pounds with her fist, once, twice, lowers her mouth to the foam.

After a minute, she steps on the bumper, slides onto the warm hood, reclines against the windshield the way they sometimes used to at the drive-in movies.

Still the tang of smoke in the air. Amazing how far it travels, how disconcerting it is.

Helen Stavros lets the beer run down her throat, rolls the bottle against the bare skin of her leg between swallows, tells herself to *please please* give it a rest for one night. Tells herself feeling sorry for people is a number-one waster of time, it's what you *do* that matters . . . but it *is* too bad, the way no one ever takes Olivia's side quite, the way they always want her to tone it down, lighten up, get real.

Imagine Linny without the mischief.

Imagine Celia without the wild heart.

Who's to say Olivia's not right?

A taste of wind finally, rustling the weeds, but the flashes of somber light come infrequently now, the clouds tumble into the valley and rip soundlessly apart.

Helen dangles the empty bottle. Thinks, *Should have grabbed two of these.*

She drives again.

East of the bridge, in a ring of dying cottonwoods, there's the Diamond T where she could score another quart . . . she remembers Celia's dictum to stay out of bars named for cattle brands, not that Celia follows her own advice religiously, or did before Thomas . . . she drives past without slowing, also avoids the Rooster . . . no warning vis-à-vis barnyard animals, but the Rooster's a dive, the neon coxcomb flickers halfheartedly, watery pink, so Helen winds her way back into Sperry, parks across Montana Street from Kid Billy's, which is where she must have been headed all along.

Earl Simmons is working the front bar. A big man with bad eyes, great rolls of forehead skin as he looks up and aims his goggles at you. Quarter to eleven most mornings he'd take a seat in the Vagabond and Helen would deliver tea and dry toast and four soft-boiled eggs . . . delicate touch for his size, she always thought, *tap, tap, tap,* and off came the white skullcaps, in went the teaspoon. He did the crossword puzzle with an ink pen. Stella Baucus used to save up words to ask him. *Quotidian. Indemnify. Architrave.* What's a man like Earl Simmons doing tending bar? She's never thought to ask.

Now he brightens at the sight of Helen, won't accept her money.

"I hardly know what to do with myself," he admits. He says he's been stopping for breakfast at Stell's, out on the highway. He shakes his head. "It doesn't do much for me, that place."

"Well, I wouldn't have planned it this way, either," Helen replies.

"Circumstances beyond our control."

"Yes."

Helen thanks him for the drink. Nice as he is, she's too prickly to stay and converse. She drifts into the back where it's darker, louder. This group that's playing isn't bad, a five-piece, not local, she guesses. She used to come here with Celia, and Celia could be counted on to extricate her from the awkward moments, Celia with her acute radar. Never been accused of being a graceful girl, Helen, one to use her femininity to advantage, but always did like dancing, dancing for its own sake . . . it's the rest she can take or leave, the rest that vexes her with its protocols and secret understandings.

By no means a grand dance floor at Kid Billy's, but it's a swirl of limbs now. Must be a hundred degrees back here, too, even in a dark nook out of the fray.

Earl Simmons comes by, escorting a drunk. Minutes later, Helen's rocking her shoulders against the wallpaper, eyes shut, feels her forearm tugged, and it's Earl again, one finger in the air, one dance, how can she refuse? An up-tempo swing tune, *Mama, oh, Mama, ain't you somethin' to see*— Helen does balk for a second, though . . . it's this spell she's been under all day. She almost says, "Sorry, I'm not myself," but she'd have to shout, and so says nothing, lets Earl Simmons guide her onto the hardwood. And he's not a bad dancer at all, carves space around them with his very presence, and it *is* better to move, to spring off her toes, to feel her hair lift and fall. *Mama, oh, Mama . . .*

Smile, Earl's face says.

In return, Helen smiles.

Flying backward, blind, her shoulders seem to recall the spasm of motion that sent Celia's T-bird hurtling, seem ready to brace themselves once more, but Earl has a good grip on her, reels her in, and the tune comes to a cymbal-thrashing end.

Earl stands apart, says thanks.

He must do this every night, single out some friendly girl, give her the swing-around, then it's back to work. So, mercifully, there'll be no trouble getting free. But now the piano produces three rising chords and it's a slow song, bluesy, irresistible.

Startling herself, Helen says, "One more, okay?"

She takes his hand, lays her cheek against the damp cotton along his collarbone. His lungs, recovering from their exertion, take in enormous volumes of air . . . she's squeezed rhythmically, in a way that seems independent of his intent, though perhaps not.

The second time they break apart, it's Helen who says thanks, says she knows he has to go up front, says in any case she can't stay, needs to cool off, so then she's in the alley where couples have spilled and sit fanning themselves on the slats of the fire escape or pressing their backs against the cool bricks. People she knows, or recognizes.

A barmaid comes out a moment later, asks, "Which one of you's Helen?" Hands her a tall-necked Pabst, says, "On the house," gives her a look to go with it. Helen wishes he hadn't done that, it troubles her to be in anyone's debt . . . at the same time she's grateful, drinks it down in three long swallows, eyes pinched shut. The music carries outside, dampened, yet persuasive enough to tempt her. She wavers, but walks away, out the alley mouth in lengthening strides, around the corner to the truck. She fishes the key from the ashtray, wants desperately to be in motion again, remembers in her mild intoxication the night she was pulled behind a boat. Someone's full moon party at Lake Seven, one of Celia's crowd. Not on skis but a plywood platter she clasped with her forearms, leaving the rest of her to slap along in the wake. The surface water was bathlike from the afternoon sun, but unpredictably they'd cut

through the bright cold rising from the lake's springs and she'd
arch up gasping with laughter . . . around and around, until
she was worn out, shaking on the dock under a terrycloth robe.
She can dredge up no other memory from that night, but starting the truck now, impatiently gunning the accelerator, she
thinks: What amazing sensations the body's capable of.

She joins the meager traffic, heads up Montana to Commerce, then over the rise alongside the golf course and out of
town. The wind has vanished, and the fields are stained with
rusty moonlight. Not so much as the first drop of rain has
come. She makes a right onto Dutchman's Grade and the road
is hers, but she's gone no more than three or four miles before
it strikes her that it's pointless, this driving around the confines
of the valley, an exercise in time killing. Killing time has seldom troubled her in the past, seldom seemed an offense
against life. Now the thought of it sickens her, and so at the
next wide spot, barely slowing, she cranks the wheel, and,
spinning up a cloud of clay dust, reverses course.

Somehow it's gotten late, for when she walks through the
back corridor of Kid Billy's again, she finds the dance floor
glaringly lit, the musicians packing. Earl and the other bar-
tender and a lone barmaid are loudly shooing people out. Earl
locks the Montana Street door with a flourish, turns his back
on it, has to let a straggler out, locks it a second time and then
his hugely magnified eyes light on Helen. "Ah, it's *you*," he
says. "You can stay." He circumnavigates the bar, bends to the
cooler and produces an icy bottle with foil at the lip. "Try one
of these beauties," he says.

Helen parks herself and watches the cleanup operation, the
emptying of the tills, the upending of chairs, feels out of old
habit she should join this enterprise, yet refrains, drinking in
short sips now, tasting the beer, which is foreign, sharp on the
tongue. She watches as the bass player approaches Earl and

Earl then counts a quantity of bills into the man's palm, watches as the money is folded and poked into a breast pocket and the man goes off.

"Well, this was a night," Earl says.

Helen nods, lays her chin on her knuckles. Finally, the first intimation of fatigue in this whole long day, but she resists, brushes it aside.

"I'm happy you came," he says, and there's no need to elaborate. He's a straightforward man and Helen believes she could like him.

"Do you ever eat after your shift?" she asks.

Some minutes later, then, they take a booth at the Park Inn, and though it's cramped and overly bright and not a private place in this hour after the closing of the bars, Earl gives no indication of discomfort.

She asks about his life.

Unhurried, wanting nothing, Earl tells her. With his bad eyes, he'd failed his army physical, though his brother whose eyesight was only marginally sharper had passed and was stationed in the Pacific. Earl took the physical again and again failed. Thereafter, he worked at the new Boeing plant in Renton, Washington, bolting down the seats of B-29s. After the war, he piled up nearly three years of college credits, before his father collapsed with a stroke and he moved home. The father had been a dispatcher for the Great Northern Railway, had devoted his free hours to documenting the family lineage on a vast network of charts and filecards. He'd married late and there'd been only the two boys. Earl's brother had died of malaria in the Solomon Islands.

Helen says she's sorry.

Earl shakes his head, brows massively bunched. "Well, it was very sad," he says. "I can't say as the old man ever bounced back from that."

He finishes his BLT, offers Helen the last few salty fries, which she accepts, having bulldozed through her own as he talked.

"You could've gone back later," she says.

"College? True, I could have. But I'd lost my momentum, I guess."

After a minute, she asks Earl if he was ever married.

"For a short time," he says.

The Park Inn's begun to thin out. The cook steps from the narrow galley, idly surveys the clientele. For a split second, Helen thinks it's Billy Krona, almost calls out, must be the skinny shoulders that fool her, the dangly arms. She hasn't laid eyes on any of them, Billy, Stella, Connie Bell, not once. It's like Nick blasted them into another dimension. She feels that heaviness again, gravity wanting to have its way with her.

"What is it?" Earl asks.

Helen tries to make a joke of it, says, "Beer's wearing off."

"It'll do that," he says gently. "Would you like to go?"

"Not yet. If you don't mind."

No, Earl Simmons doesn't mind.

Helen says, "I don't know how it was between you and your brother," her natural reserve dissolving in Earl's presence, "but sometimes I have this idea that my sisters and I are one person, split apart, four sides of the same thing . . . it's the strangest sensation." She gives him a squinty look, lets him know she doesn't go in for this kind of stuff, distrusts it as a rule, but then she's saying, "I used to watch people at the cafe, people I'd seen all my life, my friends . . . but they were other people, and I never felt that way about my sisters, that they were other people."

She frowns, says, "I mean, I know better. We all have our own, well, *fates*—"

She looks out the wavy glass, draws a breath, relinquishes it.

She had no intention of airing the Stavros family laundry with him, and even now resists on principle, but suddenly she can't stop herself, leans in and begins to talk in a low sustaining rush, everything there is to say about her sister Evangeline, her sister Olivia, her brother-in-law Mark Singer.

Earl listens with the forbearance of a stone Buddha, neither acts astonished, nor indulges in cheap psychologizing. When, finally, she runs out of gas, he asks, "And what's going to happen now, do you imagine?"

Helen gives a shake of her head: *All up in the air.*

After a moment, she catches his eye, says, "I don't know which way to look at things. Nothing matters or every last thing does."

Earl nods, as if she's veered headlong into the basic conundrum of the universe.

Helen sets her hand atop his. Gradually, it opens to let their fingers lace.

"But you know what's too bad?" she asks him eventually.

"What would that be?"

"I'm *leaving*."

"Town?"

"Yes."

Earl asks where she's off to.

She's not exactly sure, Helen explains.

"And when did you arrive at this wonderful insight?"

"Just today . . . just now."

Earl tells her, in his experience, staying's not for everyone.

When at last they step out into the cool air, Helen shoots a look to the mountains in the east. Late as it is, it's a little too early for sun. "I haven't been up all night since high school," she says. "I feel kind of loony."

"It's not bad once in a while."

"No."

They pause on the sandy blacktop, Helen lays a palm on his shirt front, bunches it, then briskly turns and climbs into her truck. Earl opens the door of his boxy sedan, slides heavily in. She guesses he'd like her to drive off first, so he can watch until she's gone, and stay a moment collecting his thoughts, but she smiles avidly through the glass, waves him on, claiming that privilege for herself.

Man in a Circus Act

Past one in the morning, Mark Singer douses his headlamps and rolls to a stop in the weeds along McLaren Road. The Stavros house is uncommonly dark as he approaches on foot, black even where the globeless bulb ordinarily burns all night above the vestibule door. Through the poplars, a dog barking, but no other dog takes up the cause. There's a gibbous moon, the color of iodine. In the backyard, he finds the ladder Helen's been using, angled against the tallest part of the house, its top rungs in thick shadow. It's a bruiser, old, wooden, with a pully to raise the extension, but the rope is missing, borrowed for another job and never replaced. On the ground, on the backs of the leaves lie chips of gray paint, oddly luminous.

Mark draws a breath, lays hold of the ladder and stands it straight up, hobbles back from under the eaves with it like a man in a circus act. Out in the unobstructed grass, he lets the weight fall on him, catches the top before it can slam the ground. He checks the windows. Nothing. Gingerly, he retracts the extension a half-dozen notches and makes for the south end of the house where there's an upstairs porch, situated off the upstairs hall, just beyond the telephone chair. Olivia's room is next door. He repositions the ladder in a knot of junipers, eases it against the porch railing, unties his boots, shucks them off, and begins to climb before common sense can haul him down.

A surprise, though, when his eyes draw even with the tarred roof: two heaps of bedding, occupied. Not what he'd foreseen at all. He continues up to where he can look down at these two bundles. The one to the left is his son, face a pale oval. Thus, the other would be Olivia, and Mark sees how it is: Amelia's bunking with Helen, Davey and his mother outside where there's a breath of air, where the Stavros girls used to sunbathe. Maybe she's promised it to him for being good. As Mark mutely assembles this information, the boy suddenly sits bolt upright, and isn't *that* spooky? It's as if Mark willed it. Nor does Davey make a sound, any disturbance to wake Olivia. His lips fashion themselves into a slow, serene grin. He comes on hands and knees, wraps his fingers around the railing.

Mark places his free hand on top, goes, *"Shhh—"*

Davey looks back at his mother's sleeping form, cocks his head to gauge her breathing with an adult savviness, returns his gaze to Mark.

"Bet you didn't expect to see me," Mark whispers.

Davey whispers no.

Mark asks, "Do you think you can climb inside real quietly?" He's about to say more, *Sorry to spoil your adventure, I'll make it up to you* . . . but he can see how it pleases the boy to conspire with him, so he settles for a knuckle swipe down the cheek, says, "Try to sleep, okay?" and watches his son's progression across the roof, the head-first wriggle through the open window. Such a temptation to envision his own young self lurking at the periphery of Morgan Singer's life, late at night, straining to hear, to be illuminated. Mark resists. He curls over the rail, assumes Davey's spot on the sleeping bag beside Olivia. She's under a thin cover. Reminds him of summer nights at the Ash Street apartment.

How he'd love to form himself to her backside, to pass his hands along her flanks. Instead, he sits hugging his own stubborn legs, and drifts, cheek against knee.

"Isn't it a perfect temperature out?" he says. "Doesn't it seem like we're on a raft?"

He wants to be talking when she wakes. He wants for his voice to scuttle down into her sleep and lead her slowly up. He describes his day, his week. Not a great deal to say, yet he says it anyway, loitering over the least detail of his life without her. He stops and takes note of the rise and fall of the sheet, and talks on. "I ought to be frantic I'm losing you," he says. "But do you know how I feel? Like the lady who lifted the car off her daughter. You see it on the news? *It was the most amazing thing. I just put my hands on the bumper and lifted and up it came.*"

Mark shakes his head. What presumption.

He says, "I'm in a strange way tonight, that's all. Feel kind of—" *Blessed*, he was going to say, but doesn't that, too, reek of hubris?

He shrugs, lets it go. Studies an empty quadrant of the sky. Then Olivia says, "I can't forgive you."

Mark says, "Hello, Liv."

"Did you *hear* me?"

"No one's saying you should."

"Well, I can't. It's not possible."

"All right," Mark says calmly.

"Why don't you leave me alone?"

Mark answers, "I'd like us to live together again."

"So you can fool me again?"

"Because it's our life."

"*Our life.* You ruined our life. You didn't want any part of it."

"I don't think it *is* ruined, Liv. I think it's more durable than that."

Olivia sits up, wraps her shoulders. "I'm going inside," she says.

"I wish you wouldn't."

She turns her head and he gets his first good look at her. He smiles, can't help it, but he keeps his hands where they are.

Olivia says, "I'd never know what you were going to do. I can't live that way."

"You *never* knew," Mark answers. "You were only guessing."

A scowl from Olivia. Is that all he's come for, to nitpick, to badger her?

She says, "Suppose it was me, Mark?"

"I wouldn't have liked it."

"Or maybe you wouldn't have cared less. Maybe nothing means anything to you."

"Look at me," Mark says.

"I don't want to look at you."

He waits, watching her profile.

"I'm not defending myself," he says. "I'm just making a proposition: You can start over with someone else or you can start over with me." He regrets how cold and plain this sounds, but there it is. Instinctively, he knows not to beg, knows you can't love a groveling man. Nor will he say the first thing against her sister.

Olivia doesn't respond, doesn't move except to wet her lips.

Mark says, "I don't know where we got so lost, but I'd do a better job of it next time."

He rises, stretches, hears his bones crack, then squats in front of his wife where she can't avoid seeing him. He says, "That's what I came here to say. Good night, Liv."

He eases over the railing and down the way he came. In the

dry grass, he replaces his boots, one, then the other. It's possible that a voice will ask him to stop, but he doesn't expect it.

Gold and Silver

Before she became insensible, Grace steered Nick through a list of women he should consider marrying once she was out of the picture. Nick nodded along, as if this were a serious conversation. "And I suppose you should think about Patsy Gershon," she said. "Or Evie St. Cyr."

"Evie St. *Cyr?*" Nick said. "Have a *heart*."

"Don't make it somebody too young, Nick. You think you'd like it, but you wouldn't."

"I might like it fine," Nick said.

It was only a reflex, this bantering, seemed to buoy her spirits. She'd aged ten years in six months. Her complexion had gone gray, a cool mist lay on her forehead as if it were a rock at water's edge. Other times she was afraid he would forget her. No way on God's earth, Nick assured her. He wasn't marrying again, either. "Once was plenty," he said. "You took the starch out of me."

"I used to put the starch in, Nick."

"That's a fact," he said. "Oh, yes."

She was the same about being held now, wanted it, didn't want it. On occasion, his touch sent an unbearable current across her skin. Others times, she craved his body heat, couldn't he just lie under the coverlet with her? They avoided the grand retrospective, discussed the day-to-day. The lapping of waves.

Then, in the space of two weeks, Grace lost her faculties. Her mood yawed wildly, she bared her teeth at Nick. "I know *you*," she said one afternoon. "You sidewinder." Nick loitered at the bedside, said, "Ah, Gracie, it's okay now . . ." He brought the girls in sparingly, clumsily forewarned them, relied too heavily on Linny to deal with Olivia and Helen. One night he dozed in the chair, dreamed he was lugging Grace down Second Street in a fireman's carry. She was mute, bound in sheets, weighed nothing. It was a brilliant summer's day. People turned and stared, but he wouldn't look at them. He bent instead to his wife. The swaddling burst and she began to blow away, like milkweed.

The first thing he did was have a man in to hang new paper in the bedroom. Gone the fleurs-de-lis. Gone, also, the skirted makeup table. The two black-framed etchings of Scottish castles he removed to the rear of his closet. He expected trouble from the girls, Olivia in particular. He prepared himself to say, "Liv, I can't keep it like a shrine, I got to live in here," his voice not too plaintive, he hoped, "I'm only forty-seven, honey. I can't help it, I've got a long—" But no one challenged him, no one complained to his face. Perhaps he had Linny to thank for that, too.

He expected it would be unbearable to talk about Grace in the routine fashion everyday life demanded, expected to drill into wells of sentiment, of fury. And yet, through repetition, it grew possible. Bleary-eyed, fueled by instinct, he kept the business running, kept his girls from falling apart, vowed not to use Grace as leverage on them. He told Linny, "You ever hear me start off a sentence, *Your mother would have wanted* . . . I give you permission to kick me."

In private, he thought of Grace's freckled, pearlike breasts hefted in his palms, the plane of skin that extended from sternum to pubic bone. It had softened with the girls, but never lost its sleekness as she lay back, nor did any of the births require it to be parted with a scalpel. He thought of her pref-

erences, her arsenal of endearments, her cries. He remembered the loop of blue yarn that would go on the outer knob
of their door as a signal, and Celia's unabashed, "Have a nice
nap, you two?" He let himself be aroused, fought shame,
arrived at the view that he was the sole proprietor of these
memories, that if he did not exercise them, they would cease
to exist.

And the arguments, yes, against better judgment he thought
of those, too. Early on, he and Grace haggled over the
Vagabond's finances, over Nick's reticence. She called him a
tightwad. It was the goddamn Depression, what did she
expect? But he wasn't going to have the home front polluted by
battles over money. Growing up, he'd witnessed enough of that
to last a lifetime. Yet, there were other traps . . . crevasses fallen
into, wearily climbed out of. She could be grotesquely unrea-
sonable, unfair. You had to pick your fights, but Nick picked
badly where Grace was concerned. He'd take offense, and
away they'd go. An hour later, he'd be unable to say what had
set him off, remembering only the path of the fight, the switchbacks where they'd either pressed on or succumbed to their
affection. After she was gone, picking through this store of old
complaints felt as unseemly as stroking himself to the mirage
of Grace as a healthy twenty-two-year-old. But almost as irresistible, as hopelessly necessary and fruitless.

He'd meant what he said about remarrying. Still, he thought
he should keep an open mind. Six months passed, a year,
another year. His friend Albert Sowerwine told him a young
guy like him needed to get back into the hunt. That seemed the
prevailing view. Nick said he would when he felt like it, and he
didn't feel like it yet. Albert backed off. Nick thought of Grace
if not constantly, then in waves that would leave him short of
air. He was so lucky to have found her, to have abandoned himself to her on such little evidence. And that they still had some-

thing genuine to show for themselves after twenty-four years, wasn't it amazing? Maybe this was why he'd been willing to trust Olivia when it came to Mark Singer, why he squelched the primordial urge to tell her, "I wish to Christ you wouldn't rush into this, sweetheart."

In any case, he began to believe he wouldn't mind a woman's company. Hadn't he always liked women, never minded—despite his theatrical grousing—that fate had set him down in a warren of females? Had he not told Grace each time, his heart unimpeded, that he was happy she'd had another girl, and honestly didn't give a damn if they never had a son? All true. He was in his fifties now, not utterly over the hill yet, he supposed. No one would blame him. When circumstance permitted, he manned the Vagabond's till, surveyed the clientele, started, as Linny put it, to *circulate*. He remembered how he'd stood chatting with Emily Cotton, remembered her blaze of white hair, but she seemed to exist in a realm of time more remote and antique than even Grace's. Now and then, he would find himself having a drink with someone, escorting someone to a harvest dinner or motion picture. There was not the crushing awkwardness he'd feared. Neither was there momentum, intimacy. Companionship was all right, there was nothing wrong with a little companionship, but after a time he stopped seeking it out.

Tonight, Nick cranks off the porcelain *Hot* and *Cold*, steps from the shower into slats of gold-tinged light. An August evening in this surprisingly difficult summer of 1961, eight-thirty, quarter to nine. He checks his cuticles for vestiges of garden dirt, raises his feet to the stool one by one and inspects the turtle shells his toenails have become. He runs a hand through the pewtery mat of chest hair, yanks it to the point of mild pain, presses his belly against the sink, and decides, as long as his beard's softened, he might as well shave. Hasn't since Tuesday, and Helen gives him that look, *Please don't let yourself go*— So, in slow circles, he lathers with the brush, pilots the safety razor around his Adam's apple, steadfastly avoids engaging his eyes in the glass.

Taps, rinses, shaves again.

From the end of the upstairs hallway, the shrilling phone. He takes another pass across his cheek before remembering he's alone in the house. He lashes a towel to his midsection, steps out onto the carpet runner. The towel comes undone, falls, he doesn't go back for it.

He grabs up the receiver, says, "Yuh?"

"How's my old dad?"

For a confused instant, he takes it to be Celia, but realizes then it's his prodigal. Long distance, coins rattling down. He swallows back a dose of stomach reflux, says, "Stark naked, if you'd like to know."

"Let me picture it," Linny says.

Nick says never mind that, where is she?

"Well, I'm at a safe distance, I guess you could say."

"There is such a thing?"

An extended silence from Linny.

"You all right?" Nick asks.

"Swell."

"Drinking?"

"Not at present."

Nick collapses into the chair, feels the cool brocade on his flanks.

"I guess you outdid yourself this time," he says.

"You think so?"

He doesn't honor this with a reply.

Behind him, the window is open, screenless from the recent traffic to and from the porch roof. The air that seeps past his wet scalp has the exhausted sweetness of burnt sugar, but he himself, though muscle-sore, is not exhausted, feels curiously alert, ready.

He says, "I wasn't all that sure I'd be hearing from you again."

"It's your lucky day."

"Let's not make me take a stand on that."

From Linny's end, the tick of an earring as the phone is repositioned.

Nick says, "So what would you like, a casualty report?"

Linny denies this is her purpose, says she was just having coffee in a little place, just had the urge to hear Nick's voice . . . but if he'd rather not, that's all right, she's a big girl.

"Stay on the line, you," he says.

"Yeah, okay. I got a few quarters here."

Nick stares down the dreamlit corridor, clears his throat. He says, "Your sister's going to Chicago," waits a second longer than necessary, says, *"Helen."*

"Somebody die?"

"Naw, it's not that."

"She's moving out, you mean?"

"Seems to be the story," Nick says.

"What's she want to do *that* for?"

"Now there's an odd question, considering the source."

Nick notes what sounds like a sigh from Linny, or an uncharacteristic shortage of words.

He explains that their cousin Stephen who runs a catering outfit has agreed to take Helen on until she finds what suits her, that she's talking about going to school next spring, that she seems a changed person.

"No fooling?"

Nick says, as it happens, he's not fooling.

"She there now? Suppose I could—?"

"She's here, but she's out someplace in the truck, if I'm not mistaken. Maybe you could try later."

Maybe so, says Linny Stavros.

Then the operator, more silver tumbling into the phone's vault.

Nick encounters a brief silence of his own, says finally, "You know, I didn't expect you girls to hang around here indefinitely. Not really."

Linny asks him if there's going to be a big send-off for Helen, asks when it is.

In as unencouraging a voice as he can manage, Nick tells her.

He braces himself, digs down with his free hand and reconfigures his lank old equipment, settles back. There's not a whole hell of a lot left to add, but he says, "You're in Frisco?"

"Close enough."

"Funny, I wanted nothing more than to get my butt out of the city," Nick says. "Same with your mother."

"That's how it works."

"I guess," Nick says.

Then he says, "And you're okay."

Linny answers, "I've been better."

Nick says, "I ought to brain you," and suddenly he's too ruined to speak.

Farewell

A front blows through: charcoal-bottomed clouds, squalling wind that tears off still-green leaves, sends up roils of field dirt. Headlights appear, the air temperature falls forty-two degrees in the course of one sunless afternoon, and finally it rains. Mark comes out in the morning and finds his car window down, the driver's seat drenched, has to drape it with a tarp for the ride to work. Along the road south of town, spotted horses standing head to tail in the lee of billboards, hay sheds. A hawk on a phone pole, neck feathers plumped. It rains steadily for three days and not until the third day does the air seem clean.

After the rain, another convulsive wind, then a vast sea of mild, dry air.

One afternoon toward the start of September, Mark returns from work and finds the TV set going, Olivia and the kids at home. The countertops are obscured by brown sacks from the grocery. "Laying in provisions?" he manages. Olivia replies by loading his arms with things for the bathroom, asks if he'd mind putting them away.

Toilet paper, Ipana, Dr. Bronner's, talc.

A supper of sloppy Joes, sweet corn that Davey has meticulously shucked and desilked outdoors. He's had a haircut, leaving a thin white border around his tan. Watching his son eat, it occurs to Mark that, in his distraction, he never took Davey for a last tour of the Vagabond. Nothing to be done about it now. His son catches him staring. "I can't believe you're already a second-grader," Mark says.

Davey with that shy, long-lashed smile, as if aging were a feat of great accomplishment.

Mark gazes across at his wife, asks where she got the corn. Olivia nods in the direction of the produce stand down by the viaduct, and doesn't seem at all put out by the triviality of his question.

After supper, a walk up Paxson Road, four Singers along the margin of crumbling blacktop. A bur-snaggled Irish setter appears out of the field grass, inspects them, jogs along beside. Toward the last, Amelia rides Mark's shoulders, her heels making a hollow thump on his chest.

A starry evening, approaching cool, their first in the same bed since June. Mark's habit of late is to strip naked, but tonight he leaves on boxer shorts, flips back her side of the sheets in a fashion he hopes is read as friendly and no more. He hopes she won't be compelled to say, "Don't get any big ideas."

She comes in wearing a long chemise of white cotton, laundered to near-transparency. Dark-tipped shapes swaying beneath it.

"Everyone asleep?" he asks.

Olivia nods. She gives the bedroom a cursory look, *Oh, yes, I do recall this place,* extinguishes the light.

"Good night," Mark says.

Olivia rolling and settling. Mark rubbing his ribs in the dark. It's so quiet he can hear the juices when she swallows.

"I wanted to ask you something," she says at last.

Like a gust raising whitecaps, these words. Mark answers, "What's that?"

"I wondered if you were feeling sexy?"

"Sexy? Are *you?*"

"No, I don't think so."

"That's all right," he answers. Instantly, he's stiff as a length of pipe.

"You'll have to give me some time."

Mark says she can have all the time in the world, though he suddenly finds the expression chilling, horrible.

Olivia says, "Mark, this is the hardest thing I've ever done."

"I know that. I do."

She could tell him he knows nothing, that he's the prince of knowing nothing. She passes up the chance.

He says, "It won't be the last hard thing for either of us."

"No, it won't."

Thereafter, every day's an experiment.

Every day has *always* been an experiment, only he didn't know it. Not that earthshaking a revelation, so why does it hammer him? Why does he feel so raw, like a hatchling?

Every day with its questions:

Who are you, Mark?

What use is desire?

Where to from here?

Sunday, they wake late. Olivia gets out cereal for the kids, and comes back to the bedroom. "You're not going to church?" Mark asks.

"I don't think so," she says. "Not this week."

"What about next week?"

"I'll see."

Whatever Mark's qualms about the Covenant Church, its hold over Olivia, he lets them lie.

She sits on the bed, slips down the straps of the chemise, says, "Would you rub a little cream on my back . . . it's so dry."

Her skin doesn't seem all that parched, but never mind. The light in the room is pearly, merciful.

"That enough?" Mark asks.

When Olivia doesn't answer, he dips in for more, rubs again. She's lifted the tumble of hair off her neck with a forearm. Mark puts his lips there, tastes salt. He reaches around front, eyes closed, circles with his fingertips, feels the flesh go bumpy under the slick of lotion, imagining how she looks, but not looking, not yet. It's another few nights before he approaches her, and by then he's ravenous, he's beside himself.

They drop Amelia off with Helen, and Davey at a friend's, then drive across Sperry to Daugherty's Steak House, where Mark has made a reservation, though it's an ordinary Wednesday and the restaurant isn't crowded. They're seated in one of the scalloped booths in the back room. Daugherty's is famous for its huge sirloins and T-bones, its surf and turf, but the waitress tells Olivia there's prime rib tonight, she had a piece herself and it melts in your mouth. Mark says, "Get it if you want."

"What about you?"

Mark says, sure. Two prime ribs.

How long since they've spent an evening like this? He can hardly sit still, wanting to be home again. Willfully, he slows down the headlong rush of things, watches Olivia lading fork-fuls of prime rib with horseradish, watches the smudge of shadow along her collarbone as her lungs fill.

"It's good, isn't it," Mark says, remembers Thomas Balfour, *You know how a taste hits you just right?*

Olivia looks him in the eye and smiles, a smile purged of regret, or so he would like to imagine.

Their waitress is back several times, this pleasant, intrusive girl with the blotchy skin, the tiny locket at her throat, asks, "You celebrating, you two?"

Mark says actually, they are.

So do they want mud pie? She's had a piece of that, too, it's incredibly rich. Or what about coffee?

"No, but thank you," Olivia tells her with a certain ambi-guity, a certain slyness, "we need to go."

And then, at last, their clothes are off. There's a scratch of cool air at the screens, a stub of candle quavering on the night table. Mark stands by the bed in full view of Olivia, one hand idling on his belly, and he doesn't believe he can restrain him-self another instant. But now it comes to him—suddenly, the way, suddenly, sickeningly, he remembers he's going to die—it comes to him that Olivia's had a surprise waiting for him all the time she's been home, an exquisite payback, a humiliation to mete out that will equal her own. And this, he believes, is its moment.

"What are you *looking* at? Mark?"

His heart's flailing, but his hands have gone as dormant as sash weights.

"What is it? You're scaring me. Honey?"

The bed shakes as she sits up and urgently reaches for him. He couldn't have had it more wrong if he'd tried.

"Come here," she says, fierce and direct, taking hold of him. "Come *here*."

And so she engulfs him, locks her limbs about his, says, "You're here and nowhere else."

And Mark is.

No announcement is made at work, though Ike seems to know, has a sixth sense. All summer, Mark could swear that Ike's been about to cough out a withering assessment of him, but suddenly that's long in the past. Besides, Ike has other fish to fry. One morning, Roddy's not with him, nor is he the next. Ike offers no enlightenment until the third day, when he discloses at coffee that his nephew no longer works for them. It emerges that Roddy is in jail in Sandpoint, Idaho: DUI, malicious destruction of a sheriff's vehicle, resisting arrest, et cetera. His companion, the blonde girl from the convertible, has lost her teeth, an eye. "That dizzy fuck," Whitey says. Monday, a kid named Lewis Qualls joins Conlon Construction, an addition that may or may not be permanent. Ike's rejuvenated with the change of weather, wants them to frame out three more of these matchbox houses before the snow flies. Qualls is a round-faced boy of twenty-four, handy with the tools, hard to rile. "Sweet Lew," Whitey starts calling him and Qualls takes it. Ike assigns him to Mark, tells him to stick close and keep his eyes open.

A few mornings later, Ike takes a meditative bite of cruller, brushes the sugar from his fingers, begins telling Lewis the story about the boy who fell through the stairwell. Whitey sits opposite, rocking forward and back in a state of near bliss. "You remember that kid, don't you, Singer?" he asks.

Mark nods, soberly. He turns to Qualls and says, "Whistled 'The Irish Washerwoman' morning to night." He demonstrates. A breathy whistle, tongue against his palate.

A sly piece of smile out of Ike Conlon. "So where was I?"

"The cellar," Mark says. "Shirt off. Goose bumps. Boy's arm twisted wrong."

"Right, right. So finally," Ike says, hitting his stride again, "I reach my hand up under the kid's head, I feel my fingers slide on this gooey slime—"

And now September.

The house at McLaren Road has a fresh coat of dove gray paint, matte black for the window trim. The juniper beds along the foundation have been pruned and raked, the ladder stowed, and the Saturday of Helen's departure has arrived. The train leaves from Stillwater midevening, and therefore an early supper is scheduled. Mark cleans himself up, finds Davey a clean shirt, swipes his son's face with a washcloth, wets his hair and passes the brush through it so it stands up. But Olivia seems to take forever. Mark checks the clock on the stove . . . already they're fifteen minutes late. He looks at Davey, shrugs, the boy shrugs back. The two of them watch Amelia crabwalk around the hassock in the front room. Finally, Olivia appears, wearing a cream-colored sweater that must be new, slacks with a razory crease, her black hair ribboned at the neck. Eyeliner, a little scent he notices as she passes. "You look good," he says without premeditation.

A placid smile from Olivia. "Thank you."

The four doors of the Chevrolet opening, four bodies getting in. Mark ferries them across Sperry, down the willow-strewn hill, steers sharply into McLaren Road, the Coasters on the radio. The drive's already choked with vehicles: Nick's, Helen's truck, Thomas's gray Thunderbird, a buffed pale green Oldsmobile that must belong to Helen's guest, and, off to one side, among the knobby roots of the Norway maple, a runty black rig of English manufacture, possibly the last car on earth he'd expected to lay eyes on today. His foot stutters on the gas, but Olivia's hand is at his knee. "Why don't you park here behind Thomas," she says. Once he rolls to a stop, Davey throws open the rear door, and the kids bolt. Mark turns toward Olivia, mouth open to say he knows not what, but she's already climbing out with the foil-topped salad bowl. She turns back, bends to her window and says, "Grab the present, okay?" and strides off toward the backyard.

Mark sits a moment in the scattered light, scoops up the little box for Helen, turns it in his hands. A wind-up travel alarm with sliding, corrugated lid.

He gets out, follows his wife.

On the cloth-draped picnic table, a bushy display of carnations, citronella candles, unopened cards in colored envelopes. Mark deposits his package, lifts his face to scan the assembled, but before he can conduct an exhaustive inventory, Helen has him by the bicep, says she's glad he's come, asks forthrightly how he is.

"I can't believe you're going," Mark answers. "I'll *miss* you."

Helen's mouth in a lopsided smile. "Oh, don't go squishy on me, Mark." She's in kneesocks, a blue corduroy jumper with big pockets. Won't wrinkle too horribly on the train, he imagines. She has a raw, happy look, almost greedy. One of the Stavros girls after all.

"Just stating a fact," Mark says.

On the almost-still air, the smell of coals, bratwursts, charring chicken breasts.

Helen says, "I have no idea what's going to come of this. I guess that's the point."

"I guess it is."

Before their conversation can stray, she says Mark has to meet her friend, leads him over to Earl Simmons. The man has glasses like the rondelles in a church window, minute crusts of blood under the chin where he's raked himself with the razor.

Mark sticks out a hand.

"Pleased to know you," Earl says heartily.

And he *does* look pleased. Ought to feel like the odd man out, but he acts genuinely delighted to be among them. If he's gotten the lowdown on Mark Singer, it seems he couldn't care less.

So Mark stands trading talk with Earl. Out of the corner of his eye, he watches Olivia migrate to her father, who's hunched over the stonework grill, sees her plant a hand on Nick's back and speak into his ear. Sees Nick park his cigar, nod repeatedly, and stare down.

Then it's Celia and Thomas seeking Mark out, Thomas his usual courtly self, and Celia *her*self, impish and carnal and full of life . . . even fuller than Mark suspects, for in another three weeks Celia will announce her pregnancy, and this will be Mark's first niece, a rangy, wise-cracking girl by the name of Carolyn Grace Balfour, but for now, in deference to Helen, and possibly a little superstitious herself, Celia holds back this distracting news, says to Mark, "You thirsty? I brought you a beer," slides an icy bottle into his hand.

And she, too, asks how he is.

This solicitude, Mark thinks. He tells Celia he's been worse.

"I'll bet," Celia says.

After a moment, she catches Mark's eye again, makes him lean down, and says softly, "She's in the house."

Mark squeezes his lips, nods.

He takes in Celia's bright, moist smile. Given the choice—Linny here versus Linny elsewhere in the great world—it's abundantly clear how Celia Balfour votes.

And Mark's ballot? Mark's ballot?

Mark looks up in time to see Olivia mounting the back steps, disappearing into the vestibule, the kitchen.

At the grill, Nick working the tongs. He turns, holding the

loaded platter. It takes him a second to register Olivia's absence, but you can see his shoulders sag, you can see how he sets the plate down before the sausages roll off. And what he's thinking: *A simple farewell for Helen, was that too goddamn much to hope for?*

Mark flashes a look around for his kids, but they're right here, Davey hugging Aunt Helen's waist, Amelia cross-legged on the grass, sipping at a root beer, one of the Stavros tiger cats nuzzling her leg.

Mark finally makes his way to Nick, says, "Strange day."

His father-in-law would as soon give him the evil eye, the back of the hand, Mark imagines. But Nick just shakes his big head. "It is that," he agrees. He glances warily at the house, emits a voluminous sigh. He rips off a strip of tinfoil and covers the meat. "I guess we'll just hold off a minute on eating," he says.

An air of preoccupation settles over everyone. Earl Simmons adjusting his trousers, Celia toeing the ground with her sandal, Thomas exhaling smoke into the amber light and embarking on a story to fill the vacuum, "It was a night a lot like this, the end of summer . . ."

Mark drinks, wipes his mouth, drinks again.

He says, "Nick, I want to tell you how—"

But Nick cuts him off, clamps a hand on the knob of Mark's shoulder. His voice gravelly and low, he says, "Wouldn't you give anything to be inside there, a fly on the wall?"

Catches Mark completely offguard, this comradely tone. He coughs out a helpless laugh, stands grinning, weak in the knees from the sudden relief.

Nick blinks his great watery eyes, says, "You'd learn things then, you'd see how things worked."

The two men in long ribbons of shadow, staring. The Stavros house, its new paint aglow. Looks perfectly inert, no sign of the declaration taking place within.

At last, the screen door slaps and Linny Stavros traipses out. Long-legged jeans with a showy buckle, black shirt flapping at the neck. She has kisses for Celia and Thomas as she makes her way across the mown grass. An arm-pumping handshake for Earl Simmons, a quick laugh tossed back at whatever he's just said, and then she approaches her father and brother-in-law where they wait, one beside the other.

For Mark, a rueful, disheveled smile. She touches her cheek to his, says, "Hi, love," pulls back, withdraws to arm's length.

Before Mark can speak, she turns and faces Nick, gives his aproned chest a pat, says, "Jesus, what *smells* so good?" She uncrimps the tinfoil, picks off a shred of burnt chicken, sticks it in her mouth, feigning ecstacy. Then she ambles over to have a word with her sister Helen, who'll soon be leaving for the train.

Nick stares after her, remembers eventually to shut his own mouth.

But Mark's watching the house again. Moments pass. There's a touch of breeze now, shadows of the birch leaves jittering on the glass-walled vestibule. What a startling, sweet evening on earth. And here comes Olivia, down the steps and crossing the lawn toward them all, almost gliding, shoulders back, arms folded at her waist. She looks radiant. Undefeated, Mark's tempted to say. The triumph not over Linny, it turns out, but over the forces that fling people apart.